GW00643743

EVIL

TIJAN

Edited by The Word Maid and proofread by Chris O'Neil Parece, Paige Smith, Pam Huff, and Kara Hildebrand.

This one is dedicated to all the readers who loved Evil when I wrote and published it online so long ago, and for those that kept asking me to finish it! I really hope you guys love the ending as much as I do.

Thank you again, so much.

1

When I was grabbed from behind and thrown against my locker, I wasn't surprised to see Matt Rettley's smirking expression. He was heavily muscled, striking blue eyes, and blinding blond curls to match. Matt might've been the high school football quarterback most girls' dream to squeeze, but to me—he was the aggressor.

And a part of me liked it.

"What?" I asked. He had my hands pushed up against the lockers. I glanced at them and wondered at the different skin colors. Of course, I didn't have a skin color. I wore black, all black, all over. And his hands were golden tan since summer was just around the corner.

"What do you mean 'what?' You know what." Matt pushed closer. "I saw you eyeing me in the cafeteria today. You don't eat. You don't think I know what that's about? You trying to be all skinny for me? You think it makes me hot?"

One of his hands slid to the back of my neck and filtered through my long black hair before it rested on the curve of my back. He pulled me close, and bent to whisper into the crook of my neck, "You just breathe, and I think it's hot. Right, baby? Do I do it for you, too?"

I glanced over his shoulder, felt my brother's approach, and whispered, "Maybe if you died."

Matt tensed and then shoved me against the locker again. As my head hit the metal, I saw Kellan rip Matt away, hurling him against the next locker.

It was odd. I never saw Kellan's approach, but I always felt him. Just like he always felt when I needed him.

I watched as Kellan threw Matt against another locker, snarl something into his ear, and rear back to throw a punch. I felt the crunch of bone more than I heard it and knew that my brother had just broken another umpteenth jaw.

As a teacher turned the corner, Matt rushed around the other corner. No one wanted to get the Bradens in trouble.

"Kellan and Shay Braden, why is it always you two? And if it's not the two of you, it's your other two siblings. All the time." Mr. Mirchak approached, shaking his head. "Who'd you fight this time, Kellan?"

I should've felt something, maybe remorse, but there was nothing. Matt had assaulted me. Kellan felt it and protected me. And if Matt chose to run away, then that was Matt's decision. But still...I should've felt guilty.

Kellan drew to his full height of six one and squared his lean shoulders against the portly forty-something teacher. He shook his head and drawled, "Do you see anyone, Mr. Mirchak?"

The balding teacher shook his head. "I never see anyone, Kellan. That's the problem. But I know that someone's going to show up with a busted eye, maybe a shoulder. I don't know, but there's always something." He turned away, but mumbled over his shoulder, "...too damn scared to say a thing..."

Kellan waited until the teacher had turned the corner before he flashed a smile. "What do you think?"

I rolled my eyes and kicked my locker open. "You didn't have to break his jaw."

"Right." Kellan fell against the locker beside mine and studied me intently. "At least this way, he'll shut up all the time. I'm getting tired of his mouth. The guy thinks he knows you too much. He doesn't know anything."

"Still..." I muttered as I bent inside to grab my book.

"Still," Kellan mimicked me and yanked me out. "Why didn't you do something, Shay?"

"What are you talk—?"

"Don't. Not with me," Kellan interrupted. "You could've stopped him long before I came around the corner. You knew I was coming. Why didn't you stop him?"

"Maybe I wanted to hear his rhetoric on how hot I must be for him."

"Don't be funny, Shay. You're not the funny one, remember?"

I smirked. "That's funny. I don't think that role's been taken in our family."

Kellan's hand tightened on my arm. He pulled me closer and bent his head to my ear. "You always wait for me. Why?"

Maybe I couldn't bring myself to do what he enjoyed. Maybe I liked knowing he'd always protect me or that someone would protect me. Maybe...maybe I enjoyed the sick pleasure knowing that someone like Matt could never really hurt me, though he didn't know that fact. Or maybe...I whispered, "I don't know, okay?"

I didn't know. I had ideas. I had possible scenarios, but the only truth was, I could've easily broken Matt's hold on me and I didn't.

"It's done, I guess. No harm." He caught my swift look. "No harm done...to us."

"That's better." I grinned and eyed the book in my hand.

"Are you going to class?"

"I don't know." I should. I was the "good" student, but there was something tempting about the summer wind. Living in Minnesota made it difficult to stay away from the summer lakes. The water always beckoned...

"Vespar just texted me. He and Giuseppa are heading to the river," Kellan commented as a bell rang. The doors burst open, and all our classmates streamed into the hallway.

I always forgot the last period was a short period during our last week.

"Decision made." Kellan grunted and grabbed my bag for me. As he threw it over his shoulder and stood upright, I watched as all the students move around us. Matt was one of the few that braved an encounter with us. He was the top of his food chain so he felt it was his duty. I understood that, but the truth was, no one would dare stand against Kellan. And if not Kellan, then Vespar was just as formidable.

The Braden siblings were famous in our little community of Poehler, but not really known—by anyone.

When I caught the wolfish looks from some girls on the yearbook committee, I taunted, "Leah still hasn't gotten her clutches in you? I'm surprised, brother dearie. She's been giving you the look since last summer."

Kellan rubbed his jaw, but his eyes were intent on me. He ran a brisk hand over his head. "She's got nothing new that I want. I've been inside of her too many times. I'm getting tired of it."

My eyebrows arched at that, and I whistled. "What happened to 'never kiss and tell'? I didn't think you were the type." But Kellan was the type. He didn't give a damn, not when it was over. He'd spew anything I wanted to hear, and he'd only spew it to me.

Kellan shrugged. "Let's go. We've got only a few hours before the sun's gone."

I sighed. I loved the summer. I loved the water. But I also

knew what my siblings would do when the sun went down. And I wasn't really up for that. Besides...my fingers were itching to feel the painter's brush between them. And I had a tingle in my back. I always knew to heed that tingle when it came on.

"I'm gonna opt out. I've got things to do." I tried for casual, but Kellan shot me a dark look. I waited, tensely, for him to question my decision. I'd tell him if it came to it, but my time in the painting studio had been my private time up to now...

"Okay."

Relieved, I stood there as Kellan raked one more scrutinizing look over me before he turned and left. It was remarkable to watch everyone instinctively move aside for him. And it wasn't because of his rakish good looks. Although that helped. Kellan, Giuseppa, and Vespar were all tall with the blond good looks they inherited from our mother.

Not me. I stood a couple of inches below them with black as night hair that teased just below my shoulder blades. Giuseppa had a long mane of golden tendrils. They were just wavy enough to give her a whole goddess look. Not my hair. It was straight black, but it seemed to sparkle underneath the right light. Kellan always said that it seemed to lure the guys.

It seemed to have lured Matt Rettley in, but Kellan was right. I hadn't met a guy that I couldn't handle. It was just if I chose to handle them or not. It drove Kellan crazy. Not Vespar. He just sniffed and marched the other way. Secretly, I wondered if Vespar was a little jealous of my closeness with Kellan. But then again, Vespar and Giuseppa had formed their own clique.

That was us, the Bradens. Gorgeous, mysterious, and a little dysfunctional.

And as I turned to head toward the art studio, I wasn't immune to how the same students moved for me, too.

"You've come to grace the studio walls?" My art teacher, Mrs. Ullen, smiled as she swept open the door.

I stepped inside and took in the new paintings that decorated the art room.

"They're nice. Whose are they?" A student did each painting. I recognized a few handiworks. Some were roughly outlined while others were given a detailed swoosh of the hand. The paintings were of animals, sports, and even balloons. I perused each of them as Mrs. Ullen waited in silence. She walked beside me, her arms crossed over her chest, wearing a billowy dress that dwarfed her tiny frame.

I paused at the end of the room when I saw a handful of paintings hung. Each of them was bold, dark, and encased a chilling image of a demon. Each black form had two red eyes that sent shivers down my spine. I almost felt the fire that was reflected from the demon's hell. And the very last one took my breath away. It was the same demon, but this time a slight slant had been given to the eyes so that it looked... My eyes widened as I realized the implication. I turned sharply and rasped out, "Who did these?"

Mrs. Ullen's smile never faltered, but I caught the slight tensing around her eyes. She swept a hand toward the graying bun her hair was loosely pulled into, and she mused, "You don't like them?"

They were beautifully done. That wasn't my issue. I demanded, "Who did these? Who did this one specifically?"

Mrs. Ullen didn't need to look. She knew which one I meant. "These didn't come from a student here, Shay. I hung these two weeks ago. It's been a while since your last visit here."

I didn't visit. I painted. And I knew there was a reason why Mrs. Ullen wanted me to study the paintings.

"I want you to take the last painting down."

"Shay, really. I don't understand..." And then her eyes caught and held on the last painting. I saw the realization before I heard the swift intake of breath.

"That last one looks like Kellan. I want it taken down, and I want to know who painted it."

"Shay—"

"I'd like to paint, Mrs. Ullen. I'd like you to keep selling my portraits in your store, but I really don't want that painting hung on the wall. And I really want to know who the artist is."

Mrs. Ullen looked flabbergasted. And no wonder. I usually came into the art room, perused through the pieces she displayed that week, and then quietly went into the studio room that was kept locked. Mrs. Ullen had taken note of my talent early in elementary school. She had proclaimed my doodles as masterpieces and then introduced me to a blank painting canvas. The relationship had been cemented that day. I painted whenever I wanted, and she sold them in her private store. No one knew except the two of us. It was respected by both, but this was the first time I'd spoken against my collaborator.

"Oh dear, of course. I didn't even notice—but then again, you always see what I cannot. I'm sure the artist didn't intend anything by the painting. It's a total and accidental coincidence. I'm sure of this, Shay. I'm so sure of this. Of course, I'll take the painting down. I know how close you are with your brother."

As she hurriedly moved forward to unhinge the painting, I tried to calm myself. I didn't care if it was accidental or not. Something fierce and angry burned inside of me at the idea of a demonic portrait of Kellan...though it may be true at times.

"There you go, Shay. It's down. I'll keep it behind the desk covered until he arrives for his paintings again. I'm so sorry again, Shay honey. I'm sure your brother isn't even..." But her voice trailed off when our eyes met. Everyone knew Kellan's reputation, and it wasn't an angelic one.

"Still." She cleared her throat. "I'm sorry again, Shay. Did you come in to paint this evening?"

I nodded, mutely, still a little shaken from the fierceness I'd felt over the painting.

"I'll unlock the door for you, Shay honey. You know how to leave the school if you stay late. And with that, I'll leave you alone." She hustled out of the room, and I heard the click of the studio door unlocking a moment later. When I heard her approach, I quickly moved to the second door and timed it so that I exited the room as she re-entered.

And then I was in the empty hallway, still shaken, but the tingle urged me ahead. It was stronger than it had ever been before, and I quickly moved to the studio door. I swished through and breathed in freedom as it locked shut behind me. That was when I turned to survey the room.

Three empty canvases were perched on easels.

I forgot everything else.

2

It never ceased to amaze me how the world went away when I painted. It was like everything clicked off the second my hand picked up that brush. And then I'd blink awake, maybe four hours later, and stare, befuddled, at a finished product.

This time wasn't anything different.

I caught my breath as I stared at my handiwork. The general background was a brown color, almost sand-like. There was a mass of clouds, a beautiful storm that looked like it had just started, and three angels that hung in the air, mesmerizing. They seemed to pierce through me as I stared at each of them. Their wings were folded in, white with long feathers, and their robes sparkled from some unseen light.

I didn't know what prompted this painting out of me. And to be honest, I never understood why I painted what I did, but this one took my breath away. It was like someone else had used me to paint it. I didn't feel like I could take credit, but it didn't matter.

I bent and pulled the masking cover over it. I made sure each of the prominent tacks was pointed out so that the cover wouldn't rest on the painting, just around it. And then I glanced at the clock.

Five after nine.

Great.

I'd been painting for longer than four hours.

Cursing underneath my breath, I grabbed my bag and left through the door. It would automatically lock behind me, so I didn't give it a thought. As I hurried down the far east corridor and descended the back stairwell, I hoped like I always did that the alarm wouldn't sound when I pushed on the exit doors. They never had, but it only took one time. As I pushed through, I breathed in relief when no alarm splintered the air.

I was safe...once again.

The air was chilled, like it should've been on an early summer night. It didn't help that I hadn't gone to school with a sweater or jacket.

I tried to warm my arms, but it never worked. I was still trembling when I got to my car. As I blasted the heat, I sat back and pulled out my cell phone. Two missed calls from Kellan and four text messages from Matt.

Lovely.

The first one read, ya beatch, ur gonna pay for ur bruda be back 2morrow dun worry.

The second one wasn't much different, and the last two promised payback.

I rolled my eyes and shifted the car into gear. As I drove through the backstreets of Poehler and headed out of town, I saw Leah and a few others leaving one of the pizza places, like a normal teenager enjoying time with her friends.

I'd never been a part of that world. None of the Bradens had. And for some reason, it never bothered us. We were meant for different things. Still...a part of me wished things could've been different. That I could've grown up as a normal girl with a normal family and even a normal boyfriend.

When I slowed and turned onto the gravel road that led to my home, I knew it was useless to wish that.

I wasn't normal. No one in my family was, but it would've been nice...to know what normal felt like.

We lived in a three-story brick house. And as I parked to the left of the garage, I cursed when I saw that every single light was off. That didn't mean everyone was asleep, not in my family. It meant that they were outside, probably down by the river.

Still...it was a little reprieve for me.

I let myself in to the empty house, kept the lights off, toed off my sandals, and moved into the kitchen. The bare tile felt cool underneath my feet. As I opened the fridge, I pulled out a container of orange juice and then screamed.

Kellan stood right behind me, a foreboding expression on his face.

"Oh God." I laughed, weakly, as I set down the orange juice. "You gave me a heart attack just now."

Kellan cocked his head to the side, his eyes studious on mine.

When I shut the door, the fridge's light was replaced by the moonlight. It fell over his face and gave him a shadowed, mysterious look. Anyone else would've shuddered in scared anticipation. I just shuddered because it was cold.

"What?" I asked. Kellan had something to say, I could tell. I didn't have the patience to play his games.

"Where were you?" he asked, his voice low and gruff, almost raw.

"I had things to do. What are you talking about? I told you that." I wanted him to leave it alone. I didn't want to tell him about the painting, not after so many years of secrecy.

"No, you didn't tell me anything. And I knew you didn't want me to ask, just like you never want me to ask." Kellan moved forward and leaned against the fridge. I knew he didn't intend it, but his stance seemed predatory.

"I saw Leah leaving the pizza place tonight. You sure you want to miss out on that?" I asked nervously. I downed the rest of the orange juice, and when I turned toward the sink, Kellan grabbed my arm and hauled me back.

"What?" I asked. Kellan had never been intentionally rough with me. I'd never seen it, but I knew he had it in him. In fact, something told me that he had a lot in him that I wouldn't want to know.

His fingers tightened on my arm. "What were you doing tonight?"

I looked at his hand, almost distantly, though I felt the pain intimately. "Don't ask me that."

"Why? Are you going to tell me the truth?"

I looked up and met his gaze. His eyes were a piercing blue, so beautiful to look at, but I swallowed and steadied myself. "I would lie. And I don't want to lie to you."

Kellan didn't remove his hand, but he used it to draw me closer. "What do you mean?"

"I don't..." I looked in Kellan's eyes. He wasn't looking for some weak truth. He was looking for something deep, infinite, something that would hold true no matter what trials endured. So I lied for the first time, "I went to see Matt Rettley."

"Why?" Kellan hadn't bought my lie. His hand didn't tighten or relax either.

I glanced at his hold on my arm. His fingers were strong, too strong, but we both knew he couldn't hurt me. Slowly, almost gently, I slid a finger underneath one of his and yanked it backward. Kellan held his breath, but let me hold his finger at bay. He tilted his head and narrowed his eyes. They seemed to sparkle in the moonlight.

"Why, Shay?" Kellan demanded with a rough edge in his voice.

A shudder went down my spine, but I tightened my hold on his finger. "I wanted to make sure he wouldn't say anything. I wouldn't want my brother getting in trouble for me."

"You don't want me to get hurt?" A ghost of a smile flashed over his face.

I smiled, and then I yanked his finger the rest of the way until the bone snapped. Kellan didn't move, not an inch. When it was done, after a moment of silence, he rasped, "Are you going to break the rest of my fingers?" He still had his hold on my arm, but his fingers had loosened their grip. I shrugged off his hand and stepped back.

A chill slammed into me, and I hugged myself to ward it off.

Kellan watched. He didn't say a thing.

Softly, I murmured, "I just lied to you." I didn't know what compelled me. Maybe it was that I'd broken his finger, I'd hurt him back. Or maybe it was because I'd lied for the first time and I needed to expunge myself. I wasn't sure.

But I saw that Kellan already knew I'd lied.

I added, "I didn't go to see Matt Rettley, but I'm not going to tell you where I was. That's for me. And don't put your hands on me again." As I turned and headed upstairs to my room, I couldn't shake off a sense of dread. Something had happened, something that felt off, between Kellan and me.

I hadn't left him with the knowledge that I could and would hurt him, if need be. No. Kellan had left me with the knowledge that he allowed me to hurt him. He stood there and just let me do it. But...why?

I shook my head as too many chills washed over me. Kellan had always been my protector. He'd been beside me all my life. He would've been the big brother that any little sister would idolize, but the problem is that those girls didn't know who their big brothers really were, or what they were capable of.

Kellan was a lot of things, but I needed to reassure myself that he'd always protect me. That was my bottom line... I couldn't be concerned about it, not anymore. When I pushed through my bedroom door, I sagged in relief. Within my four walls was my sanctuary. It was mine and mine alone. No Kellan. No Rettley. No Mrs. Ullen. No one. Just me.

The door burst open, and Giuseppa threw herself onto my bed.

Guess my sanctuary was easily penetrable.

I turned from my desk and sighed. "Can you leave? Please? I'm asking nicely."

Giuseppa laughed, her blue eyes sparkled in evil mirth, and her smile widened as she threw out her arms to stretch on my bed. Her long golden curls became entangled around her arms and within my white laced bedcover, which starkly contrasted underneath the black bikini top and bottom she wore. Nothing else.

"Aren't you cold?"

"I'm drunk, Shay. You should try it." She giggled and hiccupped. "Oh. Oops."

"Go to bed, Gus. Your own bed. Please." I slumped down in my desk chair. The wood creaked, protesting, underneath my weight. I groaned. The chair would have to deal with it. I was dealing with my drunken, scantily-clad sister. As I bent forward to open my bag, I muttered, "You're not passing out in my room. You snore, for one. And two, you want Kellan to wake you in the morning? You want to go running for me? I'm all for that."

Giuseppa bolted upright and exclaimed as she brushed her curls back from her heated face, "Speaking of Kellan—what'd you do to him? He looked like he could commit murder or something."

"Why do you think it was me?"

"It usually is. He doesn't get that pissed with me." She shuddered. "And hell no. I am not going running for you. That's your sick obsession that I don't understand. It's not like we have to work for these bodies."

My heart froze. Everything froze. I froze.

I hated hearing those words.

"I'm sorry. I forgot that you hate talking about how we're different. Whatever. I'm out." Giuseppa stood up and strode to the door. Just as she reached it, she swiftly turned, her blonde curls swung so that a strand hung just off her lips, and she rested her hands on her slim hips. Her black bikini showed off her perfect body...the body that she claimed we didn't have to work for.

I lifted deadened eyes to her face. I knew what was coming.

"You need to deal with it, Shay. We're different. Our entire family is different. We're not human. We don't have to play by their rules. I think it's seriously weird that Kellan indulges you by going on these 'runs.' I don't get it. I don't get why he indulges you at all. You're so...out of all of us, you are the most powerful and the weirdest one. You never even use—"

"That's enough." Kellan materialized from behind Giuseppa. He wrapped an arm around her mid-section and lifted her into the hallway. I could hear her rant, "Stop, Kellan. Stop—"

"Gus, stop. Hush." I closed my eyes, but I still knew what was going on just outside my door. Kellan had placed his hand over Giuseppa's mouth. He was making soothing sounds, but none of it worked. It enraged more than sedated her.

"No!" She ripped his hand away. "I'm freaking tired of it. Where was she today? That's right, you don't know. None of us know where she goes. You should know, you're more powerful than the rest of us except for Shay, who doesn't even use her powers. But no..."

There was silence. I felt my heart skip another beat. And then I heard a more muted Giuseppa, like she'd lost her fight. "I think I'm drunk. I think I'll go to bed."

"That's a good girl." I heard Vespar murmur from down the hallway.

Kellan stood in my doorway and watched until another door clicked shut.

I didn't say a thing. I didn't need to. We both knew Gus would be sleeping it off in Vespar's room the rest of the night. If I weren't related to them, I'd assume they were incestuous. They had a weird best friend/sibling relationship. Vespar was often the only one who could quiet Gus.

"I think he uses his mind tricks on her," Kellan offered his two cents. He flashed a sardonic smile and sauntered inside to sit where Gus had recently been lying. I hadn't moved.

I finished pulling out my homework.

"She's right, you know."

"Can we not?" I groaned, but I knew what was coming.

"We're not human, Shay. Stop pretending we are."

"Kellan, don't..." I said.

"I'm not saying that we have to have a conversation about it. I'm just saying, you gotta own up to who you are someday. And that day's coming soon, Shay."

"Kellan, stop." I reared back. I was ready for a fight. Suddenly, I *wanted* that fight. I could feel the energy in my body. It tingled right down to my fingertips. I wondered what I'd see if I looked at my hands, if I'd actually see the power there.

Kellan fell silent. He was the one to rear back this time. He stood to his fullest height, his eyes thoughtful, and then he sniffed the air. An evil smile lit his face, his golden features, and his shoulders straightened. He was ready for a fight, one that he lived for.

A part of me died inside because that fight was with me.

"Are you ready?" He moved forward, just an inch. "I can feel it in the air. I can feel you, Shay. You're everywhere. Everyone in the house knows it. You're enraged. They can feel it, and they cower."

I narrowed my eyes and slammed the door shut behind him.

Kellan didn't even jump. I felt his adrenaline kick up another notch.

"This is what you want? This is what you live for? You want to fight me?" I whispered.

"No, Shay. I don't want to fight you. I want to make you alive. I want to see what you can do."

"Why? Why is it you?" It was always Kellan, since I was a little kid. It was never Vespar. Never my sister. Not even my mother or our father. It didn't feel right. When we grew up, it was only Kellan."

"What do you mean, Shay? Who takes care of you? Who makes sure you eat? Who makes sure you get a ride home from school? Is that what you mean? Why is it always me who pushes you? That's what I'm doing right now. I'm pushing you. Let go. Feel your powers. Show me what you can do."

"Show me what you can do."

Those words weren't right. They didn't sound right. I shook my head, and the fight left me. I didn't understand it, but something rebelled against Kellan. It was like he wanted me to do something and I couldn't, not on command.

They were correct, though. I knew we weren't human. It was why I knew I could've easily removed Matt Rettley's hands from holding me against the locker, why I could've stopped him. It was why I had felt Kellan's approach before I saw him. It was why... It was possibly why I painted masterpieces. But it didn't matter, not in that moment, because in that moment I was a student.

I tapped my books. "I need to do my homework."

Everything was gone in that moment. The air was replete,

sucked of emotion, and I actually saw Kellan's chest fall in disappointment.

"I don't think I can go running in the morning. I'll be up late studying. There's a test in college psych tomorrow, you know..." I trailed off.

Kellan just sighed and left.

I was okay with it. I had homework to do. In some ways, I wasn't sure if I was a coward or if I was courageous.

3

Dew still stuck to my car. The morning was chilled. A light smattering of chirping birds could be heard in the background as I arrived at school the next morning. I took a moment and remained in my seat. I wasn't quite ready to face another day as a Braden. It didn't use to bother me so much, but...things had started to change, somehow, unexplainably.

Pulling the mirror over, I sat back and studied what I saw.

I had a heart-shaped face, with slightly reddened cheeks that came naturally. My cheekbones seemed to stick out, which drew the eye to my lips. A curve filled out on my top lip, and the bottom was slightly plush. And my eyes, dark eyelashes over frostbitten green eyes, and coal black hair that framed each side of my face.

I looked good. I knew it, but I didn't care. Giuseppa was gorgeous. She was one of those golden Greek goddesses, and she loved it. She used her looks to get anything she wanted, and if her looks didn't work, she'd use her powers. She'd probably slept with half of the guys in school, and most of them didn't even remember. Gus was the ultimate female player, but no one even considered slamming her with labels such as "slut" or "whore." Gus was just Gus, and she wasn't considered on the same level as the human girls, who would call each other "slut" or "whore."

Gus used them, enjoyed them, and made them forget. There were no ramifications afterwards.

I wasn't sure, but I assumed Vespar did the same thing. He was just more discreet about it.

And Kellan...Kellan slept with who he wanted. If he changed their memories, that was up to him. No girl dared make any demands after a night with him. She wouldn't have lasted long enough for the words to even escape her lips. His look alone would've filleted her, but I knew he altered some memories. I'd felt it in the air, like he'd felt my power last night. I always assumed that his sexual exploits, the ones that turned bad, were the recipients of erased memories.

Maybe, maybe not.

Matt Rettley's scamper was the same as everyone else. No one wanted to mess with Kellan. If they did, those people tended to be changed for the rest of their life.

And me...I stared in the mirror. I looked different from them. I felt different from them. But was I different? I had the same powers, more powers, but I rarely used them. I felt like I couldn't, like I hadn't a reason for them, not yet.

I eyed my clothes. I always chose black, though I wasn't sure the reason. And I always covered every inch. Sometimes I wore jeans, like I was wearing today. They were faded blue that I paired with a tight black long-sleeved shirt. Why did I cover my skin? It wasn't because I was pale to my siblings' tanned skin. No, it was because something new had started to arise in the last year, something that I didn't dare tell a soul, especially my siblings.

I pushed up one of my sleeves and looked down. My wrist was pale, like normal, but three inches above, a black circling tattoo had formed. Some days it was there, and other days it wasn't. I hadn't asked for it. I hadn't performed any spell for it. I had no idea what it meant, but it was on my arm anyway.

It scared the crap out of me. I was the only one with it.

"Hey!"

I looked up in time to watch a body thrown across the front of my car. It bounced and dropped to the ground outside my door. I hurried out and saw the body was a skinny boy with scraggly blond hair. He looked like he hadn't showered in a week, and there were two holes ripped in his red T-shirt. The jeans were skin tight, not designer tight, but washed too many times tight. They rested an inch above his socks and sneakers.

He looked up in horror, and the look doubled when he saw who I was. As I closed the door and stepped to the side, two athletic-looking guys raced around and braked at the sight of me.

I was a Braden after all.

"Sorry, Shay." One of the guys rushed out, his chest heaving underneath a blue polo shirt.

The other guy ran a ragged hand through his own brown mop of curls. "Yeah, sorry. We didn't know you were in the car. We weren't thinking."

"So, if it was someone else's car and someone else had been in it, you'd still have thrown the boy? Do you do that a lot? Throw people at cars?"

The first guy flushed. "No, I mean...look, this isn't...I mean..."

"Shay." Kellan stood on the other side of my car. He'd materialized like he always did. As he gazed questionably at the two guys, he came around to join us. When he stood above the boy on the street, Kellan looked once at me, confused, but the look disappeared. He was amused, and he only leaned against the car, just behind me. As I looked from my brother to the other two, images of a panther keeping company with hyenas came to mind.

It wasn't too far off from reality.

"Um, I mean...hi, Kellan."

"Pete." Kellan tucked his head, content to let me handle the situation. Whatever situation it was, I wasn't quite sure.

"Look, you can't throw people at cars." I decided what the situation was. The boy was an obvious victim. The two idiots were bullies, and I was the one who needed to stop it.

A part of me cringed, knowing that Kellan wouldn't have cared either way.

It didn't matter. I'd just decided my role, and I clarified it again as I repeated, "You're bullying him. How old are you?"

Pete looked like his mouth had become glued shut as his eyes skirted from me to Kellan and back again. The other guy had yet to make a noise since my brother's appearance.

"His name is Scott," Kellan informed me. He didn't move from his leaning stance.

I kept my back to him. "Why would you even throw—what's your name?" I turned and glared my question. The boy seemed to tremble, but I wasn't sure if it was because Kellan's feet rested just around his, entrapping him, or if my attention was too much too handle.

"What's your name?" I repeated slowly.

Pete jerked forward. "Look, uh, this is just...ah hell."

I was starting to get irritated. "What's his name? Does he have a name?"

Scott came alive. "His name is Luke. We were just...we didn't mean anything bad by it. The kid was just in the wrong place at the wrong time."

"Like my car?" My irritation was growing, and in the back of my head I knew that Kellan was enjoying it. That sparked my irritation into anger.

I drilled holes in Scott and Pete, but something paralyzed them. They couldn't move, couldn't speak. They just stared, in horror. Luke had been sniffling during the entire exchange, but even that quieted. Everything just stilled, and my anger was nearing its exploding point.

It was like a battle had been waging inside of me. I wasn't sure what I was supposed to do. And then I decided to do the right thing, to save the boy, but nothing was happening. They wouldn't talk. I didn't know what to do because I knew Luke would be bullied again the next day, maybe even the same afternoon.

Kellan was loving it.

I took two threatening steps toward Pete and Scott. "You will leave Luke alone. You will be kind and courteous to him from now on. You will befriend him. You will do this, and you will be loyal to him, to each other, until you die."

I felt a spark ignite from my hand and explode in the air. Just as quickly as everything had quieted, everything slammed back into reality.

Pete and Scott's terror morphed into friendly smiles. Each helped Luke up and threw an arm around his shoulders. As they walked toward the school, Kellan noted, "That was...a nice thing to do."

"We're nice people." I grabbed my bag and headed toward the school.

Kellan kept pace beside me, his hands stuffed in his jeans. "We're not nice people, Shay."

"Shut up."

"We're not people, Shay. And what you did just there, a normal person couldn't have done that."

"Shut up." I didn't want to hear about what I'd just done. I didn't *know* what had come over me.

"You just bonded those three guys for life. You did it with magic, Shay. You don't ever use that stuff."

"Shut up, okay?" I shrugged him off, but Kellan caught my elbow. We turned a quick corner, another, and he shoved me against the wall.

"What is your deal?" I pushed back at him. "I thought this is what you wanted. You want me to use my powers, like you do, right? Like Gus and Vespar? Isn't this what you wanted last night?"

Annoyance flashed over his features before he gripped my arm tighter and leaned close. "You're on edge, Shay. Your powers don't come naturally to you like they do to us because you don't use them. We use ours all the time. I'm not going to accidentally kill someone if I get a little angry."

"Yeah, you wouldn't want to kill someone...on accident."

Kellan stiffened. I grew wary as fury formed in his eyes.

"You have something you want to say?" He grew quiet. Too quiet.

A chill slithered down my spine. "You're right, Kellan. We don't do nice things. You're a demon. We're all demons."

His eyes pierced mine. "We're not demons, Shay."

"No, we just come from demon blood. There's a big difference, isn't there?"

Kellan pulled me from the wall and against him. "Our mother was conceived by a demon. Yes, we have demon blood in us, but that doesn't make us demonic or evil or murderers. It just makes us not nice people, but we're not demons, Shay."

I kept quiet. He was reassuring himself, too.

Kellan took a breath, brushed some hair away from my face, and tried to compose himself. He added, forcing a lighter tone, "And you're wrong. This isn't what I wanted last night. I want you to stop denying who you are. It's dangerous. You snapped just now. You altered those guys for the rest of their lives. If you'd stop denying yourself, you wouldn't have done that by accident. You need to control yourself."

Holding my breath, I unwound Kellan's grip from my arm and pushed him back a step. He teetered backward, then took another step away.

"Fine, you're right." My voice was unsteady in the wake of

such intensity. "I'll...practice my powers. I won't do something like that again. I promise."

Kellan didn't say anything. He turned and nodded once, with his back slightly turned from me. He ducked his head and pushed his hands into his pockets.

I knew what that meant when he took that stance. He was off, and he needed to re-center himself. I shook my head, more to clear my thoughts than to deny what had happened. But then again...what *had* just happened?

Kellan shook his head. "I'm not really sure."

"What?" I looked up, confused.

"You just asked what happened. I don't know why you snapped. What were you feeling?" He swung those composed sapphire eyes to me again. The old Kellan was back, smooth, controlled, and oh so dangerous. He wasn't riled any longer.

I narrowed my eyes at him, thinking it hadn't been hard to push Kellan's buttons.

He doesn't get that pissed with me.

Gus was right when she'd said those words.

"Shay?" Kellan prompted.

"Oh yeah. Uh...what was I feeling?" I shrugged, "I don't know. I guess...I wasn't sure actually. I just wanted—I was frustrated. I wanted to help that kid, but I knew I really couldn't. Those guys would be beating him up later this afternoon and then you were there...I don't know. I just 'snapped,' I guess. It won't happen again."

Kellan nodded and pulled me in for a hug.

I closed my eyes and rested my head against his shoulder for a second. He was a lot of things, probably none of it was good, but he was my brother. And I knew that Kellan would do anything for me. Anything.

"Anyway," I pulled away and muttered awkwardly.

"Go ahead." Kellan read my mind and gestured around the corner. "I've got some things to do. I'll see you in humanities."

Humanities it was. That wasn't until seventh period, the only period I shared with Kellan and my other siblings. Kellan was a senior. I was a junior, where Gus and Vespar were both sophomores—twins. We tried to share one elective class a semester, and humanities was the chosen class this time.

I turned and left. I didn't want to ask what he'd be doing the entire day. I didn't want to know. And really, a big reason why I snapped was the pressure I always felt from Kellan. It was for the best if he was gone, for right now.

4

"That's new," Giuseppa drawled as she stopped by my locker.

I turned and looked. Sure enough—Scott, Luke, and Pete were walking down the hallway. Both Scott and Pete had their arms on Luke's shoulder, leaning in as if sharing a joke.

We weren't the only ones watching. Everyone in the hallway stopped to stare.

"It's the talk of the school," Gus informed me. She flipped her golden curls over her shoulder and hugged a book against her blue tank top. She eyed me, knowingly. "It's almost like someone magically told them to be friends."

Rolling my eyes, I retorted, "Shut up. I already got an earful from Kellan this morning."

"Yeah, well, you should listen to him. You changed their lifelines permanently. That's serious, not something I could pull off. I know that much. But still, Shay, there are others who are tuned into that stuff. They'll know a big player's in town now."

I scoffed at the idea of being a 'big player.' "I'm hardly that,

Gus. I just... It's not that big of a deal. He's not getting his underwear stuffed into his mouth anymore."

"Whatever. It's kind of funny, though."

"What is?" I was wary.

She gestured around the hallway as three slim silver bracelets jangled around her wrist. "Look at them. They don't know what to do. Two big jocks are now buddies with one of the nerds. Classic, Shay. Classic. It's like all their asses were turned upside down."

I wasn't sure about the imagery, but Gus thought it was funny. Just then, as my sister continued to laugh uproariously by herself, Leah and two other girls approached us. Or, well, Leah approached us cautiously. The other two stayed back, a few yards away.

Gus immediately stopped laughing as she eyed Leah down, hostile.

Leah fidgeted with the sleeve of her top. She wore a violet wrap-around light cloth shirt and kept tugging down the end of her sleeve, only to push it back up, and tug it down once more. The girl was terrified.

"Um..." She eyed us nervously and pushed forward bravely. "I was wondering... Do you know where your brother is?"

Gus stood to her fullest height, all five feet and ten inches. Comparing the two, Gus was the supermodel with her willowy figure, but I knew Leah was popular among the school. She was shorter by a few inches, slim, and her hair hung in two brunette braids that rested over her shoulders. There was a reason why Kellan had chosen to sleep with her, more than once.

"If he doesn't call you, I wouldn't go calling him," Gus warned thickly.

Leah backed up a step, but remembered her need. "I need to talk to him. He wouldn't talk to me yesterday, and I really need to talk to him."

"Why? If you're pregnant, it's not his. I guarantee that."

Leah flushed. "That's not what this is about. I just really need to talk to him." She glanced over her shoulder. I saw both of her friends give her supporting smiles, but neither of them budged forward. Leah was on her own.

"If you think you're dating him, you're not." The hostility increased in Gus, but before she could say anything else, I intervened and pulled my sister behind me.

"This would go a lot easier if you told us what you wanted from Kellan. We might help you."

Gus growled, which drew attention from every male in the hallway...who wasn't already watching.

I elbowed my sister as Leah tugged her sleeve down again. "Um, well, Kellan said that he'd help me with this thing if I needed it. And, well, I guess...it's like, it's now, you know?"

"Not in the least," Gus muttered through gritted teeth.

I rolled my eyes, resigned. I understood Gus' reluctance to help. Bradens didn't help, not usually. And no one ever sought Kellan out, much less for us to help in his stead. Still...I'd started the day out with a theme of helping. I might as well continue...?

"What do you need help with?" I willed the girl to bolster her courage and just blurt it out.

"Um..." She still faltered and then rushed out, "My stepdad just got home from a business trip. He's a drunk and he..."

And everything clicked. Even Gus perked up. We both knew what Kellan had offered to do. I finished for her, dryly, "And Kellan offered to rough him up if your stepdad hurt you, didn't he?"

She nodded, grateful.

I felt Gus' glee as she asked, "What'd he do to you?"

"Kellan?" Leah asked, confused.

Both of us flinched. "No, you idiot. Your father. What'd he do to you?" Gus cringed again.

"He did some stuff. Could you call Kellan for me? I don't

have his number. I don't even know if he has a phone, but...I...it can't happen again. Kellan said he'd stop him."

"We'll take care of it. Don't worry." Giuseppa was all smiles now. It wasn't a sight Leah was used to, nor myself, but I was pretty sure it shocked Leah the most as she instinctually retreated three steps before she stopped. Her friends quickly moved backward with her.

"I..." Leah wasn't sure what to say. Her eyes skirted between us again.

I smiled, or tried to smile, though I was a little apprehensive about what Giuseppa had in mind. "He'll be taken care of by tonight."

"You'll talk to Kellan?"

"We'll do it ourselves," Gus muttered underneath her breath.

"He'll be told. Promise," I tried to reassure her.

"Okay." Leah jerked a nod before she quickly melted among the rest in the hallway.

"We're not telling Kellan, right?" Gus asked anxiously. She was the one to eye me nervously now.

"I just told her that he'd be told."

"Yeah, but you didn't say when. Let me handle this, Shay. Please. I haven't had fun in a while."

I tried to figure out what my sister intended to do. I stared her down, despite the innocent look she flashed my way. I knew my sister, and I knew she wasn't going to pray for him. I warned, darkly, "Do not kill him. Do not do anything that'll bring attention to us."

Gus rolled her eyes and retorted nastily, "Right, Shay. You should be the one talking after what you did today. And no, I don't intend to do anything like that. But the guy will leave his stepdaughter alone after I'm done with him. Promise."

"You're not going to kill him."

"Promise," she repeated forcefully.

"Fine," I relented and was rewarded with a flash of perfect teeth. As she turned to leave, I called out, "And no Vespar involved."

Gus braked, didn't turn around. And then continued, but not before I heard a few choice words.

The bell sounded, and I heeded. The rest of the day was like usual. I watched, silent, as everyone else played their social games. The quiet ones stayed with their cliques and sent furtive glances at the popular ones. The geeks did their own thing and managed to avoid all contact with any jock. The popular girls whispered together or hung off the arm of their boyfriends. I caught sight of Leah one time, and she managed a tight smile my way. All of her friends looked my direction and then bent their heads over their table. The guys looked and quickly averted their gazes.

I wasn't a part of their social hierarchy. According to my bloodline, I was supposed to use them as pawns. I knew Giuseppa and Vespar did. I knew they loved the game. They loved the "mind screwing," how they put it. And I knew Kellan did it, but his appetite seemed a bit deeper. I wondered if he was happy with the shallow mind playing with the Leahs in our school.

I'd never wanted to do that. I'd never felt compelled and, if anything, I wanted to do the opposite. I wanted to stop it.

I felt a burning on my wrist and touched my sleeve. I felt the tattoo burning my skin. I wondered if it was rotating or staying in place. It moved at times, like when it knew I was paying attention to it. And other times, it was just there, like a reminder for something. I just didn't know what.

When I got to humanities, the tattoo stopped burning. Thank God.

I dropped my books and slumped into my usual table. We sat on the left side, by the windows, and in the middle. The populars liked to sit in the back, which was fine by us. It never mattered because my siblings surrounded me.

Vespar and Giuseppa slid into their table, just in front of me, and bent their heads close together. Kellan dropped his books beside me and slid into his own chair. He turned, studied me intently like he always did, and then lounged back in his chair.

Just then, Mr. Hawkins strode into the room and dropped his lecture book on the table before he took up a marker and turned to the board. "Okay, class. Tell me what you know about religion."

Silence scattered over the class and their conversations. And then, after a beat of silence, Leah spoke up, "I'm Catholic. Is that what you mean?"

Another girl raised her hand. "Was this part of our reading? I thought we were supposed to read chapter seven in our book? I don't remember any discussion on religion there."

Mr. Hawkins ignored her and looked at Leah. "Yes, Leah. Catholicism is a form of religion. You're correct. Now tell me about being Catholic." He smiled encouragingly and pushed up his thin wire-rimmed glasses. He tugged down one of his sleeves from his white polo shirt. His bicep muscle flexed, momentarily, and then it relaxed as Leah spoke up, falteringly, "Uh...I guess...I give confession."

"Purgatory!" Scott yelled out laughingly.

"Yes, Mr. Lorrells, but there's more to Catholicism than purgatory. There's so much more to religion than Catholics. Tell me something more class, please."

Kellan looked at me, long and hard, and then spoke up, clearly, "It's the intellectual battle for a soul."

Everyone was shocked, just as myself. The Bradens didn't talk in class discussions. We weren't called on, and we were never even required during a class reading. And now, here Kellan spoke up, our leader.

After another beat of silence, Mr. Hawkins gathered himself and rasped out, "Yes, Kellan, but I was looking for something more."

Kellan shrugged. "It's the idea of where the soul goes after death. It's about if the soul can be corrupted during life or not."

"And what do you think?" our teacher challenged.

Kellan smiled tightly and glanced sideways at me. "I think everyone's already corrupted, but there are some who don't agree."

Mr. Hawkins caught the glance and trounced eagerly. "Shay, what do you think? Do you think souls can be saved? Not corrupted?"

I was furious with Kellan, but I wasn't sure what to say. I was caught off-guard, "I think souls are just a prize to some. I think they can be saved, yes."

Both Giuseppa and Vespar turned around in their chairs, wide-eyed, as they looked at us, at me. I refused to flush underneath their scrutiny. Kellan had baited me for a specific reason. I wasn't going to back down.

"Do you think they're worth being saved?" Kellan challenged me further.

Everyone in class listened raptly. Never had a battle between the Bradens, much less Kellan and myself, been publicized. A pin dropping could've been heard in the silence between our dialogue.

"Am I worth being saved?" I asked him, no one else. I didn't care the class could hear.

Kellan shifted uncomfortably in his seat, but he replied, monotone, "Any soul has a choice, Shay. What do you choose?"

I grinned faintly. "Do I choose hell now and heaven later? Or do I choose heaven now, for the pleasure, and get hell as my reward? What would any sane person choose?"

"But that's the issue of this discussion. No one is going to choose hell first. Everyone wants the easiest, the quickest.

Everyone wants to be gratified now. You know they're going to choose heaven first."

"And get hell as their reward?" I asked lightly, a little hoarsely.

"That sounds like my diet," one girl exclaimed.

"Bethany!" Mr. Hawkins laughed, a little relieved from the intensity in the room. "What does your diet have to do with our discussion?"

"Nothing, really, but it's the same," she piped up brightly. "I can choose to eat Dunkin' Donuts now—heaven—or choose to eat my one serving of cottage cheese—hell—to get heaven later. What do I want to choose? The donuts, of course. What should I really choose? The cottage cheese."

"Is that what you want, Bethany?"

"Hell no. I want to lose ten pounds, but those donuts taste like heaven."

"It's called discipline!" one of the boys shouted out cheerfully. "I might want to get laid now, but I'm hoping heaven is all sorts of sex!"

Another boy laughed. "That's got nothing to do with discipline, Kent. That's called rejection."

"Well, if you'd put out, Brian, I might go to hell right now." Kent laughed good-naturedly.

The insults flew between the two. Before long, the class had separated into their own conversations. Mr. Hawkins was called over to a table for personal questions, and it was soon chaos in the room. That was, until Kellan suddenly spoke up, another first—to initiate a discussion—when he asked, "What if there wasn't heaven or hell? What if it's all to play with our minds?"

Silence descended the room. Everyone turned toward Kellan and then to Mr. Hawkins, who narrowed his eyes, pushed up his glasses, and folded his arms. His toned arms bunched underneath his shirt as he asked me, "What do you think, Shay? The two of you seem like you've put the most thought into this. Do you think there's a heaven and hell?"

I closed my eyes a moment. I felt my siblings' gazes. I felt their own intensity at what answer I'd give. And then, as my tattoo started burning again, I opened my eyes and stared right into my brother's authoritative gaze. "I know there is."

"Well." I felt Mr. Hawkins' excitement at an actual debate, especially one between two Bradens. "Can you explain more on your matter-of-fact statement, Shay?"

"Yeah," Vespar scoffed. "Those are big words coming from a high school girl."

Someone sucked in their breath. Someone else whispered, "Holy cow." Never had a Braden called out another Braden.

I felt Kellan's anger brimming beside me and knew it wasn't directed toward me. I also saw how Vespar glanced at his older brother, but he didn't backpedal.

Giuseppa grew still.

I leaned forward and spoke clearly, "We both know I'm more than a high school girl."

Vespar snapped his mouth shut, but not before he snuck another look at Kellan. Then he turned back around in his chair. The small challenge was officially closed, and I was the victor.

I just wasn't sure if I wanted to be.

5

A ll hell broke loose after class.

Well, not immediately after class, but as soon we left school. Kellan told me to go straight home, that he'd deal with Vespar. However, when I drove down our long winding gravel road, I saw that he hadn't quite "dealt" with our brother. Vespar was smoking, waving agitatedly in the air, and pacing back and forth by the river. Giuseppa sat on the bank, her knees drawn against her chest, and her head tucked between her legs.

I hadn't gone farther than two steps before Kellan's car zoomed and braked beside mine. Dirt flew in my face, but I didn't see it. Some of it nicked my leg, and blood was drawn, but I was intent on Vespar. Never had a Braden disrespected another in public. It wasn't going to fly now. I took another step and found myself hauled back.

Kellan was there. "Let me handle him."

"No." I shoved off his hand. "He pissed on me. I told the truth, Kellan. He didn't like it, for whatever reason, and he humiliated me! Me! Not you."

"I'll deal with it. He won't listen to you. He'll fight. He won't fight me. Let me do this, Shay."

"No!" I was out for Vespar's blood. I swung around, ready to charge, and found myself face-to-face with an equally enraged Vespar. His eyes were wide, pupils dilated, and when he shook a finger in the air, I saw the actual air move with it. I wondered if the trees swayed as well.

"You don't say that! You don't play with our lives like you did in class!" Vespar yelled at me. Giuseppa stood to the side, anxious, but still alert. Kellan fell to the side, and I surged forward. "He asked me a question. I told the truth!"

"How do you know, Shay?" Vespar laughed mockingly, bitingly. "How do you know there's a heaven or hell? How do you know when no one else knows?"

"I know because—"

"You know because you're a demon! Just like us, Shay. We're all demons. We're all going to hell. That's how you know, but are you going to tell them that? Are you going to—" Vespar interrupted heatedly. He shook his finger with each word until he stood an inch from my nose.

I took it. I held firm, and then I cut him off, "What life are you so worried about, Vespar? You can't die. You're a demon. We all are. We don't die!"

"Enough!" Kellan roared and stepped between us.

He didn't touch us, but his hands sparked, and we were thrown backward. Vespar went farther than me, and as I landed, a little unsteadily on my feet, Vespar fell to the ground. I quickly strode to where Vespar lay. "I spoke the truth. That's all I did. No one's going to think we're demons. No one's going to ever consider it, so you're safe, Vespar. Your little hide is safe because that's all you're really worried about. You don't care about me. You've never cared about me."

He looked up, dazed, but I saw the anger still there. His blue eyes snapped back at me as he cradled a hand on his chest, where Kellan had zapped him. "Humans can't hurt us, but don't you think there's something worse for us? We're half-human, but we're half-demon, Shay. We can go to hell. That's our rightful place—"

"Not if we're smart. Not if we..."

Vespar laughed coldly and rolled to his feet. "Not if we what, Shay? Not if we ignore all the sick, dark stuff we love? Not if we...what? I'd like to know. We've got a nature inside. It's called evil. We're evil. You're evil, just like us. You just fight what's inside of you better than the rest of us, but there's worse for us, Shay. Worse than just dying."

I frowned, caught off-guard.

Giuseppa stepped forward with her eyes narrowed and her hair pulled into a hasty ponytail. She murmured throatily, "They can send messengers after us, agents after us. You have no idea, Shay, because you never want to know. You don't want to know what we are, what you are. You're one of us. You need to start acting like it."

Messengers? Agents? A cold shiver slammed down my spine as I remembered my painting. Three angels were descending—I painted that after seeing Kellan portrayed as a demon. It didn't mean anything. It couldn't. I shook my head and rasped out, "It's no excuse. Just because our mother had demon blood—"

"Has," Giuseppa interrupted firmly, coldly. Her blue eyes studied me as if seeing me for the first time, like she was seeing something she'd never seen before and didn't like it. She stepped back, retreating, and repeated again, "Has."

"What?" I frowned, scratching absent-mindedly at my arm. The tattoo was burning...

"You said 'had.' Mom has blood. She's not dead, Shay," Vespar snapped back. "And you still need to hear us. You can't go talk about stuff like that. There are people, things, around that are more open-minded than most. They believe in stuff like us, like demons. They'll figure it out and send messengers after us—"

"—if they're smart, they will," Kellan finished for him darkly.

I looked at him, confused. "You want that?"

Kellan shrugged. "We're demons. If they're not coming after us, I'm going after them."

"Do you know who it is?"

"Does it matter?" Gus laughed shrewdly. "The minute they open a channel and summon something, we'll feel it and be all over them." Her eyes twinkled in anticipation.

I felt a shiver down my back, but suppressed it. This was my blood.

"Why do you always talk as if Mom is dead?" Vespar folded his arms over his chest.

Why? I opened my mouth to explain and stopped. I had no idea. "I...I never see Mom or Dad. They're never here. It's only us all the time." It had never been them. It had always been the four of us.

Giuseppa frowned. "They're here all the time. What are you talking about?"

Kellan stepped in between us and folded his arms over his chest. His eyes sparked. "I think that's enough. Vespar, don't ever challenge another Braden in public." Vespar opened his mouth, but Kellan finished, "Or be prepared for me to challenge you."

He shut his mouth with a snap. He raked his eyes over me and then Kellan. With a disgusted sound, he grabbed Giuseppa's arm and yanked her with him when he stalked to his car. Ignoring her protest, he shoved her in the car and took off, spitting gravel from the tires. When they were gone from eyesight, Kellan sighed. "Vespar will leave you alone from now on."

I didn't say anything at first. I spoke the truth, and Vespar couldn't handle it. But then I felt their darkness inside of me. I felt it twist around my soul and squeeze, if I had one. This was the family that I came from? I felt like I'd just gotten a bucket of boiling water thrown in my face.

"Shay."

I whipped my eyes to his and saw concern. "What?"

"What were you just thinking?"

"Why?" For some reason, I didn't want to tell him. For some reason, I didn't trust Kellan anymore and that shook me more than anything else. "Nothing. Why?"

"Because the garage just lifted off the ground."

I twisted around just as it landed with a crash. The cement was cracked as well as the bottom portion of the garage. "I didn't even...I don't know how to fix that."

Kellan stepped forward and waved a hand in the air. The garage was lifted again, and every crack was fixed. He set the building back down as if nothing had happened and then studied me again. I felt his gaze on me. It was heavy, as if wet cement covered me head to toe, and it was drying rapidly. A lot of different emotions were swirling inside of me, but I focused on one thing. I needed Kellan away from me. My head couldn't get clear if he was around. He always got in there and muddled everything up. I spoke hastily, "Leah came to my locker today."

He frowned more fiercely, but I felt a shift in his concentration. "What about?"

I wet my lips. "Her father hurt her. She asked us to tell you because..."

"I know why." He sighed. "I have to take care of that as soon as possible."

"You can go now. I'll be fine."

"I don't think I should leave you alone."

"No." I shook my head and hugged myself to ward off a chill in the air. It felt like it was trying to slip inside of me, winding around my legs, arms, neck. "You can go. I'm going swimming. That'll help me relax. I'll be fine."

Kellan stared at me, and I knew he was trying to read my

thoughts. I didn't think he could, but I clamped down on everything in my body. A wall slammed in place, and I figuratively
shoved him out. "Okay," he murmured slowly. "I'll go."

I held my breath when he turned and walked away. It wasn't
until after his car had driven off and was gone from sight did I
let it out raggedly. When I jerked forward a step, I wasn't
surprised at how my legs shook. Then I reached for the door
handle on my own car, and I saw that my hands trembled even
more so. As I cursed, I attempted twice to open my door until I
finally managed it. When I crawled in and shut my door, I
slumped forward and rested my forehead against the steering
wheel. It felt cool to my skin, and I pressed my cheek against it
to calm down. Then I turned, and my eyes opened slightly to
look at the house.

My house looked like it always did: tall, three stories high,
with a deck that wrapped around it. What was different was the
front window. Two people stood there, watching me. They
hadn't been there two seconds ago, but they were now. Their
eyes were large black holes, and the woman had white hair that
wrapped around her waist. Her mouth opened, and her hand
stretched to me as if she had a warning for me.

It wasn't the sight of them that jolted me. It was their pure
darkness that rushed at me. It was as if they'd come from hell
and wanted to take me with them. I screamed and jerked
upright. When I reversed the car, I slammed down on the accel-
erator and shot out of the driveway. It wasn't until I was miles
away before I slowed down to a normal speed, but my heart
kept racing. I knew demons existed. I knew ghosts existed, but
those two weren't either of them. Whatever they were, they
were worse. And I knew instantly they were more powerful
than I was.

"You don't have to be like them," a voice whispered from
behind me.

I whirled around, but there was nothing there. Then I

sensed all around me, in the car, out of the car, above, underneath since magic could come from anywhere. I couldn't detect anything. Magical spells always left a trail. Then I heard the voice again. "You've been given a reminder. You keep ignoring it."

I sucked in my breath and tried to concentrate on driving. The voice didn't send chills down my spine. In fact, I wasn't alarmed at all. I was more intrigued and cautious. "Who are you?"

There was no answer. I waited a few more minutes, and there was still no response. When I pulled into my school's parking lot, I turned off the engine and listened to the silence for a while. My heart pounded loudly, but my hands no longer trembled. I waited for the voice again, but there was nothing. So I asked softly, "What reminder?"

"The bracelet."

I pushed back my black sleeves, but my wrists were bare. "I don't have a bracelet."

Nothing. I waited ten more minutes, but there was no answer.

"Who are you? What do you have to tell me?" My heart pounded thunderously in my ear. I focused on that voice, only that voice. Everything in me strained to feel where that voice came from because it touched something inside of me. And that same something told me it didn't come from a foe, but from an ally, a very powerful ally. "Who are you?"

I held my breath and closed my eyes. The ticking from someone's watch pounded loudly in my ear. When I opened my eyes, I saw an older man across the road. He walked beside his son, and they were headed back into a house. The voice didn't come from him, but it was connected to them. I just didn't know how.

My phone vibrated in my pocket, and I was startled.

I gasped, and my eyes flew open. That was when I realized

that I'd never opened them in the first place. I looked around and only saw my school's parking lot. There were no houses nearby. The older man and son had been a vision. Somehow, I'd conjured them in my mind because they were connected to the voice.

My phone vibrated again.

I cursed because something snapped in me, and I knew I'd lost whatever connection I'd had to the voice. "What?"

"Hey, bitch." They sounded drunk on the other end.

"Who is this?" My patience was nearing an end.

"None"—hiccup—"ob your bidness."

When I looked at the caller ID name, I sighed. "Matt. What do you want? You need to leave me alone."

"Whatss your perblum?"

"What's my problem?" My translation was a little rusty. "Is that what you said? You called me, Matt. You're drunk. Say what you have to say and let it go after this. That's my warning."

"Your werning? What werning? You gib me a werning?" He laughed and then hiccupped.

My patience was running low, seriously low. I felt the vision of the old man slipping from my grasp, as if I could hold on to it. "Matt! I swear to your God that this is enough. One word and my brother will be at your throat. One word, Matt."

He was quiet on the other end except for his heavy breathing. Then he choked out, "Oh yeah? Well, he can just try."

The call ended after that, and I sighed. I didn't sigh because I was tired of Matt. Humans rarely annoyed me. I'd always been surprised at the patience I had with them, considering my bloodline. I sighed because I knew Matt had become a problem. If I didn't tell Kellan about him, Matt would feel that he'd overpowered a Braden. No one overpowered us. No one could, and if one thought they had, then he'd start on Kellan or one of the other two. I was fearful what they would do to him then. The chances of Matt graduating alive had just grown slim, very slim, unless I took care of him myself.

The school beckoned to me. The painting studio wanted me to come in there, and I knew I had something to paint. I almost wanted to go just to see what would be the end product, but I started my car again. Matt wasn't going away, and he'd have to be dealt with. Quickly.

"Don't," the voice whispered this time.

I turned the engine off. "What do you want from me? Who are you? I know that you mean well."

"Don't."

"Who are you? What do you mean I'm not like them? What is my reminder for? What is my reminder?" I didn't search out through my powers this time. I sat there and waited, hoping it would answer.

"Don't..."

Goose bumps rose on my arm, and my tattoo burned my skin. I hissed from the pain and clamped a hand on it, trying to stop it. Then my phone vibrated again. This time, I looked before I answered and saw it was Kellan. Instantly, I took a few deep breaths. I needed to be calm before I talked to him. He'd know right away something was wrong and would push until he knew about Matt or the voice.

"Kellan."

"What happened to you?"

I clamped my eyes shut. "What are you talking about?"

"Don't lie to me. I know something huge just happened. What was it? Tell me, Shay."

"Kellan, there was no—"

"Tell me!" he yelled.

My eyes popped open, shocked. "Why do you think something's wrong?"

"I just know, Shay. What happened?"

"Matt called me. He threatened me."

Kellan was quiet on the other end for a minute. "That's it? Matt scared you?"

"How do you know I was scared?"

"I felt it."

He felt it? I couldn't feel him, but Kellan might never get scared though. "How did you feel it?"

"I just did. It was Matt?"

"Yes." I whispered the word because I felt as if I signed over his death warrant. I should've held strong and not said a word, but Kellan had gotten a sniff. He was like a bloodhound on a trail. He wouldn't have let up until I'd given something to him, and I wasn't going to tell him about the voice. Something in me clamped steel walls around that secret. No one was going to be told that secret. If they tried, they'd have to kill me first. Then I wondered, as I realized how strong my conviction was, why I was willing to die for a voice inside my head? It was an ally, but why did I need an ally? Who was I at war with?

6

I turned my car around. Kellan was going after Matt, and no matter how evil Matt was, he was still human. Something inside told me painting would wait. This was the right thing to do, which was ironic. It was dark out when I turned my car down Matt's driveway, and I knew my brother was there. I felt his anger in the air. It surged everywhere, and then it switched dramatically.

Kellan knew I was there, too.

When I turned my car off around a bend on the driveway, where my car wouldn't be seen from the road or home, I wasn't surprised when Kellan stepped out from the woods. The driveway was a mile long, and it was cloaked by the forest.

"You came to do this yourself?" His voice seemed to glide toward me.

Shivers went down my back. "I came to stop you. I know what you're going to do."

"He's a problem. He threatened a Braden."

"Kellan." I sighed.

He stepped closer. "He threatened you."

"And if Giuseppa had been threatened?"

"She'd do it herself. He'd already be dead."

I swallowed a tight knot in my throat. "Kellan, you can't kill him."

"Why not? They'd kill us."

"With due reason. We're not exactly normal...things."

He was bored. "Let's get it done. I still have to get over to Leah's unless those two did the deed for me."

That wouldn't surprise me. "You can go. I'll deal with Matt —go handle Leah's dad. You're the one who said you'd do it."

"Deal with me? How are you going to deal with me?" Matt asked from behind us. We whirled around. I was shocked, but Kellan had a feral grin on his face. He'd known Matt was there, had probably been following him, and then came out when my car stopped. That was when I narrowed my eyes. "I thought you were drunk."

Matt shrugged. "I was. I'm not anymore. Does it matter?"

Kellan smirked. "I wanted him sober. I want him to feel what's going to happen to him."

Matt didn't react. He didn't seem fazed at all, even scared. There was a zombie look in his eyes as he swayed on his feet.

"You put him in a trance?"

"I did what I had to do. He was passed out in his own piss. I took him out, cleaned him up, and now he's ready to wake up."

I closed my eyes and groaned. "Don't wake him up."

"I thought you didn't want him in a trance."

"You know what I mean." If Matt woke up, then Kellan really would have to do something with him. He'd find himself in his driveway with us, sober. I wouldn't want him to make his own assumptions as to how he got there.

"Trance or no trance. What do you want, Shay? Choose."

"I'm choosing for you to shut up."

"Just," he seethed. "Watch your powers. I don't enjoy being silenced."

"Okay..." I looked at Matt, who'd been standing there. He

looked from one to the other, but the look on his face made me twitch inside. He trusted us. It was similar to a child's trust in their parent. "Kellan, leave."

"No." He moved to stand in front of Matt.

"I mean it." I touched his shoulder, but drew back, surprised. His muscles were tight, clenched together. That was when I felt a force within my brother that I'd never noticed before. I knew he was darker than the others, but this was the first time that I felt it.

It didn't sit well with me.

He didn't move.

"Kellan. I mean it."

"No, Shay. I know what you're going to do. You don't want me to hurt him, so you'll promise me the moon right now. You'll say something about you doing it yourself, and you're going to try to distract me with Leah, that I should be helping her instead. It won't work. I know all you'll do is try to wipe his memory. For someone who doesn't use her powers, you're dangerous, even to humans."

I was quiet for a moment, and Kellan relaxed slightly. Just slightly. Then he raised his hand to Matt, and I murmured, "You don't think I can do it?"

"What? No."

But it was too late. Kellan whirled around just as I lifted my hand in the air. I didn't do anything great. I thought one word, but tried to put extra oomph in it. *Forget!* Then the air zapped. It felt like a tidal wave of electricity washed over us. When I looked up, Kellan was staring at me with something that looked like fear in his eyes. Matt was on the ground. And I was...I looked down. I was floating in the air.

"Oh!" Immediately, I crashed to the ground.

"Do you know what you just did?" Kellan growled.

"Thanks for helping me up," I grumbled as I stood and then dusted off my pants.

He ignored me, staring at Matt. "I wasn't going to kill him, Shay. I was going to make him hurt for a while, and then I was going to turn him into our bitch. He was going to live life normally, but he'd always do whatever we wanted him to do. That's all I was going to do to him. Swear. Now, we have to sit back and see what you did to him. The most I do is wipe memories of certain events. I've never killed anyone." Kellan looked and stared directly in my eyes.

When I stared back, I saw multiple layers in his eyes. The first was human. It was what anyone would see. The second was more demon, but it was what he thought was the truth. A part of him really thought he was telling the truth, that he was only going to turn Matt into our servant. Then I looked past into the third and fourth layers. There were more behind them, but I saw what I wanted to see.

Kellan wasn't as in complete control of his demon as he thought. He had killed, but he either didn't know or he didn't want to tell me he knew, not at that particular time. A part of me knew it didn't make sense, but it was what it was. Kellan was telling the truth when he said that he was only going to brainwash Matt a little. Not completely. That was something, right?

"What do you see?" Kellan asked quietly.

"What?" I shook out of my own trance-like stare.

"You were looking into me, Shay. What did you see? I have a feeling you see something no one else does."

Something in his voice caught my attention. Narrowing my eyes, I studied him again. Kellan didn't move. He didn't twitch. There was an extra meaning in his words that I'd never heard. "What are you saying? What do you mean by that?"

Then it was gone. Kellan smirked and withdrew. "Figure it out." When he looked at Matt, he groaned. "Look at him. You turned him into an actual zombie."

"No, I..." My voice faded when I saw what he saw. Matt had a blank expression in his eyes. He lay on the ground with his hands resting together on his stomach. His chest still moved up and down so we knew he was alive, but there was nothing in his mind. I'd turned him into something like the living dead.

"I..."

Kellan cursed and then barked out, "Get up!"

Matt stood. He didn't move stiffly, but like normal. His eyes were so blank.

"You will remember your life. You will live your life as you did, but you will stay away from any Braden. Do you understand?"

Matt never blinked. He didn't say a word.

Kellan cursed again and then slammed his hand into Matt's forehead. As he did, he muttered something under his breath. The same energy sparked in the air, and Matt's body jerked alive. His back arched. His feet lifted off the ground. And then everything was frozen for a second after. Suddenly, Matt's body fell back to the ground, and he let out a strangled cry. As he fell, moaning, Kellan turned to me. His eyes were hard. "Go home."

"But."

Matt looked up, blinking away tears in his eyes. "Wha...who?"

"Go, Shay!"

His command bounced off me. It would've compelled someone else, possibly even our siblings, but I merely looked at him in confusion. "You fixed it?"

"Go. Do your painting."

I turned without thinking. When his words registered, I stopped and whirled back. "You know?"

"I've always known." Kellan gentled his voice and bent to help Matt back to his feet. He spoke to me as he watched Matt tentatively start to walk toward his home. "I know everything about you, Shay. One of these days you'll realize why it's me and no one else."

"What?" He knew about my paintings... Did he know about the ones of him?

He sighed and walked past me. "Come on. Let's go."

I watched as he got into my car, in the driver's seat, and then opened the passenger door for me. I got in reluctantly. "I feel like I have no idea what's going on anymore."

Kellan patted my arm and then wheeled the car around. "I'll even drop you off at the school. When you're done, I'll come get you."

As he drove, I watched him. Who was this new Kellan? As of a day ago, I would've never thought he'd be dropping me off to do my paintings. I would've had a heart attack even thinking about that possibility. And now it's happening. What else had changed?

A different thought occurred to me. "Do Vespar and Gus know?"

"About what you paint?"

He knew what I painted!

Kellan shook his head. "They don't know a thing. It's why they're so angry. They know we're keeping them in the dark about something."

My mouth was so dry. "About Mom and Dad?"

"What about them?"

I sensed a sudden stillness in him, but asked anyway. "Is it true? Are they around, but I can't see them?"

He hesitated for a moment. "Yes. They're there."

"Why don't I see them?"

"I don't know, but my guess is because you don't want to see them. You have the power to do that."

I looked down at my hands. They looked so human, clasped together as if I was praying. My skin even looked a little tanner, not the normal complete pale that I'd always been. Then I felt the tattoo burn on my arm. It started to circle my skin again.

My voice was hoarse. "Why would I not want to see our parents?"

Kellan didn't answer for a moment. When he did, his voice was soft. "I don't know, Shay. I can't answer that for you."

When we pulled into the school's parking lot, I didn't reach for the door handle right away. Instead, I looked at my brother and saw he sat guarded against me. He didn't want me to see something about him. I wanted to ask him what it was, but I knew I didn't dare. So I asked instead, "You know what I paint?"

"I know." He looked down.

"Do you know why?"

To this, he smiled. "Are you asking me why I think a demon would paint angels? Hell if I know, but there's gotta be a reason. Right?"

"You're not scared? Gus and Vespar would freak if they found out."

"Gus and Vespar are terrified of you. Period. Anything you do will freak them out."

It hurt hearing that, but it was true. "You aren't scared of me?"

"No." He looked up and met my eyes. He wasn't guarded this time, and he let me see into him again.

I hesitated, unsure if I wanted to look again, but when I did, I saw that the demon had grown still. The third and fourth layers in his eyes almost seemed loving. Peaceful. Suddenly it was too much for me.

The inside of that car was too overwhelming, and I couldn't handle being there so I reached for the handle and shot out. I took a few steps away when I heard Kellan say quietly, "I should be, though."

I paused for a second and then kept going. When I got inside, the car was already gone, and I breathed in relief.

"You shouldn't keep company with demons."

A surge of alarm shot through me, then out of me. Light

exploded down the hallway, and it highlighted who stood in front of me. It was a guy who looked my age, a bit older. He had brown hair that was slightly long and tucked behind his ears. His cheekbones were set high, giving him a classic model-type of handsome. When he smirked, I saw that he didn't care how powerful I might've been.

The light turned off then, and we were in the dark again.

"Who are you?" I asked.

He laughed. "You know who I am."

I didn't, and then I did. "You painted those other ones of Kellan."

"Yes."

"Why?"

"Why not?" He laughed again. "He's a demon. They're all demons. Why are you with them?"

I frowned. "They're my family."

"No, they aren't. They're demons. You're not. Why are you with them?"

Wait—what? "I'm not a demon?"

7

His eyes pierced through me. "You've always known you weren't one of them. You put a blanketing spell over yourself to stop from seeing it and dealing with it. What are you doing?"

"Who are you?" I wasn't a demon? I'd known this whole time? I heard what he said, but I couldn't think of that then. Who was this guy, and why didn't I feel like he was dangerous? How did I know he'd painted those of Kellan?

"You're not ready. You can't handle this yet."

He sounded as if he was saddened because of that. Then, when I felt like he was going to leave, I jerked forward. "Wait! Tell me who you are. I have to know."

"You know who I am, but I can see you're not ready to let yourself know. If you really want to know, ask Kellan."

Kellan knew? Before I could ask anything more, he vanished, and I was left feeling cheated of something. And then I hadn't turned the other way before Kellan spoke behind me, "I thought he might show tonight."

"What?" My voice was wrangled. What the hell was going on?

Kellan stepped forward in the darkness, but I saw him clearly as if it were daylight. His eyes were overcast, and his shoulders slightly slumped. "Because of the spell you did tonight. You turned a human into a zombie. Do you know what kind of power that takes? He thought you were ready."

"You turned him back." And he'd done it so easily.

"I know who I am. I know what I can do. I know what I'm supposed to do. I know what I can't do—not you. You don't know any of that."

"That guy told me that I'm not ready to know."

"What does my opinion matter? I'm not your brother, remember?" Kellan stepped closer and asked softly, "Isn't that what he said?"

I swallowed tightly. Painfully. "He said that I'm not a demon."

"You're not."

"How can you—how can you be casual about this? He told me that I'm not one of you, and you're acting like you don't care. It's like we're talking about if we should walk the dog or something." My chest was starting to hurt. My heart started to pound faster. And I knew something was coming, something I wasn't ready for.

Kellan felt it, too. I saw how his nostrils flared and felt his excitement. He was the predator in that moment, ready to pounce on whatever burst through the gate. I felt him whisper against my skin, "I am anything but casual, Shay. You can feel it from me. I can feel you, too. I know that you're holding back. You always hold back."

"You get mad at me when I don't." I felt him behind me, beside me, in front of me. He hadn't moved one step, but I sensed him circling me, measuring me. "What are you doing?"

"It's the demon. He's reacting to you." His voice was curt.

My body started to tremble, shaking back and forth. My heart picked up its pace, and my chest hurt. Opening my mouth, I tried to let out a cry in pain, but nothing came out. My voice had been choked off.

Kellan watched a few inches away with cold eyes. His watched mine.

"What's happening to me?" My throat felt like I'd swallowed thorns that slowly were going down, dragging from within, tearing into my skin.

He shook his head and moved back.

I felt his withdrawal and lurched forward. I needed him close. I needed him. When my feet remained in place, everything ricocheted inside of me. It was like I was slamming against an invisible cage, one that was inside of me and Kellan didn't care at all. He almost seemed to enjoy my suffering.

He bent his head, and his voice glided toward me in the air. "You can't hide from what's demanding to come out. The more you're with me, the angrier it will get."

"Kellan?"

I felt him leaving.

"Kellan!" I could no longer see him. "Where'd you go? Come back."

I was left with a whole host of "what the hells" going on in my head. The painter knew me. He knew Kellan. Kellan knew him. They both knew that I wasn't a demon. They knew more than what they shared tonight, and somehow I also knew this other information, too, but wasn't allowing myself to know it. Again—what the hell?

Then the man from my vision spoke to me. "You will learn. You are still a child."

His voice haunted me, but I couldn't see him. I couldn't see a ghost, and I was thankful for that little bit, which was ironic, considering I'd grown up in a demonic family.

When Kellan left, the mounting anger stopped inside of me. I didn't feel like I was inside of a cage, and instead, I was alone in a darkened hallway of my school. I could've convinced myself there'd been no painter, no Kellan, no haunting voice. Just me. I was merely a student. Human. But the overwhelming peace that entered me when I heard the old man's voice was too strong for me to ignore.

My relief when I heard that I wasn't a demon was too powerful. There was something inside of me, something I couldn't control. Kellan was right. I felt like a ticking time bomb. It was a matter of time before I exploded. There'd be no more answers that night. Sighing, I did what I always did when an urge was blasting inside of me. I painted. Four hours later, the result wasn't what I expected. My last painting had been of three angels descending. The painting before that had been a trail in a forest. This one was of me. I wore a cloak that was pulled over my head with my face peering out. There was a light behind me, and I was half-turned toward it. A shadow of something was coming out of the light, and my expression in the painting was that I was reluctant for some reason. I should've been scared. Kellan told me that I was scared of everything.

As I turned to leave, I took the canvas and lifted it to place on the floor. When I did this and stepped back, something in the bottom corner caught my eye. One of my hands in the painting was half-turned, as if I was about to reach out to the light. The other hung down on my other side, in the darkness. The end of it was dripping in blood. Something horrible was going to happen. I didn't know what, or how it would happen, but I'd have a hand in it. Literally.

Shivers went down my spine. I couldn't shake them even after I left the school and called Kellan to pick me up. When he arrived, the shivers only got worse. I was almost trembling as I got into the car and struggled to buckle my seatbelt.

Kellan spoke roughly, "You don't really need that."

Oh yeah. My now numb fingers let it fall back.

He added, "One of these days you'll forget you're not human."

"I'm part human." I was sure of that.

He didn't respond, and the silence grew between us. I felt like I was being suffocated again. Kellan had this effect on me. As we drove, neither of us spoke. I was slightly fearful he'd ask what I had painted, but then again, I wasn't sure if he really knew. All I knew was that I didn't want to tell him. For some reason, I wanted it kept private to myself. But then again, until this evening, everything I had done had been kept private. I had been in fear of Kellan finding anything out about me, of this—I wasn't sure either. Maybe it was because his demon was so powerful. Maybe I still didn't completely trust Kellan. Had I ever trusted him? Was I sure that I could trust him now?

"I can feel your thoughts. They're irritating me," Kellan growled in the darkness.

Glancing over, his side profile seemed attentive to the road, but I knew it was a lie. Everything in his body was tuned toward me. The human eye could be deceived so easily. I commented lightly, "I'm surprised you can't read thoughts."

"I can't read yours. I can read others."

"Like Leah's?" My heart skipped a beat when I asked. That situation had been bothering me since I first learned about her stepfather. And I couldn't help to wonder if he'd still gone over there—or what had he done?

Kellan didn't respond for a moment. When he did, his voice was rough. "Why don't you ask what you really want to know?"

"Fine." I took a breath. "Did you kill him?"

"I didn't even go over there."

His answer came so swift, too swift. "What do you mean?"

"I was going over there, but I felt something was wrong with you. I didn't go because of that. I changed course."

"You came for me?"

"You know I did. Why are you acting like this?"

"Like what?"

"Like..." Then he turned and watched me intently. "Like you're trying to figure me out. What is it? What do you want to know?"

Never had Kellan been so upfront with me. It blew my breath away for a moment. "Just like that? Anything I ask you, you're just going to answer?"

"I can see it's bothering you, so yes. Within reason, I'll answer whatever you ask of me."

"Why?" The question blurted from me, so quickly. He'd always been closed off, gone his separate way. Even Vespar and Gus didn't feel they really knew him.

"Because I can feel how important it is for you. That's why. You need more reason?" Annoyance flashed in his voice. "You only get a few questions. Pick wisely."

"You said I could ask you anything."

"I lied. You get three, three questions and I will be completely honest. I changed my mind."

I didn't think twice about one. "Am I actually a Braden?"

"As far as I'm concerned you are."

I nearly growled. "You didn't answer my question."

He shrugged, still driving. "I'll answer as best I can. I won't keep anything from you that I think you'd want to know."

"How can I not be a demon and still be your sister?"

A grin flirted at the corner of his mouth. "Is that your second question?"

I balled my hand into a fist and snapped, "I want to hit you. It's the same question. Answer it. You told me you would."

Kellan sighed, fighting back a grin. "Fine. Are you a Braden? Yes. Are we all Bradens? Yes. We all grew up together."

He still didn't answer my question. Somehow, his answer was a riddle, and I couldn't decipher it in that moment.

"What's your second question?"

Oh no. I'd just caught on to his game. "I'm not going to ask right now."

"What?" He threw me a look from the corner of his eyes, surprised.

"I get three. I asked one. I need time to think of the last two. There was no time restriction on the questions."

"Wha..." His mouth hung open for a split second. Then it snapped shut. "Fine. You can ask the other two anytime."

I could tell he was annoyed, but impressed. Good. That was what he got for keeping who knows what else from me. I wanted to ask about the painter. I wanted to ask if he knew what I was since I wasn't a demon and how long had he known. I wanted to ask if anyone else knew. There were so many questions, but I also wanted to know if Gus and Vespar were still my siblings. If Kellan was actually my brother. Since I didn't want to waste the last two questions, I was determined to answer as much as I could by myself. I needed to pick those last two questions carefully. Kellan wasn't normally a sharing being. I knew this honest side of him wouldn't last.

A mile from home, Kellan brought up another topic I hadn't considered. "What are you going to say to Vespar and Gus?"

"What do you mean?"

He sighed. "They can't know about you. They won't understand."

I narrowed my eyes. "Again. What are you talking about?"

"You don't look the same. Your new revelations tonight changed you. They'll notice. They'll want to know why."

And therein lays the problem. Gus and Vespar couldn't know, but know what? "They can't know I'm not a demon? Because they wouldn't be able to handle that, would they?"

Kellan chose his words carefully. "They're already on edge. You saw that this morning. They're scared that you might alert people about us."

"Like messengers?"

"Or others."

He was being evasive again. It was starting to piss me off. "Why can't you just tell me what the problem is? What are you hiding from me?"

"Are those your last two questions?" He grinned and then saw he shouldn't have joked. "Relax. Sorry. They're not as powerful as you or me. They have good reason for being scared. There are beings more powerful than them around. They could come here, and Gus and Vespar might not hold up against them very well."

"They're scared of being killed?"

"Or tortured. Witches, anyone who knows demon lore, knows our laws and how to get around them could hurt us. Some people enjoy hurting a demon. They think they can because we're essentially dark and evil."

"You guys are evil."

Kellan's jaw clenched, and his knuckles tightened on the steering wheel. "Regardless, our brother and sister don't deserve to be tortured for fun. No one deserves that."

"Isn't that what you do?"

He didn't respond, and the tension was suddenly thick in the air. His anger boiled. I felt it snap at me. And I knew the demon wanted to harm me, but Kellan fought it back. We kept driving, and he still hadn't replied until we got to our driveway. When he did comment, it wasn't about that. "You can't say anything to them about tonight. Matt. Your visitor tonight. Your paintings. None of it. Nothing."

"They can't know about Matt?"

"No, you're right. We dealt with Matt tonight. They'll know that he's been altered. They'll want to know why. We'll tell them the truth about that."

As we drove around the house and parked in front of the garage, I asked, "What about Leah tonight?"

"What about her?" Kellan turned off the car and glanced

toward the house. All the windows were dark, but we both knew our siblings were up. In fact, I knew they were watching. Gus stood in front of the living room window, and Vespar was framed by his bedroom window on the second floor. Both watched with somber expressions.

"What happened to her?" I asked him the question, but I saw the answer was with our other siblings. Blood. I felt it dripping from their hands. Of course, I couldn't see it, but I sensed it. It was there, and it had changed them. Somehow.

"Leah will be fine," Kellan said shortly and got out of the car.

"They killed her father, didn't they?" Who else knew? How could this be covered up?

"Stepfather," he corrected me, walking in front of me to the door.

My feet stopped in their place. Kellan knew they had killed him. He probably knew their intent in the first place, where they were headed once they left that afternoon. I saw that he didn't condone it. In fact, he approved. Then my eyes widened, and I asked, hushed, "Did you tell them to do it?"

"Shay."

I saw that he had. Something fell away inside of me. Maybe it was truth, maybe it was loyalty, maybe it was idealism? "I thought you had changed from today. I was wrong. I was *stupidly* wrong."

"What's the problem? It's not like you don't know we do this sometimes."

"You could've wiped his memory. You could've broken his legs. You could've—you didn't have to kill him."

"I didn't kill him."

"You had them kill him. His blood is on you, too." I gestured to the house, to our siblings, and then back to Kellan, to his hands. "I can't believe...after tonight..."

Suddenly, my anger raised a notch. My stomach churned on

itself, and I lifted surprised eyes to my brother. My hands lifted upward, and I saw my skin trembling. Something was growing inside of me, and it was angry. It was angry with Kellan. I felt the same hatred from before—what he had initially warned me. Whatever was inside of me hated Kellan in that moment.

"You need to go." Kellan jerked forward a step.

"No!" I stopped him. "Don't come close. I might—" I was scared of what I could do in that moment.

"Shay, you need to calm down." His tone was quiet, soothing.

"Why?" The word wrung out of me. Why did he care? Why now?

"Because you're going to hurt someone if you don't. The ground is shaking." He was completely still, frozen in front of me.

My eyes snapped open—I hadn't realized I'd closed them— and I felt it rumble beneath us. I could do that; I could make the ground move. No, it was whatever was inside of me. That was making everything storm around us. The elements answered to it.

"What am I?" I choked out.

Kellan looked at me with grave eyes. He knew I'd just used my second question.

8

The question hung in the air between us. I wanted answers, and I could see Kellan didn't want to give them. Then his eyes snapped past my shoulder, and he murmured, "They're coming. They can't know."

As soon as he stopped, the door opened behind me, and Gus asked, "Are you guys coming in or not?"

"Why?" I turned around. "You think we're going to sit down for a game of checkers?" I tried to hold back the bitter sarcasm, but I couldn't.

Her eyes widened in surprise.

Vespar stepped around her, his shoulders tense. "What's your problem? You were high and mighty before. What brought you down?"

The question felt like a challenge. He was still angry with me, but I didn't care. There was blood on their hands, and I could smell it. The stench churned my stomach. It sickened me. And I said as much, "You disgust me."

The air swelled around us in tension.

Vespar's eyes sparked in eagerness. A malicious smile flashed for a second. "I disgust you? What did I do this time?

Let's remember that I'm not the one giving out our secret to the
world."

Gus touched his hand, but he flicked her away.

Something started to stir inside of me. Maybe it was revulsion or just plain anger, but Kellan moved ahead of me before it
started boiling. He murmured, "Let's go to bed for the rest of
the night. We can calm down and talk tomorrow."

"You're going to let her talk to me like that?"

Kellan bristled. "Shay can say whatever she likes."

"Right."

"As do you." Kellan moved another step forward. He was
almost directly in front of Vespar now, staring at him
steadfastly.

Vespar narrowed his eyes. The anger shimmered just
underneath the surface, ready to burst out, but it never did. He
fought a battle inside of him and jerked around with his hands
clenched in fists. "Come on, Gus."

A sly smile flickered over Gus' face, but her eyes caught
mine. Her face went blank immediately, and then Vespar jerked
her behind him. As he dragged her into the house, her eyes
held mine. Something akin to fear and amazement flared
briefly. Then the door slammed shut behind her, and it was
only Kellan and me outside. We heard doors slam shut, and
then there was silence. It echoed around us. Eerily.

Kellan sighed. "Why did you have to bait him?"

"Same reason I'm not happy with you. You let them kill
someone."

His eyes found mine, searching. "Are you kidding me? I
know you might feel like you're holy now because you found
out that you're not a demon, but you've known your whole life
how we operate. This isn't the first time they've killed. And
Leah's stepfather needed to be ridded from this world. Trust
me. She wasn't the only girl he's hurt."

Shivers went down my back. "What are you talking about?"

"He raped three of her friends. They all wanted me to do something about him. He'd hurt more. He'd hurt you, if he could." Then he added, softer, "Besides, Vespar needed to hurt somebody."

"He wanted to hurt me."

"I wouldn't allow that."

My eyes clung to his. "Why not?"

His eyes closed, and I felt a wall slam between us. As he turned away, I already knew he'd retreated from me. "We should go to bed. I am a little tired."

We had another day of school before the weekend. Sometimes I wondered why we attended school, but Kellan always said a part of us were human. We should live as much as we could as humans do. And he was right, though we had demon blood in us didn't mean... Who was I kidding?

I remembered the painter's words. *"They're demons. You're not."*

Kellan started to go inside, but when he saw that I didn't follow, he turned back. "What's wrong?"

"I'm not one of you." I whispered those words and stared at him. A part of me wanted him to refute those words. I wanted him to say that I was. We both knew he couldn't. "I'm not a demon, so does that mean I don't have demon blood in me? Who am I, Kellan? You told me that you'd answer my questions. That's my second one."

Exhaustion appeared on his face as he stepped close and took my hand. He whispered back, tenderly "I will answer you, but not now."

I opened my mouth to argue, but he shook his head.

"I never agreed on a time restriction. I will answer that question, but not yet. And you are one of us. You're family." His hands squeezed mine once before letting go. "Come on. You can sleep with me tonight."

Something calmed inside of me. The human world didn't

approve of something like this, but something more primal existed in us. I still felt it, even if I wasn't a demon. Being close to another, to one whom you trusted, calmed us. I remembered Kellan's other words. *"You can't hide from what's demanding to come out. The more you're with me, the angrier it will get."*

He spoke now, as if reading my mind, "You quieted it. It's sleeping, or you've turned it off."

What is inside of me? My eyes clasped together tightly as I thought that. I put a hand over my stomach, as if calming the storm inside.

"Shay," Kellan spoke, now in front of the house.

I hadn't noticed that he'd gone ahead of me. "What?"

He gestured inside. "Come on. I want to sleep."

My head bent forward, and I followed, feeling meek for some reason, as I followed Kellan up the three flights of stairs to his bedroom. He kept the loft on the top floor. The rest of us had the three bedrooms on the second floor. As I climbed up the stairs to his room, my eyes caught sight of his king-sized bed. Images of girls writhing around in desire flashed in my mind. I barely held back my revulsion.

Kellan laughed softly from his bathroom. "I can feel your thoughts again. I've never brought a girl here, Shay. This is a sacred place."

Later, as we had both gotten dressed and ready for bed, Kellan lay beside me. I felt his heat curled against my side. Something felt right, but something didn't at the same time. He said softly in the dark, "You don't have to be scared of what's coming in the future. You're my family."

The way he said *'my family'* sparked something powerful in me. It was as if he laid claim to me or would die protecting me. I wasn't sure what he meant, but I wasn't brave enough to ask. A part of me was scared of his answer to that question, so I remained silent with my hands curled in the blanket.

"Sleep," he murmured next.

I closed my eyes, and a contentedness filled my limbs. I felt sleep invade my body, and when I woke, I felt refreshed, as if I'd slept for an entire week. I glanced at the clock. It had only been four hours. I looked the other way and saw that Kellan was gone. His space was empty, and his shower was running.

It was an odd feeling in the pit of my stomach as I tiptoed out of his room and down to mine. It was like I was hiding a secret, but when I was about to enter my room, Gus spoke from the hallway, "You don't have to feel ashamed."

I glanced back and saw she was in Vespar's doorway. "What do you mean?"

"You slept in Kellan's bed last night. It's not the same for us as it is with humans. It's not about sex, but comfort." She straightened to her fullest height. Then she tossed her blonde tendrils over her shoulder. "Vespar is my brother more than Kellan is. More my sibling than you are. You're feeling human emotions right now, but why you stayed with him last night wasn't human."

I swallowed painfully and tried to understand what she meant.

She sighed. "We're like animals, Shay. It's natural to sleep beside each other."

As she said that, I knew she meant it. However, there was something else in her. Anger. Resentment. Jealousy. Before I could start to try to figure out which, she smiled tiredly and waved over her shoulder. "See you at school, Shay. I'm sure all eyes are going to be on us now."

I'd called out another Braden in a class. She was right. They were all right. It wasn't done, but I hadn't understood why I had done it. I'd felt a sense of urgency at speaking the truth at that moment. Now, I knew that I'd wanted to break free from the Braden name. There were rules that went with being in our family, but I wasn't totally one of them. I was different. Some-how. I felt that a part of me wanted to act on it, as if setting it in motion that I really wasn't one of them. Then I remembered what else Kellan had said the night before. *"You're my family."*

I might not share the same blood, the same demon blood, but he was right. I was still family to them... Wasn't I?

"Look at you. He's got his claws in you tight, doesn't he?" Vespar drawled, leaning against his doorframe. He smirked. "You don't even know what kind of spell he's working, do you?"

"That's enough." Kellan appeared from the stairway, dressed in jeans and a simple white T-shirt.

The corner of Vespar's mouth curled upward in an ugly smile. His eyes flashed an emotion I didn't want to name before he turned and shut the door behind him. If he might've slammed it, it wouldn't have shocked me, but when it closed quietly, softly, a shiver passed through me.

"He's trying to get in your head. Don't let him," Kellan murmured, now beside me. His voice was soft as he watched me, studying me.

I straightened in my doorway and moved back a step. "Why would he want to get in my head?"

"To stop us from getting close." Kellan tilted his head to the side. His eyes seemed to be piercing through me. "If the two of us formed as close a bond as those two, can you imagine how powerful we'd be?"

My head jerked back. "What are you talking about?"

"I'm talking about war, between you and me and them."

"Why would you say something like that?" My voice was husky.

"Because that's what he's thinking. He knows we're close, but not as much as those two. He's fearful of what might happen if we do become that close. It's what he would do. That's what he's thinking in his head."

Kellan smiled sadly and straightened away from me. He held on to the doorframe above my head and tapped it absentmindedly with his finger. "That's how Vespar thinks, Shay.

That's not what I intend. It's not what you intend, but it's what he's filling her head with. He thinks there might be a time when the lines are drawn, and he's scared what side I might choose."

"So, he already knows I'll be on the opposite side?" Why didn't this surprise me?

"No." Kellan touched my shoulder lightly. "He's scared of you, but he's more scared of me. He's afraid I'll go against him... and if you take my side, we're unstoppable. The only saving grace he has is that he hasn't gone against me, and you haven't come into your powers yet."

The whole idea of siblings against siblings didn't sit right with me. I curled a hand over my stomach, as if warding it off, but it didn't matter. My stomach still rolled over on itself, sick once again.

"I can drive you to school..." Kellan murmured.

"No," I barked out, hoarse. "I'll drive myself."

"Okay." He didn't ask why, but I felt like I'd hurt him somehow. As he turned and went downstairs, I watched him go. His shoulders were strong, tense. His waist was trim. Gus was right. We didn't have to work for our bodies, but I felt that if Kellan had been fully human, he'd still have the same body. Then, with my hand still curled around my waist, I turned into my own room. After dressing in a light fabric black sweater that hung down to my knees and black tights that stopped just above my calves, I darted downstairs and to my car. I wasn't hungry. I was never hungry, so it didn't matter if I ate or not. My body didn't need a lot of food. It didn't need caffeine either, but I still enjoyed the taste of coffee and lattes in the morning. Once I stopped to get one, I was ready for the day. And as soon as I got to school, I felt it in the air.

Something had changed. Something was different with our school. When I went inside, everyone parted for me as they always did, but there was a different feel surrounding everyone.

"It's because of Matt," Gus answered my question when I

got to my locker. I looked up, my bag halfway in, and she
shrugged. "He was the reigning human here. You changed him
—you and Kellan—now everyone feels it. They don't know
what they're feeling, but they are. You see his little football
buddies?" She nodded in their direction.

I turned to look. There they were—four of his best friends
who always surrounded him, doing whatever Matt told them to
do. Today, they stood apart from him. They talked to each
other, laughed with each other, as Matt stood just to the side
with a confused look on his face.

Gus grinned. "He doesn't even know what happened."

Vespar strolled toward us in that moment, and I turned with
my back to my locker. My eyes caught his, and a challenge hung
from him. My throat was tight, but Gus laughed as he passed
by. "He thinks you did this on purpose, like you want to shove it
down his throat what you can do. Not me. I think you did what
you always do. You got angry and did something on accident,
then Kellan stepped in and fixed it. Am I right?"

Was she ever?

"I think it's funny," Gus went on to say, still leaning against
my neighbor's locker. Her bare shoulder touched the metal, but
she didn't seem to mind. She wore a halter-top and tight blue
jeans. "They're all clueless to what's happened. Their esteemed
leader can't be their leader anymore. Now, we get to watch
them squirm and figure out who's the next leader. Mark my
words. Two guys will throw down by the end of the day. It's just
like Kellan and Vespar. One day, they're going to throw down.
Vespar would love to now, but he knows Kellan can kick his
ass."

My eyes went to hers. That meant that... Kellan's words
suddenly haunted me. Did he know? How long had he known?

Gus smiled brightly. "No worries, sister. I'll always love
you." Then she sauntered away, flirting over her shoulder with

a few guys who watched her go, her hips swaying back and forth.

I turned to close my locker, but something tingled in the back of my neck. I turned and saw Kellan watching us from a distance. Leah stood beside him with some of her friends behind her. They all watched him as he watched me, studying me. His eyes were guarded, but I tried to send a small smile to him. It was like I wanted to reassure him about something, but I didn't know what. It failed miserably. Kellan's eyes narrowed when he saw this attempt, and his jaw tightened.

Leah and her friends skirted away, nervous. They all had confused looks on their faces.

Gus was right. So much happened that humans didn't know about. Their bodies sensed it, but their minds weren't in tune with their bodies. It was like they were the dumb animals, and we were the predators. We knew what was going on, they didn't.

I sighed with my textbook against my chest and headed to class.

9

The next few days were tense. Vespar and Gus stuck to themselves. Kellan stayed away from me and even the house. He didn't sleep there for the next week. I didn't ask why or where he went, but I didn't think anyone else did either. It seemed that everyone was at an impasse, and no one wanted to spark something that could change everything.

As for school, Gus had been right. Two of Matt's closest buddies were in a shoving match in the school parking lot at the end of that day. Matt stood by, dumbfounded. We'd changed him permanently, like he'd been rewired inside or taken the fight out of him, but he was no longer their leader. Instead, the winner had been Dylan Cavanagh. He was another football player, typical douche, and he walked around school with his arm on some trophy. Those girls all looked the same to me: skinny, pretty, long legs.

The last day Dylan had started eyeing Gus and me. I used to enjoy playing with guys like him, teasing, making them confused. Now, I stayed away, although I doubted Gus would do the same. I was sure she would play her usual games with him, but I didn't want to know what those were.

In the last week, I learned I didn't want to ask any more questions. The entire event of going against Vespar in class and everything that unfolded afterward had left a bad taste in my mouth. And learning that Kellan knew things about me didn't sit well in my stomach. Everything had become chaotic, and I wasn't sure how much more I wanted to take.

"Kellan's not at school again," Vespar commented as he stopped by my locker. He had a guarded look on his face, but he still managed to glance around with a smirk.

"Yeah." I wasn't sure what else to say.

"Where is he? Did you two have a fight?"

"I thought it was because of you."

"What do you mean by that?" He straightened and looked directly at me.

"You're the one he wasn't happy with. Not me. Or do you not remember last week correctly?"

A sneer flashed over his face, but it was gone instantly. "I remember you calling me out, and that he decided you could talk however you liked to me. Or am I wrong, Shay?" He leaned closer to me, almost in my face.

I glanced around and saw that everyone seemed to be aware of us. A few quickly looked away, but some stared blankly, enraptured by the tension between my brother and me. "Better watch out. You're doing what I did to you, and by the way, I didn't mean it how you took it. I didn't mean to go against you. I just..." I couldn't tell him that I wanted to break free, break away from the Braden rules. Vespar would think that was even more of an insult, like I was better than him, than the Braden name.

Vespar rolled his eyes and shifted so no one could see our faces. He spoke in a low voice, "I stand by what I said at the house. You're pissing on us, and you don't care. That makes me mad, but Gus wants us to make up. She wants things right, so fine. Whatever. As far as I'm concerned, you and I are fine. I hold no ill will toward you. Okay?"

It felt more like an order than a truce offering. I nodded, though. "Fine."

Relief rolled off his shoulders, and he straightened. A little more bounce seemed to be in his frame again. "So, really, where is Kellan?"

I shrugged. "I don't know, Vespar. I wasn't lying. He's not happy with you."

His eyes narrowed. "What do you mean?"

"What do you think I mean? You disrespected him to his face. You told me that he had his hooks in me. You don't think he didn't hear that? He's staying away for a reason, and things were fine with him and me. It's you. I'd be worried if I were you."

He frowned.

Giuseppa chose that moment to throw an arm around her brother and laugh as she poised next to the lockers. "How are things going? Are we all a loving family again? I certainly hope so." When neither of us commented, her eyes danced between us, and a small frown appeared. "What's wrong? What now?"

Vespar shoved her arm off and stalked down the hallway. Dylan chose that moment to turn into our hallway, right in front of Vespar, with his arm around a different girl. He stopped, saw a Braden coming his way, and glanced to the side. Then his shoulders straightened, and his feet stayed firm. Vespar saw it all as he kept approaching, reached out, grabbed Dylan's shirt collar, and slammed him into the lockers. Two girls screamed and scattered out of the way.

"Oh God," Giuseppa groaned. "What did you say to him?"

I watched as Vespar punched Dylan and then threw him onto the ground. None of his friends rushed to defend him or even help him from the floor. Then my brother continued on his way, his shoulders seemingly less tense.

I arched an eyebrow. That was interesting. "I just told him that Kellan must be staying away because of him, not me. Kellan and I were fine."

"What?" Fear sparked in her eyes. "You said that?"

"It's true. Vespar was out of line, not me. I spoke the truth, and then Vespar called me out. You think that made Kellan happy? Then he called out Kellan later when he asked why he let me talk to him that way. That's like a slap in Kellan's face. Then the next morning, he told me Kellan had his hooks in me. He heard him. Vespar's got a problem, and he knows it. I can't believe he said half of what he did."

She froze, and the fear grew. "You're right. Oh my God." She glanced over her shoulder, as if she could see Vespar, who had already vanished into another hallway. "What's he going to do? He didn't think that out at all."

I shrugged and exchanged my books. "It's not my problem."

As I started to leave, Gus blocked me. "Yes, it is. Our brothers can't be fighting. Do you know how bad that is?"

Not as bad as it's going to get, I thought to myself, but gave her a clueless look. "What are you talking about? You're the one who said this would happen anyway. You said that Vespar would do it now, but he knows Kellan would kick his ass."

"They could kill each other. And I was joking. Kind of."

"Or Kellan could kill Vespar. He can't touch Kellan, and everyone knows it. And why would you joke about that?"

She swallowed tightly. "Come on, Shay. Please do something. Say something to Kellan. Please. I can't have us broken up. I love Vespar, but I need you two, too. It's the four of us against everyone else. Don't let something happen to that. You can stop this."

"Why not you? Answer my other question."

"Because...okay. Yes. I think Vespar wanted to fight Kellan last week, but he doesn't anymore. He's over it. I'm over it. And I really was joking. I really don't want us to fight. That would be horrible. And because Kellan loves you more. Everyone knows that. He's almost obsessed with you. If you weren't his sister..." She shuddered. "You get my drift."

I did, and I wasn't fully comfortable with that. I didn't have a good feeling about it, but another side was... I wasn't going to focus on that. It didn't help anyone. I could also tell that a part of Giuseppa hated admitting that to me.

"Shay."

I sighed in surrender. "I'll find him after school and see what's really going on."

She relaxed. "Thanks."

Then I gestured to Dylan, who had gotten back to his feet and stood in a circle of his friends. He was throwing dark looks our way. "What about him? I don't want to turn someone else into another zombie."

Gus smiled. "I'll take care of him." She didn't have good intentions from the way she said that, but I needed to pick my battles. The old Gus was back, appeased now that everything was going to be fine.

"Just don't kill him," I murmured under my breath before I left for class.

"There are other ways." My sister sounded more excited than she should've been.

Kellan wasn't at school that day, and I didn't have hope that he'd show up later in the afternoon. I sent a few text messages to him, but he didn't respond. When I called, it went straight to voicemail. As I was leaving, trying to figure out where I might start looking, I wasn't expecting to find Dylan Cavanagh, so I almost bumped into him when I reached for my door. Before I made contact, I managed to jerk backward. "What are you doing?"

He straightened from my car and stood over me, reaching his fullest height. "I have a bone to pick with your family."

He rubbed a hand over his jaw where Vespar had punched

him. I saw it had darkened even more and was now an ugly shade of black and purple. "Really?"

"Yeah." He puffed up his chest. "It's not right that you guys get to walk wherever you want, do whatever you want. Kellan's been gone from school all week, and no one will say anything about it. You guys aren't special, so you shouldn't be treated like that. Vespar's going to get his ass kicked, too."

"Really?"

His eyes narrowed. "Yeah." He expected me to cower before him. I wasn't at all, and that wasn't adding up to him. "Me and some of my buddies are going to take down your brother. You might want to warn him."

"Really?" I scoffed for the third time.

"Yeah."

Then I smiled. "Good luck with that. Now, move."

He did, but only because he was confused. As I drove away, I saw my sister swaying her way to him in my rearview mirror. Her hand lifted to trail over his shoulders, and he was already entranced by it. Shaking my head, I kept driving. No matter who did it, somehow Dylan would be put down like he was a dog. I had no doubt that he'd come to school the next day with his tail figuratively between his legs.

They always had to learn.

When I got to the house, instead of going to my room, I went to Kellan's. It felt strange going up there without him there and especially because the last time I'd been there had been when I'd stayed with him. The place seemed to hold his presence in it, even though he wasn't there. I felt him everywhere. Strongly. Suppressing a shiver, I glanced around and tried to focus on what I needed to do. I wasn't sure what exactly I was looking for, but I wanted some idea of where he might've been. Maybe he had written down some information...maybe not. I doubted it, but I was willing to try. When I didn't find anything, I wasn't surprised. My brother was a very clean person/demon. Then I sighed and gave up. As I went to my own room, something was nagging at me, almost tickling the back of my neck. It was like I was forgetting something...

Then I groaned and called my sister. When she answered, I asked, "Has Leah been at school this week?"

There was silence and then, "No. I didn't even notice."

"He's probably there. Don't you think?"

"Are you going over there?"

"I guess. I mean, I have to, right?"

"It'd be good if you talked to him soon."

"Okay." I nodded. "I'll go over there."

"Okay." Her voice sounded curt, as if she had been interrupted.

I asked, "What are you doing?"

"Nothing," she said quickly and hung up.

And that meant she was doing something. I shook my head and left again for my car. I could only handle one of my siblings at a time. As I went outside, Vespar was walking toward me. His eyebrows shot up. "Where are you going?"

"Nowhere." I threw that over my shoulder as I passed him swiftly. He turned to ask again, but I shut my car's door and quickly reversed to drive away. Vespar still stood there as I turned onto the road. I could feel his confusion.

As I drove to Leah's, I tried to remember the way. I'd only been there once to pick up Kellan. I never asked questions, and he never offered any answers. He'd reeked of sex, though, and a part of me didn't want to find him in the same manner. As I pulled up to her house, I tried to sense Kellan from my car. I sensed him good and plenty. His presence wrapped around me like a blanket. It was powerful, so powerful that when I went to the door, I half expected him to answer it himself. He didn't. Leah did, looking pale and gaunt. Her eyes had a scattered look in them, like she was in the middle of a stampede and didn't know where to go for safety.

"Is my brother here?"

Before she could answer, Kellan asked from a back room, "What's wrong?"

Leah vanished into a back room, and I turned to scrutinize my brother. He looked tired. Why did he look tired? I asked as much, but he clenched his jaw and countered with, "Why did you come here?"

"Because Gus asked me to find you."

"Why?" He narrowed his eyes and rubbed his jaw, but glanced toward the room Leah had gone into.

I looked, too, and wondered what had happened between them. Why was he here? What was wrong with Leah? "Is this about her stepfather?" Then I looked around again and saw how sparse it seemed. It was as if only Leah lived there. I couldn't feel anyone else. "Where's her mother? Her real father?"

Kellan grimaced. "Our siblings got too excited last week."

I waited for more of an explanation, but he didn't offer any. "That's it? What does that mean?"

"It means..." He weighed his words. "It means that when they came here, Leah's stepfather wasn't alone. Her mother and real father were also here. They'd all been having an argument, but Vespar didn't care. Neither did our sister."

I reeled from what he said. That meant...no wonder the blood had affected me so much. I'd tried to become numb this past week because of that night. I didn't know what to do, or if I should do something. I asked, shaken, "So...what are you doing here?"

"I'm trying to make her better." Kellan still watched the door, as if he could see her through it. "She asked me for help, to stop her stepfather from hurting her. She didn't ask for this. She's hurting even more."

"Wipe her memories. You do it all the time."

He shook his head. "I can't. After what we did to Matt, I

can't do more magic. It'd alert too many things we don't want to come here."

Things.

Messengers.

I swallowed hard—what I had painted. Then I closed my eyes. "What are you going to do to Vespar and Gus?"

"Nothing."

I looked at him and saw he was frowning at me. "What? Nothing?"

"Why would I do something?"

"Because this is wrong! What they did was wrong."

Kellan tilted his head to the side in wonderment. "Shay, we're demons. That's what we do. We do bad things. I do bad things, too."

"But..." I didn't.

He nodded. "You do, too."

"I don't try to hurt people. And I don't have demon blood, remember? You won't tell me what I am."

He gripped the back of my head in the next instant. It happened so fast, I only had time to jump in shock before Kellan pushed me against the wall. He leaned forward as his hand had a tight grip on the back of my skull, keeping me in place. "Even if you don't share the same blood, you're one of mine. No matter what anyone might say, you're mine. Understand?"

Mesmerized by the ferocity in his eyes, I nodded. I couldn't say anything. His words seemed to penetrate inside of me and squeeze hard. It was like my entire body was under his control. Then, something shifted inside of me, and I gasped, arching my back and thrusting Kellan away from me. I was angry. It was anger and hatred boiled up in me. My hand shot up, and energy burst out of me. It slammed Kellan across the room, then I said, heated, in a stranger's voice, "Get away, demon! Die."

Kellan's face snapped up, and his eyes showed his demon. The pupils were diluted, and the entire orb was black and red. He hissed back, "Do not interfere!" Then his eyes changed, and my brother took control again. He spoke more calmly, "Shay, take control. Shay, stop it. Take over. Put it to sleep."

My body trembled, and I felt the fight inside of it.

"Shay." He flung his hand up, and something sparked me. My body hit the wall again, and when I looked back, Kellan was right in front of me. His hand cupped the side of my face. "Shay?"

I nodded. Weak. "I'm okay. What was that?"

He grimaced again and looked even more exhausted than before. "I should check on Leah."

"No." I stopped him with a hand on his arm. Something propelled me toward her room. "I can help her. I know it." I didn't know how, but I felt it. When I opened her door, Leah was curled in a fetal position on her bed. She had wrapped a blanket over her and didn't move, not even when I sat on the edge of her bed. With a hand placed on her arm, I closed my eyes, bent my head, and something warm went through me into her. I didn't know what it was, but it felt right. As it ended, I looked back up and knew that Leah slept in peace.

She looked the same as I had entered the room, but everything had changed. I didn't know what I did, but I knew she'd be fine. Somehow, her parents' death would make sense to her, and she'd be all right now.

I went back and closed the door behind me. Kellan stayed where I had left him, tense. Then his eyes seemed to search mine, into me, when he asked, "What'd you do?"

"I don't know, but I do know that you need to give me answers. What am I, Kellan? You tell me now, or I'll let loose whatever I have inside of me. Whatever that is, hates you. And I know that it wants to hurt you. It would do it now if I let it. Because I love you, and even though I don't share the same blood, I am still family to you. I won't let that happen, but I can't hold it off much longer. It's getting stronger, Kellan."

He nodded, closed off to me. "I know."

"So what am I?"

Resignation clung to him. "You're the opposite of what I am."

10

"I'm an angel?" Even as I asked that, I was wondering to myself if I actually believed in them. I had thought I was a demon.

Kellan shook his head. "You're a Nephilim."

"What's that?"

"Part of your blood is from a messenger, yes. Part of you is human. That's the part that's mine." He spoke with the same force as before.

It stirred inside of me, but I controlled it. I wasn't going to let it out, not when I was finally getting answers. "I'm...how... there's a lot that I don't understand, Kellan."

He nodded, sympathetic. "I'm sorry. I am." Then he looked away. "I can't lie to you. I—"

"What?"

"Nothing." He shook his head abruptly. "I can't tell you anything more. I don't know anything more."

I was half of a messenger. He was half of a demon. Who the hell were our parents? How did we end up under the same roof? "Do Vespar and Gus know?"

"No!" Kellan laughed out, hoarse. "God no. They'd... They can't know. Trust me."

"Why?" Although I was pretty sure I knew why.

"Because they'd kill you. You know that."

I had, but it was painful hearing it. "And you? Why don't you kill me? Why haven't you tried?" I laughed. The sound came out nearly hysterical. "This makes us enemies, doesn't it? Something inside of me wants to kill you. I'm sure your demon wants to do the same to me."

Kellan quieted and watched me. His eyes seemed to pierce me, looking into my soul. It was uncomfortable and I waved a hand. "Stop it. Just...stop it. I can't handle you being inside of me."

"That's not what I'm doing. I'm trying to figure out what to say to you to make it better. I don't know what to say right now."

"You know everything." All my life, Kellan had been our leader. He'd been the strongest. The fastest. The most powerful. The one who always knew what to do, who could handle anything. He couldn't handle this and that said a lot. At the same time, it was like he'd taken a knife to my heart. I felt him stabbing me one, two, three times—like I'd been gutted. "What am I supposed to do with this information? Where do I go now?"

Something shifted in him, and he glanced to Leah's room. "She's okay?"

"Yeah. She'll be fine now."

"She won't need me here?"

"No, she shouldn't. I made it okay with her. I don't know how, but she'll be fine. She might remember, she might not. She might think of something to justify everything in her mind. I don't know, but she'll be fine. She's at peace now."

I had done that. The messenger inside of me had done that. It felt right, but strange. It also felt like I'd chosen a different side. The line had been drawn. With that action I chose the other side. Kellan might not admit it, but we were enemies. I felt it in me. A part of me wanted to kill him.

"Let's go somewhere. I'll..." But he didn't know what to say. Kellan looked around, helpless. I saw it all over his face. It was heart-wrenching. He had no idea how to make this better, and my brother always knew. Then he frowned sharply. "Why did you come here again?"

Where did I start? "Vespar came up to me at school today. He thinks you're angry with him. Then Gus pleaded with me to find you. She's scared that you and Vespar are going to fight, breaking all of us up."

He narrowed his eyes. "Why would Vespar think that I'm angry with him?"

I shrugged. "I have no idea."

"Shay?"

"I might've told him that."

A normal being would groan in frustration. Kellan flashed a smile. "Really?"

I couldn't help but smile back. "Now I'm glad. They're both on edge because of it. I was just going off what you told me, that Vespar thinks we're going to war with them."

He laughed now. "I said that because he does think it. I didn't mean today or next week. I meant in the future. He knows the lines are drawn. He knows the alliances, and you and I are more powerful than those two. I have no intention of fighting them now."

"They don't need to know that."

He quieted and asked, "Tell me the real reason why you found me."

"Matt was replaced by Dylan Cavanagh. Vespar punched him in the hallway. I think he's a little pissed. He's already started trying to bully me. He threatened us, said that we won't get away with half the stuff we do now."

Kellan sobered, watching me. "That's not why you sought me out either. Why, Shay?"

He was annoying when he did that. "I don't know. I really don't." And I didn't, not really. I could've guessed, but those were emotions I didn't want to acknowledge, especially now.

"And if I were to guess, I'm sure Vespar or Giuseppa have already dealt with him. Am I right?" Both of his hands cupped my cheeks, and he cradled my face now. "What's going on with you, Shay? Don't tell me that it's you being a Nephilim because you sought me out for a different reason. We will deal with your different parentage. I'm not concerned with it, not how you are, but I know things will be fine. That's not the reason why you came here. Tell me why."

I opened my mouth to say something, but I had no idea what. So I halted, speechless, as he held me in his hands. When his thumbs started to brush against my cheeks, caressing back and forth, I couldn't help but to close my eyes and lean into his touch. It was like I needed it. I needed him. I had sought him out because I needed this. The reality of that rushed through my whole body, and I jerked away.

Kellan didn't let go. He felt the tension in my body and instead wrapped his arms around me, anchoring me against him. We stood there, enveloped together, as he murmured into my hair, "You need to be more honest with yourself. You have all the answers, Shay. You decide where we go from here."

My hands balled into fists and rested helplessly against his shoulders. I was half-hugging him, but I felt like I was half-dying at the same time. "What does that mean? I have no idea."

"What do you want?" His breath teased my forehead.

His phone rang, and we both knew it was important. No one would call Kellan unless it was me or something life and death. He pulled away and looked at it. His voice was rough. "It's Gus."

Something had gone wrong.

We both felt it, and then he answered, "What happened?"

I listened to her nearly hysterical voice before he interrupted her, "Where are you?" A second later, after she told him, he added, "We're coming." Then he hung up. As he pocketed the phone, he took my hand and pulled me behind. "She's in trouble."

As we left the house and got into his car, I asked, "What happened?"

"Cavanagh is into demon/devil worship stuff. He had some tricks up his sleeve. Gus couldn't handle herself and killed his entire family. It's too much. We can't handle this much death on our hands. Messengers will come now."

The ride was tense. All the new revelations didn't sit well with us, or with me. What was I supposed to do now? Where did my loyalty lie? Kellan didn't say a word, and neither did I. He parked outside of a huge house that I had no doubt was Dylan's. They always seemed to come from money. Gus appeared in the door, frantic and pale. She had blood over her entire body. It dripped onto the floor, leaving bloodied footprints since she was barefoot. "I don't know what to do, Kellan. They..." She looked back, fearful. "They're all over. They all came home."

She choked off the rest and looked away.

We stepped around and surveyed the scene. Bodies were everywhere. Their eyes were all wide-open, blank. Death glazed over them.

Kellan asked, almost normal, "Where's Vespar?"

"He's home. He didn't want to come once he knew I had called you. I'm sorry, Kellan. I really am. I know that..." She didn't say any more, but bit her hand with tears running down her cheeks.

This wasn't a scene I was used to, but I felt like Kellan was. That unnerved me the most. Gus seemed hysterical, like she had done something she hadn't wanted to, but he was cold—

completely cold to what had happened. I felt a kick in my gut and knew the messenger sensed what was going on. It was angry. Again.

Kellan looked at me sharply. He sensed the messenger in me, too, but I clamped down and quieted it. It went silent immediately. He looked back to the room and asked, disappointed, "There was a child, Gus?"

She bit back a cry. "There were three of them. I didn't know. I was so—he was chanting something, and it was hurting me. When they showed up, he stopped, and I was so mad. I couldn't hold back. I didn't know they were here until... I am so sorry, Kellan."

I bit back everything and numbed myself. That was when I started actually looking at the bodies, at who they were. "He's not here. Dylan isn't here."

Kellan whirled around. We both looked at Gus. She shook her head. "I don't know where he is. I'm sorry."

"He's still alive?"

"He knew things...chants..." She looked away, still crying.

A sudden realization occurred to me. "He knows what we are."

She nodded, still turned away.

"Oh my God."

Kellan didn't say anything, but then he waved a hand over the bodies. As he started to mutter some words under his breath, Gus gasped, "What are you doing? That will bring them here."

He stopped and looked at her. "They're already coming, Gus. At least I can make this right."

She quieted and turned into a corner. Her back was to us, and she sobbed.

He continued, and something sparked the air. I felt it swirling around us, picking up speed. It was strong. Powerful. Kellan controlled it easily, as if he'd been born to do so. Then I felt it touch me and gasped. It was life—it was theirs. I looked at him with renewed eyes—what couldn't he do? He was trying to give them their lives back.

What demon did that?

Our sister still cried while he continued to mount the spell. It circled my feet, then my legs, my stomach, and I lifted my arms. With my head bent, I closed myself down and let the messenger out. It answered what was going on, how I had hoped it would, and somehow I knew the words to say along with Kellan. Both of us gave life to the spell, and then suddenly everything exploded between us. Bursts of light sparked and flew into their mouths.

It was done as soon as it had started.

When it was, when I felt their souls return to their bodies, Kellan gasped, "We have to leave. Now. They can't see us."

He darted out the door. It was going to happen so fast, and they couldn't see us. They would know we had something to do with it. I dragged Gus behind me and literally lifted her the entire way. The devastation was real with her. She hadn't wanted to kill all those people.

As soon as we were in the car, Kellan drove out of there as fast as possible. I didn't have time to grab a seatbelt, but I was to the point where I didn't know if one was needed for us. Gus lay in my lap in the backseat. She curled her head in my shoulder and sobbed. As I stroked her hair back, my eyes caught Kellan's in the rearview mirror. I could tell he was angry, but I wasn't sure why. He wasn't sympathetic to Gus—that much I could feel from him. He was furious with her. And a part of him was furious with me, too.

Then his eyes switched, and he watched behind us as he drove forward. His eyes couldn't look away. My hand shielded Gus' eyes, and I looked also. I couldn't not—something pulled at me, and then I saw the light. Dylan's entire house was illuminated. It looked like it was being raised in the air. Rays of light burst through the windows, doors, anything that would open, and suddenly it was dark again. The house seemed like it fell back to the ground, shattered, and yet with the blink of an eye —everything was normal again.

It was done. They were alive again.

Kellan watched the road again, and no one spoke. Gus still sobbed, interrupting the silence, but her weeping quieted by the time we reached our home. As we went inside, I felt Kellan's exhaustion. At the same time, his body was fully energized with adrenaline. His fury kept him from falling to the ground.

Vespar stood up from his seat at the table. Gus flew to him, and he caught her, lifting her in his arms. Her legs and arms wrapped around him, and he was the one to stroke her hair this time, comforting. He watched us both, Kellan and me, and nodded in thanks before he turned and took her to his room.

We both knew they'd remain there for the night, if not longer.

Kellan didn't say a word to me, but went to his room. I followed and sat on his bed while he went to the bathroom. Neither of us spoke, I didn't think we dared. What could be said? Whatever said was the acknowledgment of what had just happened, what would happen now. Something was coming, and I felt it in my bones. It was going to hurt us.

After he washed and showered, he stood in the bathroom doorway. Then he turned the light off, but didn't move to me. He stayed and stared at me as I stared back. The moonlight filtered through the half-closed drapes and touched the floor. A shadow from it was cast onto the bed, showing my face. Kellan was completely in the dark.

Then I asked, "What will happen now?"

"I have to kill Dylan," he answered so quickly.

"Because he knows too much?"

"Because he hurt one of mine." Kellan jerked away from where he stood and sat beside me. He hung his head forward, and I cradled the back of his neck in my hand. My thumb rubbed at a knot that had formed there. Soothing.

"Is that the only reason why?"

He sighed again deeply. "Messengers are coming. It will take a while for them to find us. Our parents put a blanketing spell over all of us so we can't be sensed by other beings."

"What do you mean?"

"Witches, other demons. Messengers. Anyone who does magic or knows about that world."

"They'll still figure out it was us."

"Yes, but it'll take them some time. We'll sense them before they know it's us."

"And you'll kill Dylan to keep him from telling them?"

"That's one of the reasons, yes." His voice was rough, angered. Kellan was going to kill him anyway, even if there had been no threat to us. And he was going to do it because he played with Gus. He hurt her. He hurt one of us.

"When?"

"Now." He stood and crossed to his closet. I looked away as he changed clothing. He had been in normal attire, jeans and a blue shirt. Now, he pulled on a black long-sleeved shirt that tightly fit him over black sports pants. They were made of soft material. When he moved across the room, I knew why he chose those clothes. I couldn't hear him. I could barely see him. They were perfect for what he was going to do that night.

After he put his other clothes in a hamper, the ones that were bloodied from the house, he stopped and looked at me. "Are you going to stop me?"

I was torn inside, and I didn't know what to say, much less do. All I knew was, I couldn't move or stop him so I remained there while he left, after he left. Then I curled into a ball on his bed with my eyes wide open and waited for him to come back.

Sometime later, my eyes snapped open. I didn't know how long I had stayed there or been asleep, but I lifted my head and saw someone in the doorway. It wasn't Kellan, so I swung my legs over the edge of the bed and asked, "How is she?"

Vespar didn't move from the doorway. He remained on the top step of the stairs. "He went to take care of Cavanagh?"

"You know he did." I sighed.

He jerked his head up and down in an awkward nod. Guilt seemed to consume him. "Good."

"Why didn't you come to help? She must've called you first."

"I can't do what he can."

His answer was simple, but I felt there was more to it. "How is she?"

He answered this time. "She's... I put her out. I put her to sleep. She can't handle what she did."

"She's not as dark as you."

"Nor you," he shot back. "You act like you're above us because you don't use your powers, but you'd do the same she did. Probably more. You can't control yourself any better than Gus can—at least she can control her powers on a normal day."

I stood now. "Do you really want to be threatening me?"

He opened his mouth, but Kellan appeared behind him. He jerked him backward and threw him down the stairs. As Vespar fell over the last step and stopped on the second floor, Kellan stood above him. "Do not say anything more. You should've been there, and you know it. Go to her. Take care of her now. At least do that."

Vespar looked at me, angry, as I stood in Kellan's bedroom entrance.

"Don't!" Kellan warned again and then swept back up the stairs. He took my hand, dragged me inside, and locked his door behind us.

"Why are you—" I started to ask.

He threw me onto the bed. "You don't either. We are going to sleep. Do nothing, say nothing."

My mouth hung open, but I closed it when I saw his eyes in

the moonlight. They were stark, in pain. Then he threw his clothes to the corner and started to come to bed. His eyes caught mine, saw something in them, and then he cursed before he grabbed a pair of boxers. Slipping them on, he crawled underneath his sheets and then lay there. Fatigued.

It didn't feel right being there, so I started to get up. "I'm going to my room."

He caught my hand and pulled me back. "Don't. Please. I need you here tonight."

A note was in his voice that I'd never heard before. It pulled at me, and I found myself crawling under his sheets with him. His hand held mine, and he turned his head to rest on my shoulder. As his eyes closed, I felt him fall asleep almost immediately. I stayed awake, watching him for the rest of the night.

11

No one left the house for four days. We weren't on lockdown, but all of us seemed to respect the need to recuperate before we headed out and assessed the damage, if there was any. Then I broke the uneasy quiet as I packed my bag and headed toward my car.

Kellan stopped me outside the door. "Where are you going?"

"I'm going to school."

Vespar came out behind him at that moment. He passed us by with only a look as he headed down to the river. Gus followed, but she kept her head down when she walked around us. She hadn't talked to us since that night; neither had Vespar. They sat with us at meals as we ate the little bit of food our human sides needed, but no one spoke. There were a lot of looks. Vespar looked anywhere but at us. Gus mainly only looked at Vespar or at her hands. Then there was Kellan and I. We stared at them, at each other, everywhere, but still no one said anything.

I'd had enough, and the urge to paint was strong. I had taken to drawing in the privacy of my room, but it wasn't the same. I needed the large canvas. I needed to shut off everything and let the painting come forth. I couldn't do that in my house, with my siblings there.

I reached for my car handle again, but Kellan took it instead. I glanced up. "What are you doing? I'll be fine." I waited to see if he'd say something about my messenger side, but he didn't. He hadn't spoken one word about that, and neither had I. With Vespar and Gus around, I was always fearful they could overhear our conversations. I didn't trust them, especially since Kellan told me they couldn't find out.

His eyes were trained on our siblings, and he nodded toward them. "What are they doing?"

"They're going swimming." I saw that he wasn't going to say anything about it anytime soon.

"They're not." He frowned. "Let's follow them."

"Kellan, no." I stood my ground as he tried to pull me behind him. "I'm going to school. Someone has to, or they'll send the cops out here to make sure we're all still alive. It's weird that all of us haven't gone back for a while and no one's called."

Kellan let go of my hand, but trailed behind the other two.

"I'm going to school," I called after him. Did he no longer care?

He waved, dismissing me.

"Fine. I'm..." I stopped since he'd gone too far.

When I parked in the lot, I knew things were different. It wasn't the same as before when we had changed Matt. And I wasn't sure if this was because Dylan was dead, but as I walked inside and down the hallway, there was no grief in the air. I should've sensed it. His death should've been known. Then, as I got to my locker, my hand reached up to open it, but I froze when I heard Dylan's laugh in the hallway. It had always been distinct, but it was even more so now.

Everything in my body went numb as I turned. I felt like it

was in slow motion when the crowd parted and Dylan was at his locker, laughing at something Matt said in his ear. The two stood close with their hands on each other's shoulders, giving their sign of bonding and approval to the other. Leah smiled beside them, eager for their attention.

It was how it had been a month ago.

I had thought... Oh God. I had no idea what to think anymore.

Leah caught sight of me, and her eyes widened in anticipation. She skirted over and clasped her hands together. "Is Kellan here? I haven't seen him in a while."

"Do you—wha—how's your stepdad?" I had no idea what to say, but I needed to know what else he'd done.

She froze. All the liveliness died, and she backed away a step. "I don't have a stepdad. You know that, Shay."

"She doesn't even have parents." Matt laughed, coming up behind her. He rested both of his hands on her shoulders and drew her against him. She tensed, but looked away, biting her lip.

"You don't have parents?"

"Foster homes, Shay. Get with the program." Then he winked. "We haven't seen you in a few days. How's it going? Where is the rest of the Braden foursome?"

I narrowed my eyes and sensed into Matt. Everything we had done was gone. I looked at Leah and then at Dylan. I thought Kellan had killed Dylan, but now I cursed myself for not realizing it before. He'd gone back and wiped all of their memories. Somehow, the death of Leah's parents hadn't been changed, and it was now known that she lived with foster parents.

Kellan cleaned up all of our messes.

I remembered the exhaustion he'd felt when he'd gotten home that night. He'd been tired before, but he'd been depleted of all energy. He'd slept through the night, then the next day. I hadn't thought about it, but I gave him some of my energy. In fact, I'd given it the very moment he'd reached for my hand that night.

"Shay?" Matt asked again. His voice had a husky flirting note to it, and I knew that he was their leader again. He was the same guy who had thrown me against the locker two weeks ago. He'd always pushed too far, edging too close to Gus and me, rebelling against Kellan's rule.

I ignored him and walked away. He didn't call after me, and no one said a word. They parted for me, and I kept walking. When I got to the art room, Mrs. Ullen perked up in surprise. "Shay! Are you here to paint?"

"Where can I find the guy who painted those canvases of Kellan?"

She frowned. "I'm sorry. What paintings are those? I don't seem to recall any of your brother."

"They were here two weeks ago. Someone painted them of Kellan, but he looked like a demon. I got upset. You said you'd take them down... Any of this sound familiar?"

"I'm so sorry, dear. I'm drawing a blank. I've only kept your paintings in the back."

"They weren't in the back. You hung them up on the wall. Right there!"

She looked where I pointed, but still shook her head with a hand now resting on her nape, looking nervous. "Shay, honey, I never hung any paintings up unless they were yours or a student's. I only hang student paintings up in the studio. Yours either stay in the back or go in the studio downtown. That was our agreement. Are you feeling okay, dear?"

I threw my hands up in frustration. "They were there. Where did they go? How did you meet that guy?"

She kept shaking her head. "I have no idea what you're talking about. I really don't. I'm so sorry."

"I need to check the back room."

Hesitant, she handed over the keys, but after I opened the door and looked through all the paintings, I didn't find the ones I wanted. They were gone, as if they didn't exist. How could all of this have happened? Did Kellan know about the paintings, too? Did he wipe her memory?

Then I cursed and headed back to my car. Of course, Kellan knew. He'd known the whole time that I had been painting. He knew what I had painted. He knew the painter, whomever he was. Kellan cleaned up everything and what perfect timing. The messengers would get there and find nothing. There weren't even any traces or lingering trails where magic usually remained after a spell had been done. I'd felt them before, but somehow Kellan had obliterated them, too.

How?

He'd have to have phenomenal powers to do that. Vespar and Giuseppa could only have done one or two memory wipes, but they still left traces behind.

I got in my car, ready to drive home and demand answers when I stopped. Two weeks ago, I quaked in fear of Kellan, too. There'd always been something more between us, like he was my protector, but I had still known how dangerous he was. Now I was ready to ask him anything, ready to tell him anything.

"He's good, isn't he? He's the best I've known."

I jerked my head up and around. The painter sat in my backseat, at ease, dressed in a white polo and khaki shorts. His hair looked shorter, and his eyes were so blue, so bright, they seemed to look through me. I felt like they, alone, were trying to give me a message that I couldn't receive.

"Did you take your paintings, or did he?"

He flashed a smile. His teeth were perfectly white, blinding. "I did." Then he laughed softly. "You thought he did, didn't you? I will admit that I only took them because I knew eventually he would. Then he'd interrogate your teacher and find out more than I would want him to know."

"Like what?" My lips were so dry.

"How long I've been here. How long I've known what he's doing. Your brother knew it was only a matter of time before I stepped forward. He knew it was coming. You are, after all, part of me, too."

"Part of you? What do you mean?"

"You come from a messenger, Shay. I know he already told you. Did he tell you which one?"

"Why would it matter? Aren't they the same?"

"A demon is a demon. The same as messengers—I can see why you'd assume, but messengers are special. They have special gifts that run through their blood. Your father is important."

"Is?" My father was alive? I kept forgetting about the parentage...about the parents I never saw at home. "Do I share the same mother as the rest?"

"The rest of your siblings?"

I nodded.

He frowned for a second and then nodded. "You have the same mother... It's the only reason why you were born to them."

I could sense he wasn't saying everything. He chose his words carefully, too carefully. I frowned. "What aren't you telling me?"

He hesitated. "Your father will be coming to town. Too much has happened here. The Braden twins have done too much damage. They must pay. You can tell Kellan it won't matter if he makes everything how it was, if he erases their mistakes. He couldn't erase Leah's parents. He didn't have enough in him to do that. He didn't have you with him, so he altered her life story. That's much easier than actually bringing the dead back to life. She would've been fine after you left her. She would've buried the memory of her parents and gone on to college, knowing they were okay and away from her for some reason. She would've been a nurse or a teacher. Now, she has baggage that she can't live with from the foster system, the mistakes that were made by social workers. She'll kill herself before the end of the year. He did that." He reached for the door and then stopped suddenly. "He did that for them. Not you. He didn't change anything for you, just them. And you might want to ask him about who his parents are. It seems to be the biggest lie he's told you so far."

I had bent my head, listening to him. Now, it snapped up. "What are you talking about?"

"The only real Bradens in your household are Giuseppa and Vespar, the twins." Then he got out of the car. By the time I clambered out my door, he had already vanished.

I stood there, half out of my car, frozen in shock. Had that just happened? Had he really showed up and turned everything upside down? Then I thought about what he said, and everything started to burn in me. He was right about Kellan. My brother—or not brother now—was the best I'd seen, too. His power reverberated out of him. He was a walking, living, breathing weapon, and I'd fallen for his hook. I'd slept with him, comforted him, trusted him. And now I was furious.

I turned my car around and sped back to the house. With a quick sweep of the house, I knew he wasn't there. Then I headed toward the river and found Vespar and Gus swimming around, laughing. They shut up as soon as they saw me walk down the bank and to the edge.

"What is it?" Vespar asked, cautious.

"Kellan!" I yelled and then turned around with my arms spread wide. "Where are you? You said you were coming down here, to watch them. You wanted to follow them. Where are you? Come out and face me. I know you can smell him on me."

Vespar and Gus swam to the bank. As he roughly pulled his shirt over his face, Vespar demanded, "What did you say? He was coming to watch us?"

I ignored him. "Come on out, brother—are you my brother? Are you our brother?"

Then Kellan appeared. He stood at the top of the bank, looking down on us. Furious. And yet, he was so still. It was like he'd been ready for this, waiting for this. When he didn't move to us, we went to him. Fine. We'd give him that. We deserved answers that he was going to give.

Vespar growled, leading the way up to him. "Is it true? Did you come to watch us?"

Kellan's eyes held mine, ignoring his brother. There was a dark promise in them. As a shiver went down my spine, I ignored it and lifted my face in a challenge. I warded off the chills and stepped around Vespar. "Are you really surprised by that? He's been fixing your messes. I'm surprised he hasn't always watched you, making sure you didn't do something so stupid that you'd attract the arrival of messengers."

Our sister gasped.

Vespar froze. His eyes snapped to mine.

Then Kellan narrowed his and asked, calm, quietly, "Is that what he said?"

"Among a lot of other stuff." I glared at him and then looked to Vespar. "I'd run if I were you. You killed too many. You've done too much." Then I looked at Gus and saw the guilt in her eyes. I wondered if she had even told him the magnitude of what she'd done, how many bodies there had been. "They're coming, and they're coming for you two. I was told that you 'must pay.'"

Vespar scoffed, "Who told you that?"

"A messenger."

The smirk vanished.

Then I smiled. "Maybe you should pack your bags."

He scowled. "We're not going anywhere."

Giuseppa shifted uncomfortably beside him.

And then Kellan stepped around them so it was just me and

him. His back was to them, effectively warding them from our conversation as he asked, "What else did he say?"

The way he moved, how sensual it was, how unperturbed he seemed to be, made me uneasy. I hesitated to ask what I really wanted to, but I murmured, with less heat than I'd had in the beginning, "You changed everything. Matt's the same. Leah doesn't know she had parents. Dylan's alive..."

Gus gasped and jerked forward. "You did?" Her hand clamped on to Kellan's arm, but he glared at her. Her hand jerked back in the next second, but she tried to act like that little exchange hadn't happened. She smiled and shifted on her hip. "That's great. I don't—you did something to him?"

"I wiped his memory. I wiped all of their memories—every one of them."

Vespar was quiet, which said a lot. I narrowed my eyes at him. "No thanks for your big brother?"

He lifted frosty eyes at me, but didn't say anything.

Kellan frowned at me, but also didn't say a word.

That told me everything I needed to know—they both knew Kellan wasn't related to us. If he hadn't insisted the other two would kill me if they realized my blood roots, I would've assumed that Vespar also knew about my messenger parentage. I wanted to say something, judge their responses, but I held my tongue. If they didn't know, I wasn't ready to fight my real brother and sister any time soon.

Kellan seemed to have been assessing me the whole time. He saw my surrender and swooped in to turn toward Gus and Vespar. "I'm sorry. I have been watching you, but only the last day. She's right—you two did a lot of damage and they're coming. I didn't want to give them any more against you than they already have. I did what I could, but you still upset the balance. We're not supposed to use our magic that much, and we've been using way too much. The consequences are coming our way."

Then he looked at me with eyes that held a dark promise. It slithered down my body and wrapped tight inside. Kellan was furious, and he wasn't going to be quiet. I only had a matter of time before he came to hash things out with me. I didn't think he was going to back down how I had.

Vespar nodded, grave. "How long do we have?"

"They'll come to talk first. They'll find us, and they'll inquire who did what. They'll figure out who the leader is, etc. They'll devise all of our roles, and then they'll make a plan on how to handle us. If we fight them, they'll fight back. They'll swoop in and obliterate us all. If that happens...then we'll have to see. We have some time." He turned to leave.

Giuseppa asked, anxious, "What can we do before then?"

Kellan said darkly, "Get as strong as you can." His eyes pierced mine for a second, and then he left. We stood behind, unsure of what just happened.

12

I hadn't even shut my bedroom door or turned on my light before Kellan grabbed my arm. He whisked me against him, and everything swooshed around us. When I opened my eyes again, I saw that we were in the woods, near a lake.

"How—you can do that?"

He stared at me. "I can do a lot of things, Shay. I'm less human than you think."

The way he said it, like it was a promise, sent the same shivers down my back that I'd always gotten around my brother. Then I sighed and turned away. He wasn't my brother. He was a liar.

I started walking, even though I had no idea where I was going.

Kellan called after me, "Anywhere you go, I'll find you. I can bring you right back here, anywhere I want, anywhere I choose. It's on my turf, sister dear. This is my time right now."

I turned sharply and glared. We both knew he wasn't talking about our actual location right then and there. "What are you talking about? Your turf? This isn't my turf? Are you trying to say that I don't belong?"

He was in front of me in a flash, gripping my arms tight. "You belong to me."

"I'm not even your sister. Am I?"

He quieted, but didn't move away. His eyes gleamed softer, but I still saw the demon was fierce in him. There was something he wanted to say, but he held back. Why did he always hold back?

"Am I?"

Then he let go and stepped away. It felt like a rejection, though I didn't understand why.

Kellan took a breath and calmed down. I watched as his body seemed to become more fluid, less rigid, in front of me and knew the demon was fighting him. The demon wanted to lash out, to do what it needed to do. Kellan took control then and looked back with a slight apology in his eyes.

"Are you going to explain anything to me?" I couldn't believe this. He still didn't say a word.

Then he did. Softly. "I am not your brother, no. We don't share blood, but we are bonded."

Finally. Answers. My eyes closed, and I felt relief flood my body. At least he was saying something honest. My voice cracked. "How long have you known?"

"All your life."

His answer blew me away. "What?"

"It's why I'm here. You're the reason why I'm here. Your mother and their father aren't either to me. I have no blood connection to the Braden name."

"What?" My entire body reeled in shock. Then that meant... "What does this mean?"

"My father is full demon and sent me to the Bradens. He wanted me here. That's all I know."

He was lying. I saw it as surely and swiftly as if I had been the one who told the lie. "You just said that I'm the reason you're here."

"You are."

"You aren't making any sense. Why aren't you making sense? What are you still hiding from me?"

He smirked. "I'm hiding a lot, but so are you."

"No—" But I was and I knew it. The reason was because I didn't trust him, not fully. I loved him. I had grown up with him as my brother, but I didn't trust him. Then something shifted in me. The messenger wanted out. I felt it rallying, shaking the cage, and I gasped when it exploded inside of me. She was so strong...

My eyes switched, and I saw everything in black and white. The only colors were his eyes. They were a vibrant reddish brown and seemed to smolder in front of me. Kellan's body was black, dark. Everything was white around us. I was white except for my own eyes. The reflection in Kellan's eyes showed that mine were pitch-black. And I hissed, she hissed, "Demon!"

His eyes went wide. "Shay?"

Extending my hand, white light burst from it and slammed against his chest. Kellan flew backward into some trees. They bent at an angle from the force of his impact. He didn't stay down. His head burst upright, and everything changed in him. His demon came to the forefront. His entire body was the same smoldering dark reddish brown.

He spat, "Messenger."

"Leave her alone!" she threatened. An ominous feeling took root in my body.

He smoldered, bristling in fury before her/us. "You leave. You're not wanted. You shouldn't be a part of her."

"I am. I will be. I forever shall be." The promise of her voice shook. It rattled the ground. The trees waved back and forth, and the leaves fell to the ground from her force. It was so strong, so powerful...

"She's his. You know this." He started to circle, the predator.

She stood upright, never the prey. "She's mine! I am in her. You cannot separate us."

His eyes were fierce, promising ways of vengeance as he kept circling, slowly, so slowly.

She stared straight ahead, head high and chin lifted upward. Her shoulders were strong, so steady, and instead of watching him rounding, she ignored him. Then, as he hissed and lurched forward, she flung out an arm. Blinding light burst forth from underneath her arm, all the way down to the ground. It was a gleaming white cloak that she had adorned, and it beamed so bright, like a sun that's too close to the human eye.

He reeled back.

"Leave!" she spoke with force. "Leave her alone, and I won't break her. I will not force my way, but you will leave her."

His body jerked upright, but a fluid look took over. His skin shifted easily, and it was Kellan in the forefront. His eyes snapped open, in control, but the same smoldering reddish color from the demon. "If you break her, I will kill you."

She snorted, smiling cruelly. "As if you have the power—"

Then his hand shot out, and dark light burst from him. It shot her backward into the woods. The messenger recovered quickly, in midair, and sent another zap of her own energy. Kellan flung his hand open, caught it, and sent it back. She gaped, floating in the air, as it hit her body. No impact was felt. She absorbed it and then lifted stunned eyes back to him. Gliding to the ground, to stand before him again, she studied him. "You are not a mere hybrid."

Kellan didn't respond, standing there and waiting.

"Why should I not open my arms and let you be blinded by my real self? You would die, right now. Your eyes would burn into your body, and the demon would never recover. Tell me why I should not do that? Your kind hates my kind. My kind loathes yours."

Kellan bristled in anger, but controlled it. "Because she needs me. I am bonded to her, and you know this. You've felt this her whole life, your whole life, and you know that if you kill me, she will be broken. You cannot survive without her."

Hatred boiled underneath her surface, but something shifted, and she was gone.

***

KELLAN

SHAY GASPED, reeling backward. She threw her arms out, trying to regain some sort of balance. "Kellan!"

Swooping in, he caught her before she fell and swiftly lifted her up in his arms. His hand tucked her head against his chest, and he murmured, "Sleep. I'll explain when you wake."

"No!" She dug her hands in his shirt, her nails scraping through to his skin.

Kellan watched, unharmed. He didn't react as she drew his blood, but smoothed out her hair from her forehead. "Sleep, Shay. It will be all right. I promise." He ducked his head down and pressed his cheek to her forehead, drawing strength from her as well. The demon was exhausted from fighting the messenger. He could feel the turmoil inside of her and sucked in his breath, angry the messenger had even threatened to destroy everything. Shay wasn't strong enough to handle the switch from messenger to human. Only one other human had survived a break as this messenger had done. They weren't supposed to break free and take control over the body. They hadn't been created for that.

"Kellan," Shay murmured drowsily. His magic was working, slipping into her, making her succumb to exhaustion.

"Sshh. Sleep."

And her eyes closed. Her entire body gave up the fight and was limp in his arms.

He drew in another shuddering breath and wrapped both of his arms around her tight. Then he whisked them through the woods and into his bedroom.

The lights were off. Since there was no moonlight that night, his room seemed darker than normal. Kellan saw everything clearly, as if it were day, and laid her down onto his bed gently. Then he sat beside her, gazing down at her in concern.

The messenger had broken free, taken over. What would be the ramifications? What would Shay remember? What parts of the messenger had become more linked to her, had broken her own sheltering spell that she cast as a child?

Kellan lifted up her sleeve and saw the circling tattoo had stopped. The strings that had formed a circle were now intertwined. They mixed together except one string at the bottom. It stood apart, silver in color while the others had taken on a brown tone. He knew Shay would be worried about this, but there was nothing he could do.

As he lay beside her, turned toward her, kept her tucked against him, his body sheltered hers, and he tucked a hand underneath her, claiming her. Then he rested his forehead in the crook of her neck and shoulder and allowed sleep to come over him. The demon inside was more than tired and would need more than his normal few hours of sleep.

I WAS RUNNING THROUGH A FOREST, but it was dark. There was no light to help me see, but something was after me, chasing me, breathing down my back. I felt it—it was too much. I couldn't ignore it, so I kept going, faster and faster. I couldn't breathe. My heart was racing in my chest. I felt it was going to explode. Each step I took, I pushed faster, harder. Every muscle was strained, and I gritted my teeth, just going farther and farther, faster and faster.

"*Your kind hates my kind.*"

"What?" I whipped my head back. Who was there?

The voice whispered again, going past me, "*She's his.*"

I braked abruptly and spun around. The forest was large, looming above me, so powerful. I felt like it wanted to shelter me, suffocate me. It didn't want me to breathe.

Then the voice came again. It was a whisper on the wind, now behind me. "*If you break her, I will kill you.*"

Then it roared, "*Leave!*"

My heart took off at a thunderous pace, and I reacted, jumping, turning, and sprinting away. Faster, faster, harder, harder. I had to get there. I must. If I didn't—someone would die. Someone was going to die. I needed to stop it. Then my heart got louder and louder. Thump. Thump. Thump, thump, thump. It took over, and I couldn't hear anything else. Trees stood in my way, and I bounded around them. Leaves and branches cut into my skin, nipping at my head, trying to blind me, pierce me. Gritting my teeth, I ignored them. I kept going. I had to. If I didn't...THUMP, THUMP.

"*I am bonded to her.*"

I stopped again and bent over, panting. My heart wouldn't stop. Then I looked up—that had been Kellan's voice. He was bonded to someone. What did that mean? To whom?

A stream of white light burst in the sky. I looked up as it illuminated the night sky. All the trees were gone. It was only me, no one else. No forest. Just the light and me and a voice above it whispered to me, "It's you. It's always you."

My eyes got wide, and the light sped downward to me. It was going to overtake me, but then my eyes shot open again, and I sat upright, gasping.

"Hey, hey." Kellan sat up next to me with an arm around my

back. He rubbed in circles, soothing. "It's okay. It was a nightmare. It's okay now."

I was disoriented, hearing his voice from a distance. Everything was going around me, too fast, too soon. I couldn't get my bearings, and I reached out, closing my hand around something strong. It was my balance. It grounded me as the room continued to spin around me.

"Wha—?" I felt my chest, how my heart wouldn't slow down. "Kellan! My heart."

"It's okay. I promise." He pressed a kiss against my forehead and rested his cheek there.

My heart started to slow, just a bit.

He lifted me up and cradled me on his chest, scooting backward until his back was against the wall. Then he rocked me back and forth, repeating his words, "It's okay. I promise. It's okay. I promise."

I gasped for breath and burrowed into him, seeking more shelter. I was only aware of his fingers on my forehead, how he brushed my hair back and kept doing it over and over. I felt my heart starting to slow down. It still pounded throughout my whole body, but a few minutes later, I saw that I was in his arms. Then we were on his bed, in his room, in our home. Finally, I breathed in and out, at a normal rate, and I was able to push up from him.

"What happened? Something happened?" My eyes searched his.

Kellan frowned, but didn't hide anything. He let me see into him, to the demon inside of him. The demon looked back at me, concerned, too. I reeled back and scrambled out of his arms. "What—your—what?"

He closed his eyes and shook his head. "I don't want to hurt you. I mean that."

"But—" I heard the whispers again. They were scratching at my consciousness. They wanted me to remember something. *"She's his."* I asked Kellan, "Who is his? What happened?"

"The messenger in you took control." He sounded in pain.

"What? Why?" Then I gulped. What had happened when I wasn't in control?

"She tried to hurt me. My demon came out, and they fought, but it was over quickly."

I jerked to my feet and darted to the farthest corner of the room. With my back to the wall, I looked at Kellan, still on the bed. "You..." My voice trembled. "You're not my brother. You told me that before—the thing happened."

He settled back against the wall and sighed. "Yes. I told you that."

I swallowed, nervous now. "What does that mean? You're here because of me."

Kellan started to stand up, but I shot out my hand. "Please don't. I'm freaked out. I can't... Just stay there. Please."

He sat back down, and I relaxed. His eyes searched mine intently as he spoke, "I'm here because my human side is bonded with your human side. I'm here because of you, for you."

"How—how do you know?"

"Because you came to me when you were a child. You weren't in control of your powers, but they were too strong back then. The messenger was mixed with your human side. The two of you flowed together naturally, and you wanted to find your soulmate. You were a child. You didn't know how frightening your powers were to others, but you came to me. My father felt your presence."

"What, like a house? Like I literally came to your house?"

"No." He shook his head, looking sad, almost wounded. "It was through magic. Your presence found mine. My father felt inside of you and found where you were, that you came from demons. He didn't understand your existence, how you could live in a home of demons when you were half-messenger, but he sent me here. For you. Because of you. I'm here because you wanted me to come here."

I gaped at him. Had he grown two heads? Had I? "None of this makes sense," I sputtered out, but it did. Clamping my eyes shut, I tried to ward of memories. They were coming at me fast, hard, too frightening for me to remember. "No, no, no, no. I couldn't. I hadn't..."

Then Kellan was in front of me. His hands took my wrists and he lifted them around his head. "Hug me. Please." He urged me closer, and then I jumped, going into him. I clung to him with my eyes closed, burrowing into him.

The memories kept coming, and I remembered being a little girl. My mother had just read a book to me. I was the princess, and I needed to find my prince. She tucked me in bed, kissed my forehead, and said goodnight. I hadn't gone to sleep, though. I crawled out and went to my window. As I placed my hand to the window, I closed my eyes and wished to find my prince. I wanted my own fairytale so bad, and I wished with all my heart. Something left my body. It sailed through the window, gliding seamlessly, and looked back once. My body remained in the room with my eyes closed so tight and my lips pursed together, sitting there in my pink princess pajamas. My blonde hair had started to grow, and it flowed over my shoulders, shining from the moonlight. I looked like I was praying, but then I looked back in the air, floating over the forests. I floated over lakes, over houses, over cities.

Then I went somewhere dark. I didn't know where, but I grew scared. It wasn't where I wanted my prince to be, and I tried to go back. I couldn't. Something had taken hold of me. It clamped a hand on my ankle and drew me close. I tried to scream, but no sound came out. Then it pulled me tighter and looked into me. Red eyes pierced through me, and I felt something behind it. I tried to peek around him, but he wouldn't let me go. He didn't want me to see, so all I could do was whimper in his hold. Tears ran down my cheeks, I felt them on my skin, and knew I was crying in my own home.

"Dad, let her go," a little voice spoke up.

I prayed he'd listen to him.

He did; he let me go. I flew back home, and when I slammed into my body, I ran to my bed and curled in a ball. I remembered closing my eyes and wishing that I would never remember that again—I never wanted to feel that terror again. I only wanted to be a little girl.

"Oh my God!" I curled my fingers into his arms. "That's when it happened, when I didn't want to be what I was. I wanted to be normal. That's when I..."

Kellan kissed my forehead. "It's when you created this." His hand lifted up my sleeve and touched my tattoo. "This banded her inside of you, but she broke free tonight. That's why the binding has changed. She's separated herself from you, from your hold."

My eyes bulged out when I saw the one silver line. It was at the bottom, separate from the rest that were now jumbled together. "I don't understand any of this. This is all too much."

Kellan lifted me and went to his bed. He lay down and pulled me back into his arms, then he rolled and propped himself above me, looking down. His finger traced the side of my face and trailed down my jaw, back up to the other side before his palm spread wide and he cupped my cheek, cradling my face in his hand. "That's what I mean when I said that I came here for you. I've always been here for you. You made that spell that night, and you couldn't see your parents any longer. You couldn't even see your mother, even though she's human. She frightened you too much because you always saw the demon that she loves. You saw that in her."

"Gus and Vespar's dad."

He nodded. His eyes looked haunted. "For a while, you

wouldn't let yourself even see them. There was too much demon in them, but then I came. Your mother let me in. She knew why I had come. She knew what you had done that day and she blamed herself. She said she shouldn't have read you that book, but she didn't know it would bring you to me. Ever since then, I've been in charge of you. You're mine, Shay."

I drew in a shuddering breath, hearing his last words. *"I am bonded to her."*

13

When I woke, I was in Kellan's bed, in his arms. He had curled them around me and held me against his chest. The sheets had been pushed off to the floor, and our legs were entangled together, poking just over the end of the bed.

"I am bonded to her."

I shivered as those words came back to me. He had looked at me, looking straight through me, claiming me when he said, *"You're mine, Shay."*

He seemed so angelic when he slept. His eyelashes were long, the tips resting on the skin underneath his eyes. Delicate. Then his cheekbones angled outward, drawing the eye to his lips.

I touched his lips and wondered what they would feel like.

Then I realized what I was doing—I was checking out my brother, no—he wasn't. Clasping my eyes shut, I buried my head underneath the pillow and let out a silent groan. Too much had changed, and I no longer knew how I felt about anything, even Kellan who wasn't really my brother, but something else entirely. It was too much, at least that early in the morning. Figuring I could sort through everything later, I knew

a trip to the bathroom was more pertinent, so I slipped out
from underneath his arm.

I took a moment to breathe once I had closed his bathroom
door. So much had happened, too much. Looking up, I gasped
when I saw my reflection. My hair had been black before, but it
was a light-colored brown now. Streaks of blonde had
appeared, and my mouth fell open when I fingered through the
strands. Then I felt my cheeks. A blush seemed to have permanently appeared on my face. My skin tone had been pale
before, and it was now a golden tan with a slight pink color
over my cheekbones.

Suddenly, my arm started to burn, and I looked down to
push up my sleeve. The silver line was still there, broken away
from the other brown ones. I couldn't believe that it had
changed, too, or maybe that was why all these other changes
had happened. I traced the tattoo slowly, wondering what other
events had changed because the messenger broke free from me.

Then a different thought crossed my mind. Why hadn't
Kellan said anything—when had he noticed my appearance
changes? I turned, intending to ask him, when I saw something
else in the mirror. My eyes widened, and I sucked in my breath.
My green eyes were no longer green. They had a smoky color to
them now. The green was still there, but in the background. I
shivered, feeling spooked.

How had I missed that the first time?

Shaking my head, not feeling good about any of it, I
returned to the room, but found that Kellan had gone downstairs. Fine—I headed to my room instead. But when I got
inside and changed into a white tank top and blue jean shorts,
someone knocked on my door. It was a tentative knock, and I
knew who that was. Opening my door and finding Gus on the
other side, looking a little sheepish, I knew my guess had been
right.

She hadn't talked to me since yesterday at the lake. From

the hesitant look on her face, how she had both of her hands wrapped in the white afghan shirt that hung on her, I was guessing she still didn't want to talk to me.

"This is going to be good," I mused, moving out and holding the door wider for her.

She came inside slowly and sat on the edge of my bed.

I turned and regarded her. "What's up, Gus?"

Her eyes had been looking around my room, skirting around, but then she looked at me and gasped. "Your hair!" Bolting to her feet, she lifted some in her hand. Then she looked at my arm. "Your—what is this?"

I shook her off. "It's nothing, just a tattoo. Why'd you come up here?"

"I..." Her eyes were transfixed on me now, but she closed her mouth and shook her head. "Oh. Okay. Uh... I was wondering what you think Kellan is going to do?"

"About what?"

"About the messengers coming and what happened with Dylan. Plus, with Kellan making everything how it was before."

"Except for Leah. Her life is worse now."

Gus shrugged. "At least she didn't lose her parents."

"At least she had parents before—"

"Who were horrible to her," she whipped back at me, glaring. Gus stood, her shoulders rigid, and she took a deep breath. The anger clung to her, but she tried to control it. When she had, she asked further, "Do you know what Kellan is going to do when the messengers come?"

"I don't know." And I didn't. "Have you ever dealt with a messenger before?"

She swallowed tightly and shook her head. "No. You?"

Yes. But I shook my head. "No."

"I bet Kellan has. He's the most powerful, except you, but do you think—?" She looked up, hopeful.

"I can't control my powers."

The hope vanished, and she hung her head again. "I suppose. Vespar's worried. He doesn't want to say anything, but I can tell. He doesn't even want to go mess with some humans. I thought it'd be fun, maybe make him feel better. But he said it'd make things worse since Kellan warned us not to do anything."

I nodded. "That's a smart move."

"I just..." She sighed, biting her lip and then crossed her arms over her chest, hugging herself. "I don't know what to do. I'm scared, and I'm worried about Vespar. You don't think... Do you think we'll survive this? Maybe we should run?"

"If Kellan thought we should run, he'd tell us. He hasn't said anything about that, though."

"Yeah, you're right." Then she looked up again, but her eyes skimmed over me as she kept looking around the room. "I made some food. Do you want some?"

"Sure." I frowned as my sister left with a little bounce in her walk. She seemed more carefree, as if she'd unloaded some of her worries on me. I had no idea how that happened, but it was Gus. Sometimes, my sister didn't make sense to me, what she thought or felt even. What I do know was that she'd go straight to Vespar and tell him about the change in my looks. He'd, in turn, go to Kellan and ask what they meant, why I looked different. What Kellan would say was a mystery to me. I only knew he wouldn't give them the whole truth, but some of the truth. Or he might give them a complete lie, but I'd follow his lead.

Then, as I went downstairs, I saw both of the twins at the table with our esteemed older brother, who lifted his eyes and scrutinized me for a moment. I felt him searching inside of me, but then he looked back at his fruit, dismissing me.

Vespar's eyebrows twitched when I sat across from him, but he didn't say or let any other emotion slip out. His eyes only slid to Gus' who gave him a grin in turn. And to this, he rolled his eyes, shaking his head, and went back to eating his toast.

"Coffee, Shay?" Gus slid a cup across the table to me.

I reached for it, surprised at the gesture, but it was knocked over when Kellan jerked the table, moving his chair closer to it.

"Hey!" I cried out.

Kellan shrugged. "Sorry."

Vespar frowned for a split second, but then he stood and grabbed the coffee pot. "I'll pour you another one, Shay."

"Actually, I was going to take her into town. We can pick up some more there. That stuff smells foul." Kellan stood and took my elbow. "Come on, I have an appointment with the principal. We're all going to be homeschooled for the rest of the year."

"We are?" Gus sounded surprised. "Can you just do that?"

"When I get him in his office alone, yeah, I can. He won't even know he's signing the papers until they're already processed. Mom and Dad called ahead on our behalf anyway."

"Where are they, anyway? I haven't seen them this morning." Vespar leaned against a counter and slid his hands into his front pockets, looking casual. His eyes weren't, as they seemed to study every word and action from Kellan.

"I told 'em to leave. They aren't safe here."

"And we are?" Vespar stood now with his hands still in his pockets.

Kellan moved so I stood slightly behind him and Gus stood also, slower. She was in the middle and glanced between her two brothers uneasily. Then her eyes shifted to mine, and I knew she was asking me what was going on. I shrugged. It was between the guys, not us.

"Right now, I think we'll be fine, but we'll see once the messengers arrive." Kellan shifted his hold on my elbow and urged me upstairs. "Go get your stuff. We gotta go now."

As I darted upstairs, I knew something had just happened between Vespar and Kellan. What it was, I had no idea, but when I grabbed my purse and bag, everyone was quiet as I got back downstairs. Kellan gave me a closed grin and held open the door. "Come on, sis. It's my treat at the coffee shop."

I ducked under his arm, and as he let it go, I heard Gus mutter inside, "I want to go for some coffee."

"Shut up," Vespar snapped at her. And then the door closed, shutting out anything else he might've said.

"Come on." Kellan took my elbow again and led me to his car. Once we were inside, I asked him, glaring, "What's with the manhandling? I can walk all by myself, you know."

He glanced at me from the corner of his eye, but didn't respond as he drove onto the street and headed toward town. After a few more minutes, I asked again, "What's going on? What just happened back there?"

He grimaced, watching the street. "No one but you drinks coffee. You don't think it's odd that he made a pot? Just for you? He gave that cup to Gus. He wanted her to offer it to you."

"What are you saying?"

"What did Gus say when she went to your room?"

"Nothing. She asked what you thought we should do about the messengers. She said that Vespar was worried."

"Vespar's more than worried. He's already figured out his plan, and that's a sacrifice. He wants to give you up, saying that you did everything."

"What?" My mouth fell open.

"I heard him planning it this morning."

"He was planning that with Gus?"

"She doesn't know. She went upstairs to distract you, make you think they're going to do what we want, but it's not true. He sent her up there to say that to you, but she doesn't know why. Gus is left in the dark, but I heard his thoughts. It's what woke me up." Then he grimaced. "And he's scared about your appearance. He doesn't know what it means, that you look different, but he's worried that it's because of your powers. You might be more in control of them."

I swallowed tightly, feeling betrayed. A whirl of emotions

was going through me, but I asked, dumbfounded, "And what about you? Doesn't he think you'd be mad about me?"

"He thinks I'll miss you, but I'd understand in the long run. He also thinks it would impress me, that he thought of that on his own. He thinks he would save us from the messengers."

"What an idiot."

Kellan grinned, but then sobered. "He suspects that I knew what he was doing. I didn't want you to drink the coffee, and normally I wouldn't care. Vespar's not stupid. He's now more worried than before since I went against his plan, either by accident or on purpose. If it's the latter, then he knows I chose my allegiance."

"And it's not with him."

"Exactly." Kellan took my hand as he pulled up outside of our school. "I want you to stay in here."

"Why?"

His eyes shifted past my shoulders, and he nodded in that direction. "Because you have a visitor."

I looked over and saw the painter. He stood in the shadows of some trees on the edge of our school's lawn. As Kellan got out and headed inside, I followed suit but went the opposite direction. When I drew closer, I saw the painter was in a hooded sweatshirt with it pulled over his head. His eyes were so bright, trying to look inside of me, but he remained where he stood. His hands, like Vespar's, were also stuffed in his front pockets. He looked casual, but the tension was thick around him, clinging to his form.

I stopped just before him, unsure what to say.

"She got out," he spoke first.

I nodded and gestured to my arm. "The tattoo changed, too."

"Your messenger side is powerful now, almost more powerful than your human side, but she's quiet. Why is she quiet?"

"I have no idea. I'm still adjusting to being a hybrid and all these new changes with having a messenger inside of me."

"She's a part of you; she's just been separated because that's what you wanted. You didn't want to be intertwined with a messenger so you separated yourself from her. You've given her an altogether separate personality because of it. It's not right, to have something inside of you that you can't control. And you don't control her. You know that, right?"

I gulped. Control her? I didn't even know she had a different personality. "How do I do that?"

"Stop denying who you are, for one. As you become more familiar with your messenger side, you'll become more whole and her personality will become meshed with you. It's the only way you can control her, if you take control of yourself."

It made perfect sense when he said it, but doing it was a whole different story. "I'll get to working on that then."

He frowned and jerked forward, but stopped and slammed back against the tree. "I'm sorry. I reacted, and I shouldn't have."

"What?"

"Nothing." He looked away and hunched his shoulders forward. "Does Kellan know what you are going to do when your father comes to town?"

I swallowed tightly. My throat felt like bark had grown inside suddenly. "I haven't told him that information yet."

"You should. You have to. He needs to know. Otherwise, everything might be ruined. You might be ruined."

Riddles. Everything was riddles. "Yeah, okay. I'll tell him."

"I mean it, Shay. Kellan has to know. He's bonded to your human side. He's been able to control his demon side because of it when he's around you, but if your father arrives, and he's not prepared, his demon might react too strongly. Someone will die, someone you'll need for your survival."

"So, you're helping me now? You're helping him?"

The painter drew back, straightening against the tree, and gave me a rueful grin. "I guess so. Yeah."

I was tempted to roll my eyes. I was beyond really trusting anyone anymore, even Kellan. I knew he was still keeping secrets from me, but I was slowly starting to believe he had my best interest at heart.

I watched him carefully when I asked, "What's your place in all this? You said before that you were a part of me, too, the messenger part? Are our messengers bonded together?" Then I did roll my eyes. "And can you at least tell me your name?"

He chuckled softly. "My name is Damien."

"It's nice to meet you, Damien."

"And my messenger side is bonded to yours in a family way."

Oh—that was...different. "So not the soulmate way?"

"No, not at all. Let's leave it at that." Then he straightened and nodded past me. "Your soulmate is back there, waiting for you. He knows I don't mean you trouble, or him for that matter." Then his eyes gleamed brightly, and he whispered, "As long as he's truthful to you, then he won't need to worry about me."

Tingles went through me at his words, and I knew he had sent them to Kellan. He wanted his message heard and glancing over my shoulder, I felt the anger start to grow with my soulmate. Kellan got the message, loud and clear, and didn't enjoy the threat, but he remained by the car, waiting.

Damien told me, "When your father comes to town, he's going to seek me out. He'll want to know where you are and what demons you are living with. Your mother has been hidden to him since she gave birth to you. He holds a grudge against her for that, but he's coming for you. The Braden twins gave him the excuse to come here. And he won't be happy about Kellan. I know he doesn't know of the demon or how you are bonded to him. Your father will be enraged and will try to break the bond."

Okay, now I was worried. "What are you saying?" Could that even happen? Could the bond be destroyed? And if so, then what would happen after that?

He seemed to choose his words carefully. "Just that it would be smart if you strengthened your bond."

My mouth went dry at that. "What do you mean by that?"

He grinned crookedly. "You can take it any way you want. Kellan will know, but if the two of you *are* strong enough, your father will know not to even try to break the bond. If you two work together as a team, you could be powerful, more powerful than you could imagine."

Well...that was nice and cryptic. I was left annoyed and slightly speechless when Damien gave me a small hug before he left through the trees. I stood there for another minute before I turned and slowly walked back to the car, back to Kellan. He straightened and asked, watching where I had left, "What did he say?"

"Oh, oh. You don't want to know." I laughed with a hysterical note in my voice.

Kellan narrowed his eyes. "What's wrong with you?"

"Oh, nothing. Just that my father is going to try to destroy our bond, and we're supposed to make it stronger. Oh, and that my father is actually coming here for me, not for Gus or Vespar. They're just his excuse to come here. Oh—I should've first told you that my father is the messenger coming here." I threw my hands up. "Surprise! I'm going to meet my dad soon. How...lovely."

Kellan arched an eyebrow and folded his arms over his chest. "Did he do something to you just now? This isn't normal, Shay."

"It's not a normal day for me. I find out about you, about

me, about my father coming, and that guy is 'family' to me. Did you know that?" I jerked a thumb over my shoulder.

He was silent for a moment and then said grudgingly, "I see your point."

That made me laugh harder. The hysterical note grew in volume until I was bent over, clutching my stomach, and slowly falling to my knees on the ground, sobbing from the laughter. Kellan watched me for another moment and bent to wrap his arms around me. Lifting me in the air, he held me against his chest while I started to sob into his shoulder. One of his hands smoothed back some of my hair while his thumb brushed at my tears while he was still holding me.

After a few moments, when my sobs had started to subside, I hiccupped against his shirt. "I'm sorry. I'm a bit not normal right now. And Vespar tried to kill me." I didn't even know how to comprehend that one.

Kellan whispered against my forehead, pressing a soft kiss there, "Vespar will be dealt with. Trust me."

It shouldn't have comforted me, but it did. When he kissed my forehead again and then bent to softly kiss my cheek, I closed my eyes and curled into him, feeling safe, even though I didn't know if I should.

LEAH

ACROSS THE SCHOOL PARKING LOT, standing inside the doors, Leah watched them from a window. Hatred boiled inside of her, and she frowned with her fingers curled so tightly into the window frame that it drew blood from underneath her nails.

Dylan came to stand beside her. Glancing from the blood under her hands and her stony face to the couple where her gaze was frozen, he sighed. "They're not who you think they are."

She clipped out, "I know."

When Shay had asked about her parents, something unlocked in her mind. Memories flew back at her, drifting in and out of focus, but they were there. She felt them. She heard her parents' laughter, her own with them. Then she heard raised voices, threats from a man's voice. His hands touched her, made her do things that brought shame to her. Cringing on the inside, Leah wanted it all to go away, but she knew it wouldn't. They were permanently there, and they shifted alongside her new memories. Nothing made sense to her, but the memories and emotions haunted her. She knew they would always haunt her, but one memory that was perfectly clear was the night her parents were killed.

Vespar and Gus had rung her doorbell, and she had answered it, thinking they were there with some information about Kellan. She'd been so excited, thinking that Kellan would come to help her. Save her. But he didn't, he sent those two and they had pushed their way inside with a sick gleam in both of their eyes. When her stepfather had demanded to know who they were, what the hell they were there for, Gus had laughed —laughed—as she flicked a knife in the air. It landed perfectly in his chest, but it hadn't been enough. The female Braden had danced to him, took the knife out, and then slit his throat, giggling when he gaped at her with his eyes wide. When his body slid to the ground, Leah's mother and real father had come out of the garage, alarmed. Then Vespar had gone mad, lunging for them through the air. He'd taken their heads— Leah trembled, clasping her eyes shut. She didn't want to remember it. She didn't want to hear their surprise or their agony, how they had begged for their lives.

"We can make them hurt." Dylan touched her arm. "Kellan

tried to erase my memory, but it didn't work. I knew a spell that kept it from happening. His power can't touch me."

"How do you know that stuff?" she whispered, choking on vomit.

"My grandmother. She told me about things like them, what we can do to protect ourselves against them. They killed my entire family."

"I saw your brother in school today."

"Gus killed them, but I think Kellan brought them back to life." He took her shoulders and turned her to him. "They can do things like that, but we can stop them. We can hurt them."

With tears running down her face, Leah frowned. "How? They're so powerful..." She looked back and felt another stab in her heart when she saw Kellan place a gentle kiss on Shay's forehead with his hand holding her cheek. It was a tender gesture, but could they feel tenderness? Did they feel love? Why did she feel comforted by him?

Dylan drew back, smiling. "I know what to do. Do you trust me?"

She jerked her gaze back to his and took a deep breath. "I want the memories to go away. I can't stand it. I'm haunted, Dylan. They made that happen. I feel like I've been ripped apart and sewn back together with a knife and rope."

"I'll make it better. I promise." Dylan took her hand and squeezed. Then he slid an arm around her shoulder and drew her against him. "Come on. We've got lots of work to do."

Leah looked back over her shoulder, but Kellan and Shay had disappeared.

14

Kellan drove through the night. At first I didn't realize that we hadn't gone back to the house. I hadn't wanted to ask because I wasn't sure what I was going to do about Vespar, but when we'd been driving for an hour, I knew we weren't going home. So I looked up and regarded him. He had a determined look on his face, like he could do anything at that moment.

Then I felt a tug in my stomach. It was Kellan, telling me he didn't want to talk at that moment, but to trust him. That's when I knew something more than learning that we were soulmates, had changed between us. Something had started to grow between us, like an invisible rope, and I felt it pull me. It pulled on me when I'd been standing with Damien. Kellan had tugged on it and I knew what he wanted me to know, that it was okay to talk to other Nephilim, and that he wasn't worried about Damien anymore. Now he pulled on it again and I knew we'd be driving for a long time that night. So I moved to the backseat and lay down, closing my eyes. I didn't need sleep, but I rested there anyway, listening to the drive, feeling Kellan and how something rock solid had come over him.

When the first light of dawn started to peek over the horizon, I sat up, realizing I had fallen asleep for a bit. Kellan still looked refreshed. Then I grinned and leaned over my chair's headrest in the front. "You look like you could drive for a week straight."

The invisible rope relaxed, and I knew Kellan had relaxed with it. The corner of his mouth quirked upward. "I needed to make sure we'd get a head start."

"From?" My mind wandered a bit, and I knew whom he meant. "From Vespar?"

Kellan nodded, grim again.

"Where are we going?"

"To get some help."

"What?" My head jerked up. "From who?"

"Another messenger." He watched me in the rearview mirror, his eyes studying me, wanting to know everything I felt. "She's friendly to some of us. She's not aligned with your father."

"Why?"

"Because you need to know answers that I can't give you. And you need to learn about what you can do. It'll help you be able to control the messenger inside of you."

I shook my head, feeling... I didn't even know. Nervous. Agitated. Scared. And pissed. "You just decided this without even talking to me about it!"

A glimmer of a smile appeared over his face, but his eyes snapped to mine, angry. "We need space from Vespar right now. Unless you're ready to declare war with him and face the consequences, then we needed to get away. He won't know where we are. He can't track us if we're driving in a car, using human transport. He definitely won't want to follow us even if he does figure out where we've gone. This messenger is not one to take lightly. She loathes demons that kill."

I sat back and muttered, faint under my breath, "And Vespar loves to kill."

"Yes." Kellan stopped the car and turned around. His eyes were fierce. "He does, he does now. He started when we were young, but now the taste is unquenchable in him. He won't stop. He can't."

"Then we have to kill him." Even as I said it, no emotion was evoked inside of me. Shouldn't I have cared? He was my half-brother.

"That's not a question. What is the question is Gus—what she'll do when we kill Vespar, if we can trust her or not."

I closed my eyes swiftly, feeling a stab of pain in my heart. He was right. Gus would go crazy if we took away her other half. She'd go mad, and she'd go dark, really dark. I bit my lip because I realized that Vespar wasn't really the one we were avoiding, it was what we'd have to do about our sister, my sister.

I felt another tug on my stomach and opened my eyes. Kellan was watching me. He was always watching me. This time he asked with his eyes if I was all right, and I nodded, closing off my emotions, pushing them down. We'd do what we had to do, and then I cleared my throat and asked with a raspy voice, "How much farther?"

He nodded outside. "We're here. This is where we're staying."

We had parked outside a small white house. Trees surrounded it, not allowing for a lawn. As I got out of the car, I heard the sounds of a small river close by. I walked around the back of the house, stepping carefully around the trees. Their roots had started to grow out of the ground and I climbed up on one that curved higher than the rest. As I did, with a hand resting on the massive oak beside it, I saw a sparkling body of water that rested just underneath a small hill behind the house. A waterfall filled it from my right, splashing onto smooth rocks that glistened underneath the water.

Kellan climbed up beside me and rested an arm behind me, placing it on the tree next to mine. I leaned back against him and asked, "What is this place? It's beautiful."

"It's a sanctuary." He touched my shoulder and turned so we looked at the house. "The house is protected. The only things the human eye can detect are the trees. No human can see the house, and no tree will fall onto it in a storm. They're magically entrusted, too. This spot is where the oldest and toughest trees live. They're alive, Shay."

I turned, wide-eyed, to him. And he grinned. "Not in the manner like they can talk to us, but they know they're here to protect the house. They'll hide it from anything we want them to. They draw their strength and knowledge from the water."

"Let me guess. It has magic in it, too?"

"A little." Kellan tapped my forehead and chuckled. Then he wrapped his hand around my waist and *wooshed* us from the trees and in front of the house to a small porch wide enough for two sets of feet. The door seemed to grow in front of our eyes until it reached to the top of the roof and separated into two doors. Kellan reached for the handle and waited. The door handle vibrated, turning underneath his hand. It stopped suddenly and the doors opened, as if the house decided we could enter. A breeze from the sudden movement rushed back against us and my eyes widened in surprise when I saw inside. The house was small from the outside, but the inside was grand.

Kellan waited on the porch as I wandered inside, gazing upward. Stairs wrapped around the house, leading to three levels inside. Then I moved back outside and saw there was only one level from there. I shook my head and went back inside. Kellan followed this time, and the doors whisked shut with a loud bang behind us.

I walked around the living room, trailing a finger over a

glass bookshelf. "This entire place has magic, doesn't it? The house included."

"It's a sanctuary for us, built to withstand darkness and good. It knows that creatures such as ourselves, who have both in them, need safety here." He placed two bags near the steps. "This was given to me by my mother, only she knows of its existence, other than you and me now."

My eyes fell on my book bag, and a sense of wonderment came over me. "You planned this last night, didn't you? You knew Vespar would do something, and you knew we'd have to leave. You had every intention of taking me away with you, but..." *Why did we go to the school?*

"I went and erased our existence with the school. I left Vespar's, but made Gus disappear, too. Your father will find Vespar's name, but no one else. He won't find you. That's all I'm concerned about right now."

My eyes lifted to him. He was watching me, gazing at me with an emotion in him that I'd never seen or felt. I'd felt possession, obsession, fury, laughter, but this was different. There was a tenderness laced with it. And a different realization occurred to me. "You're not afraid of the messengers, are you?"

Kellan never looked away, but drifted closer to me. He lifted a hand and cupped the side of my face, holding it gently. "I'm not."

But I saw something else. He *was* scared of them, but not for himself. "You're scared for me, aren't you?" I was breathless when I asked that.

He shook his head and a wall slammed down in his eyes. The rope that connected us went slack. It was still there. I didn't think even Kellan could make that connection go away now, but it was so loose it was almost as if there was no connection. Then I tightened it and watched how he stiffened in shock. "Didn't know I could do that, too, huh?"

He grinned before turning away. I let him go, releasing my hold on the connection and followed him into the kitchen where I sat. "When are we going to see this messenger?"

"She's coming to us." He was rummaging through a cupboard with his head shoved inside. His voice came out muffled.

"What?" I sat up straight. "But you just said this place was safe for you and me. If she comes then she knows where it is, where we are."

"She's an ally. We'll be safe with her. Trust me that you can trust her." Kellan kept shifting through things, moving things aside.

"What are you doing?"

"I thought some food was here. We need to eat a little bit." Then he pulled back and shook his head. "I'll have to go into town and get some things. There isn't any good food here for us."

"Town?" Where was the closest town? I just remembered trees.

"I'll have to drive there, too. It'll be an hour before I get back." Kellan sounded frustrated, but within seconds he was gone. And I was left alone in a magical house and trees that were alive surrounding it. I knew I wasn't only human, but I felt very helpless in that moment.

After a few more minutes of sitting there, still feeling shocked at the turn of events, I stood to grab my bag and headed to one of the higher floors. I wandered around, studying all the bedrooms, and settled on one in a back corner. It had its own bathroom and windows on both sides. The bed was a king size on top of a sturdy wooden base and headboard. It was a simple bedroom with quilts to make it look homey for the human eye, but warm for the demonic body, especially on colder nights. I knew Kellan would appreciate the quilts, but then I remembered the entire house was given to him. Of course, he'd appreciate them; they were probably put there *just* for him.

I looked through my bag, saw two changes of clothes, and then started poking in the closets. After finding clothes upon clothes, in my size and his, I wasn't sure why Kellan had even bothered to pack bags. However, I was glad he'd thought to pack a book. At least, I could read something if I got really bored.

Checking my phone, I saw that he'd been gone for an hour. I figured that he'd be back soon so I headed into the shower. Afterwards, I dressed in some clothes from the closet, a comfortable pair of black running pants and a loose gray top. Heading back down, I started poking around for a liquor cabinet. There had to be one. Kellan wasn't much for drinking, but I knew he enjoyed some on occasion. It seemed the appropriate thing to do in our first night at the sanctuary.

I pulled out a bottle of wine. With two large glasses in hand, I turned for the kitchen for a bottle opener, but as soon as my foot took one step forward, the house started to shake. At first it was the floors, then the walls, then the roof. Everything was shaking. Furniture started to glide across the floor, moved by the waves of shaking. I dropped the bottle and glasses onto a couch and then I stopped feeling the movements. My eyes caught sight of a chandelier in the foyer, saw that it was still shaking, and then I looked down. I wasn't shaking because I was floating in the air; much how I had been the night I'd turned Matt into a zombie. Just like then, I started to fall, but I caught myself. My eyes shut, and I concentrated in my mind. *Stay!* I barked at myself, but I started falling again slowly.

"Stop thinking, and it will happen."

The voice wasn't Kellan's, and my eyes snapped open to see an elderly woman in the corner. Her hair was silver, pulled over her shoulders to rest below her ribcage. She was dressed in a black cloak with white trim. Both of her arms were folded over each other, and the white trim moved when she opened her arms to me. "Child, you radiate the same ferocity of your father."

I landed on my feet, but jumped to a far corner. "Who are you?"

She smiled again, gently, but with a rueful look in her eyes. "I am your aunt, your mother's sister."

"My—what?"

"I know." She glided forward smoothly and smiled to herself, as if remembering fond memories. "You were told that your mother was a human in love with a demon, but she wasn't. Your *real* mother was a Nephilim, such as yourself, a hybrid of human and messenger. However, your mother's body wasn't strong enough to hold you. So they put you in that human's body. Her body had been strengthened from years of loving her demon. He had carved her out and enforced the inside of her with demonic power. None of it touched you. We made sure of it, but you were special. You were supposed to be born so we put you in there, hiding you from your father also." She sighed. "It made me happy, just getting you away from your father."

My knees gave out, and I fell to the stairs where I had been hovering over. "Wha—huh?"

She laughed then, and the sound reverberated deep within me. It was a rich sound, strong, and I felt the ancestry go into me. It went deep and took root. In that moment, I felt her in me, that we were a part of each other. Her memories rushed through me at a rapid pace. Flashes of her as a young girl, with blonde hair, came to me. They were quickly followed by images of her with another younger woman, whose green eyes turned and looked at me. I gasped, flailing backward, when I felt the other woman see me. They were memories, but it was as if she really could see me.

"She can see you. That's your mother, your true mother." My aunt had moved to sit beside me. She watched me, concerned, and touched my hand with hers. It was a warm touch, but more of her rushed into me. The physical contact seared everything else, sealing the contact, and something woke inside of me. The messenger woke, feeling her family's blood near. She railed against me, on the inside, wanting to get out.

"No—oh my God—no," I gasped, lunging forward. She was so strong, trying to break free. I couldn't hold her back, and I felt my body lurch into the air, arching backward. A light came out of me. It shone from my eyes, my nose, my mouth, even my ears. My fingertips were like flashlights, shining outward.

"Let her come. She needs to see me. She will calm down after this. I promise you," my aunt whispered, touching my throat tenderly.

I watched her, nearly helpless now, from the corner of my eye. My head had turned to the side, and a tear slid down to the corner of my eyelid. It held onto my eyelash before it slipped and fell to the floor. My aunt caught it in the palm of her hand and moved it to the tip of her finger before she lifted it back to me. As she placed it back on my eye, she murmured with a soft smile, "You shouldn't cry about this, not this tear anyway. This is a good thing. It will always be a good thing."

The tear moved back into my eye, and it was the last straw. The messenger doubled her fervor, and I swallowed, closing my eyes, when I felt my insides tear once more.

KELLAN

KELLAN WATCHED through a window in the north corner of the house. He was perched on a tree limb, and it moved close so he could better see. The house moved, too, giving him the best view of what was happening in the foyer of his sanctuary.

The connection between him and Shay had started pulsating moments before, and then it rattled with such force, so much power, that he knew what had happened when he'd been gone. The messenger had come, knowing he was away. He wasn't surprised. He'd expected it, but he hadn't expected to feel Shay's fear as if it were his own. It terrified her, consumed her so much, that he was tempted to enter to help calm her. However, his presence, one of a demon, would potentially enrage the messenger, even the one inside of Shay. It was stronger being near another of her own, especially one of her family.

When the messenger broke free once more, he felt Shay snap to him. She came across the invisible connection and rested next to him, as if perched on the tree beside him. Her body was still inside with the messenger in control, but Shay was with him, watching, too. They both held their breaths when the messenger rushed to the elder messenger. Their arms wrapped around the other, holding on tightly. Both had tears streaming down with smiles of relief on their faces.

It was a touching moment, of long lost relatives being reunited. Kellan watched, feeling disconnected from the emotional welcoming back. His connection was beside him, not in that body, so it was as if he watched mere strangers. A part of him felt as if he shouldn't be so close to his enemy, but he knew Shay would return. Then everything in him would become alarmed again, doubling in its ferocity, because the messenger had broken free once more, threatening Shay's hold over her. It threatened their own connection too because if he lost Shay, then he lost everything. But, he knew the messenger needed to be consoled by her own blood. And he was hoping that Aumae would remember her end of the bargain. He brought Shay to her, and she in turn would soothe the messenger, tell her that everything would be fine if she would trust her human counterpart. Shay's aunt was supposed to make the messenger more compliant with them, not against him as much.

He swallowed tightly, hoping his gamble would pay off. If Aumae went back on her word, taking her niece with her and forgetting the human part of Shay behind, then he would have a different war on his hands. This one would get bloody, whereas he hoped the other one still wouldn't, with Vespar being the exception.

After a few tense moments, watching how Aumae bent her head, hugging her niece, and whispered into her ear, Kellan wasn't sure how much longer he could hold himself back. He wanted to break in, force the messenger to allow Shay back in, or force Shay to take over again. He remained and then, after what seemed like an hour, Aumae lifted her head with tears in her eyes and looked up at him. She smiled and whispered the words that floated up to him, "Thank you. Thank you for giving me this time with her. She will help you. I promise you this."

As the last word was spoken, Shay was yanked back from beside him. She sailed down and into her body, where it collapsed to the ground. Kellan lithely jumped to the ground in one leap and entered through the front door. He stepped inside and saw that Aumae had moved Shay's body, now sleeping, to the couch. She sat beside her and smoothed her hair back, brushing it with her fingers.

He stopped in the living room's doorway, just watching the tender movement. "Shay already loves you. I can feel it."

Aumae bent her head, closing her eyes. Her shoulders started to shake, and he heard the sounds of crying coming from her. Sobs then started to wrack her body, and she crumbled, throwing herself over Shay. He turned, knowing his gamble had paid off. The elder messenger would help them and she had persuaded the one inside of Shay to help as well. Because of it, Shay would be strong, even more powerful than he knew. And so would he. The two of them could withstand her father's arrival now.

15

When I woke, I found myself on the bed of the room that I had chosen earlier. A blanket had been placed over me, but it wasn't needed. I was hot, really hot. In fact, I was burning up. Then I heard voices below me. They were soft, as if whispering, but I knew they weren't. It was Kellan and my aunt in the kitchen. Then, with a gasp, everything rushed at me again. The voices went from soft to loud, too loud. I clamped my hands over my ears and burrowed underneath the pillows, but it did nothing to soften their volume. It was nearly painful now. But that wasn't the only problem.

I saw everything in perfect detail as if I held up a microscope to my eye. My blanket went from looking like a normal blanket, one that I would admire the colors and textures, to the particles that made up the individual threads. I saw it all, even the dust that rested on each tiny particle. And the smells—I pressed my nose to my pillow, trying to stop from smelling so much, from the dew that still lingered from the morning to the night owls that rested miles away in a tree.

My stomach twisted over, threatening to spill out from all the smells. My entire body was on fire, protesting from all the information that I was taking in. I could feel Kellan's heartbeat, how it pounded at a regular slow pace and then picked up, sensing that I had woken. Their footsteps pounded like ten herds of elephants, and soon I felt Kellan's hands on my shoulders.

He lifted me up and held me against his chest, but it was too much. I scrambled away, crying, gasping, "Please, no. It's too much. I..." I swung my eyes to my aunt and saw the understanding in them. She knew what I was going through, and I choked out, "Help me. Please."

"The messenger has bonded with her again. She can't handle everything at once. She senses too much. It's overwhelming her."

"I know," Kellan growled and then stood before me. He tried to look gentle, but the fear was clawing at him. I felt it within him. It was clawing at me, too. He didn't know how to help me; he didn't know how to make it stop.

Then he made up his mind. "Out! Now!" My aunt went, but looked back over her shoulder before pulling the door shut behind her. I felt her concern as if it was my own and it shook me. How I could feel that? How could I know what she was thinking, what she was feeling, when she wasn't me?

Kellan gripped my shoulders and lifted me in the air. He carried me, holding me against his chest, and went to one of my windows. It was opened in an instant, and then he perched there, holding me for a moment, and leapt through the air. The trees moved for us. Some helped us along the way, brushing their leaves against us while other ducked out of the way. We landed in the small pool behind the house with the waterfall beside us.

With one hand on the back of my head, he ducked us both underneath. Immediately, everything went away. It was as if I was normal again, the old Shay who didn't know who I was. The relief was so powerful in me, I almost started crying, but I opened my eyes and saw Kellan in front of me. He held us on the bottom, anchoring us there, and he watched me, fearful. I felt it inside of me, taking root. I smiled and lifted both of my hands to grasp his face. My thumbs rubbed back and forth at the corners of his lips, and something else started to come over me.

The fervor was deep inside, but it started to climb. Then it matched with his, entwined, and twisted together to build even faster, higher, at a rapid pace. My heart started pounding. I gasped, but water rushed inside. Before I closed my mouth to stop more water from getting in, Kellan slammed his mouth over mine. His lips sucked the inside of my mouth dry, taking the water back out. He moved back once to spit it out, but his mouth was back before I fully realized he had even left. One of his hands gripped the back of my neck and the other lifted me up so my legs wrapped around his waist. He held us steady there, on the bottom of the lake. My arms wrapped around him, but I was lost on the inside of him. Everything was wrapped with him.

My heartbeat was racing so fast I was afraid that I'd combust in a moment, but I never did. Kellan calmed me down, still kissing me with a finger on the pulse at my neck. He rubbed against it, and somehow it calmed me. But then the hunger for him burst inside of me. It exploded, and I held on, weak, as if I was starving. My lips searched his.

He gripped me tightly against him, and then we were going to the surface. We broke the surface, and I gasped, pulling away. My eyes saw everything through a glaze of water still on my eyelids. It was as if we were still swimming, but I blinked a few times and brushed away the water. I saw it all clearly and then too clearly—everything until Kellan held my head in his hands. His eyes bore into mine, and he commanded, "You can control this. She was a part of you before. She's a part of you now. Accept it. Accept her. Accept everything else, even though I know you don't want to, but you have to." He jerked me against him, wrapping his arms around me in a tight hug and kissed my shoulder. "Accept who you are. Please. I need you."

My fingers clung into his shoulders, digging into them. I was trying, I really was, but everything was too much. I felt the birds as they landed on their nests. I heard the laughter from a neighbor on his phone miles away. I felt my aunt's concern in the house behind us, sitting in a corner in the kitchen with a glass of wine to calm her nerves. Her hands clenched it tightly, and her fingers were tapping the counter, in a nervous reaction. I felt everything. Still. And I couldn't handle it—then I gasped, arching upward in the water, surging against him.

"Shay," Kellan choked out, the sound gurgling in the back of his throat, as he held onto my waist when I leapt upward.

It was too much. It was all too much, and then something in him shifted—he shifted inside of me. It was his demon. He reached inside, leapt with me, and yanked at everything. It was fine—it was all gone. I still felt all the information, everything that I had sensed, but it was okay. I could handle it, and I didn't know why. I didn't know what had happened, but I realized that Kellan's forehead was pressed to my shoulder, limp. He hung on to me, as if I was holding him afloat now. He'd gone slack from exhaustion. Something occurred between us, something with his demon, because all his energy was spent.

I swam to the edge, holding him with me until we got to the bank. Then I pushed him up and rested beside him, collapsing.

A clothed foot stepped beside me, and my aunt's silver cloak bunched to the ground when she knelt at my head. Her hand came to rest on my cheek. "You should rest, child. You have gone through much." She straightened, and I heard her say further, "As has he."

We were both lifted in the air. Kellan was asleep, but his hand fell out, reaching for me. I put my hand in his, and then we were both being carried through the air to the house and to my bed. Kellan was placed next to me and his arm reached out to curl around me, pulling me close. He tucked his chin on my shoulder and twisted a leg around mine before he fell into a deep sleep.

I looked up at my aunt who had followed behind to perch on the edge of the bed at my head. She smiled in the moonlight now and combed my hair back behind my ear. "You are very beautiful. Just like her."

An image of my mother flashed through me. Pain followed quickly behind.

She added, "My name is Aumae, and I am honored to meet you, Shay. To meet both of you."

My eyelids fluttered closed, the exhaustion was too much, but I wondered whom she meant—the messenger and me or Kellan and me? Then I fell asleep, and nothing mattered.

When I woke, it was night again, and I sat up.

"How are you?" Kellan asked, perched on a windowsill. It gave him a mysterious, feline, and lethal look at the same time. Then he blinked, and all mystery was gone, rising in a fluid motion.

My heart skipped a beat, but I answered, breathless, "I'm fine. You?"

He cracked a grin. "Shay, don't lie to me. How are you? How is she?"

Then it all flooded me again, the sensory overload, the pool, the kiss, and then his demon... "What did you do to me?"

"Nothing." He stood before me as I still sat in bed. Neither of us moved, but we breathed as one. The air felt heavy, too heavy.

One breath. Two breaths. I asked, holding mine, "Was that you or was that..."

His eyes held mine, shining with a fierce emotion. "What do you think?"

I already knew—his demon had gone inside of me, but why? What did he do? What did he want? "Did he hurt me?"

Kellan snorted. "He helped you. Are you serious?"

"But—" Why would a demon help me? Help a hybrid?

"I'm a hybrid," Kellan bit out, in front of me in a flash. He braced both arms on either side of me on the bed and bent forward until his nose was an inch from mine. As his eyes bore into mine, he repeated slowly, with deadly promise, "I am a hybrid, too. I am human, and I am a demon. You're not just a hybrid, Shay. And by the way, she's merged with you. My demon helped you with that because you were freaking out, so much that you fought against accepting her. You should be thanking him, thanking me. Not wondering why we would want to help you."

Jerking away from me, he turned, but I heard him mutter, "She doesn't trust me."

"I never trusted you."

He looked back, and I waited for a few moments until he said in a low voice, "You did, in some small part. Part of you hated me, part of you distrusted me, but a part of you loves me. The part that loves me, and even more now, trusts me completely. And a part of you can't handle that. Can you?"

He was right, on all accounts. "I do love you. You're right, but I know that your demon did something to me. I don't know what he did. It can't be good, Kellan! I'm half-messenger. You're half-demon. It can't be good."

He took two steps toward me, then stopped abruptly. One hand flexed into a fist, but he forced it to relax against his thigh. "He didn't harm you. I wouldn't let him. *I* wouldn't harm you. Leave it at that."

I was speechless for a moment, staring wide-eyed at him until he turned away. As he did, the tension broke between us. A soft knock sounded on the door, and Aumae glided inside, a cup in her hand. She smiled, tucking a strand of her hair behind one ear as the rest gathered on her other shoulder, hanging low in a loose braid. Her robe touched my arm when she bent and placed the cup beside me on a nightstand. She turned and glanced between Kellan and me, then her smile beamed more. "I've brought her a cup of tea. It's very healing, especially with her changes. It will soothe her. That's what she needs right now."

Kellan jerked his head to the side and left. A burst of wind rushed at me from his sudden departure, and I closed my eyes, breathing in his smell for a moment. When I opened them again as his scent had already faded, I saw my aunt watching me with concern. She sat next to me on the edge of the bed and laid a hand on my cheek. "He only means the best for you. I can see that in him. It's so strong that there's a different aura around him. I've never met a demon like him. It's very...rare."

"She's holding back. There's more she wants to say..." a voice whispered to me. I jerked when I heard it, but I calmed, knowing it was the messenger in me—or it was just me now.

I should've asked what else she wanted to say, what she wasn't saying, but I didn't. I didn't want to hear any more new information, revelations that I couldn't handle so I lay back down. My aunt brushed back some hair from my forehead. It was a loving touch, one that I hadn't felt in so long, if ever.

Both of us sat there in silence, and then after a while Aumae pressed a soft kiss to my forehead. "You radiate now. She's merged with you, and you both look so beautiful. You look just like your mother now. It's painful to see it, but also a blessing. I miss her so."

"Where is she?" I sat up against the headboard, scooting back with my knees raised to my chest and the cup of tea in my hand.

She sat back and looked away, smiling from fond memories. "It's painful at times to think of it, but your mother passed away. It's been six years now."

"What happened?"

"No one knows. She'd gone upstairs one night, and I found her the next morning. She passed away in her bed. She'd been missing you. She felt something happened to you, but we couldn't find you."

"She felt me?"

"You were linked together because you came from her; your Nephilim was constantly trying to find hers. At first, it was so strong, but when you were little, your connection was almost lost. It dropped overnight."

I whispered, "When I was little?"

"You must've been six or so, just a little girl." Aumae bent her head, and her shoulders shook slightly.

I heard tears in her voice, and my own throat closed up. "What do you mean you couldn't find me before? You think my surrogate mother hid me or something? Like, kidnapped me?"

"We don't think so. We know so. You were put in her so she could birth you, but we were supposed to keep in contact with her. Of course, you were supposed to come back to us, but as soon as you were in her, they disappeared. It was like they fell off the face of the Earth. We couldn't do anything to find you, and we tried. We tried with our messenger side, using magic. We tried asking for help, even your father couldn't find you. They took you away, and it wasn't until Kellan contacted me a month ago that I knew you were alive. Your mother kept saying you were, that she felt little twinges from you every now and then, but I stopped believing her. I always thought she died from a broken heart, from missing you so much."

Kellan had contacted—I knew he had. Of course, he had since we'd found my aunt, but it hadn't really clicked with me before now. Kellan knew. How long had he known? Had he known this whole time that I'd been taken away from my real parents? What else did he know about me? He'd known who I was this entire time, that we were soulmates, but he'd kept it a secret from me. What else was he keeping from me?

Anger started to boil inside of me. How dare he keep my mother away from me. Did he know about her? He must've. He knew so much, too much.

"Shay, calm down."

I broke out of my thoughts and realized the bed had started to rise in the air, shaking from my anger. Immediately, I set it back down and stopped the trembling. My body stopped shaking, too.

"You're starting to control yourself better." My aunt held a hand against my cheek, brushing her thumb under my eyelid gently. "That's good. That means you're growing into yourself again."

"Kellan said we can be strong now. What did he mean by that?" I was hesitant to ask her, but he'd brought us to her for a reason. A part of me knew that I was supposed to find answers that he couldn't tell me, but there was so much I didn't know what to ask or who I should ask. I was still afraid to trust anyone.

"I can't really answer that. I just know that he wanted me to meet you. He wanted you to meet me, and you're already going strong. You've merged with your messenger side. You're so much stronger than you know, but I can see it in you. So can he. That demon of yours is one very smart, very powerful demon. He knows what he's doing and if I didn't see how much he loves you, I would fight him myself for you. I would take you away from here, away from the mess you're in, but I trust him. I trust that he knows what he's doing. You're linked to him. Anyone can see how powerful your connection is. You two need each other."

"Can a demon be good?"

"Before I met Kellan, I would've said no. But even as I say that, there's darkness in him, too. Complete darkness that only the most evil have in them. Your demon is more demon than you know, less human than you think."

I frowned, wondering what she meant by that, but then my aunt stood again. With a final squeeze to my hand and another soft kiss on my forehead, she went to the door. "I have to leave for some things. I will be back soon, in a few days."

"Where are you going?" My heart picked up a beat, feeling panic. Was she coming back?

"Just to get some items that will help you guys. I promise. I'll be back in no time. You won't even miss me." Then she shut the door quietly, and I was left sitting in bed, wondering why I felt a part of myself had just left me. Was my connection to her so strong already that I needed her with me? Was I comfortable with that connection, the feeling of needing her so much? I sighed, finishing my tea. A part of me didn't want to need anyone, miss anyone, even love anyone. It'd always been me against the world, and I didn't altogether enjoy that I was starting to lose that feeling. It usually meant that something awful was going to happen.

16

I'd been home alone for twenty-four hours when Kellan finally showed. He found me in the kitchen, making some food and brewing coffee. My head was bent over the stove, thinking when his voice broke my concentration. "Your powers have increased."

"What?" I looked up with my hands braced on the counter. He looked so good...too good. I swallowed tightly and kept myself from throwing my body against him, hugging him or doing something worse.

He grinned crookedly, a small smirk, and placed three paper bags on the table. He nodded toward the stove. "You're not using your hands when you stir that thing. And you're putting stuff away without even looking. You're starting to control your power. That's good."

Shocked, I looked around and then realized I had been putting away pans, condiments, anything that I'd taken out. I'd been doing it in the back of my mind, without even thinking about it.

"You're doing it naturally now. You don't even have to think about it, and it's already done. You're becoming a force."

"What do you mean?" What *did* he mean? It was only flour and a few mixing bowls.

"Nothing, just that it's natural to you now. You've become stronger since she's merged with you. You look at me differently, too. Did you notice that?"

"I do? How did I look at you before? How do I now?"

"You haven't always trusted me, but you've softened to me a bit, since finding out we're soulmates. Now distrust is there again, but it's more. There's a part of you that won't ever trust me, not fully. I think it's from her. She'll never trust me."

He spoke so candidly, as if we were discussing the weather. I hated that. I hated how casual this seemed to him and I turned, hissing, "How dare you talk like that—as if it's okay that I don't trust you. I should trust you. It should bother you that I don't trust you—" My words were cut off as Kellan lunged at me, growling. He pinned my arms against the counter behind me, pushing his body against mine, his eyes peering down into mine.

He wanted to dominate me, and a part of me wanted him to. I bit back what I'd been about to spew at him when I saw the fury in his eyes, brimming just under the surface. Then he leaned closer, nipping at my lips with his. I gasped, arching against him and felt him between my legs.

He whispered against my skin, tilting my head up with a hand beneath my jaw, on my neck, "It doesn't bother me that you don't trust me. I'm a demon, Shay. You're not supposed to trust me, but you should love me. It would bother me if you didn't love me." Then he licked my neck, lingering at the corner of my mouth and sweeping in, taking everything from me as he savored the kiss. "But I know you love me. You love me so much that you can't handle it. You're terrified of what you feel for me and that's why you're scared about not trusting me. You belong to me, and you know it. A part of you has already succumbed to me. Stop fighting it. Stop fighting us."

His hand smoothed down my arm and curved around my waist, pulling me closer against him. Then he lifted one of my legs so it entwined around his, positioning him, ready for entry. Our clothes were the only barrier stopping him from entering me.

One of his hands gripped my neck, lifting my chin again, and his eyes watched me all the while. Peering inside of me, judging, waiting.

"What do you want?"

He smirked. "What do you think? I want you, all of you."

My hands were helpless as they clung to his arms, holding myself upward. "Why? You knew about my family. You kept me from them. Why would you do that?"

His thumb inched upward and dipped into my mouth, hooking on the inside of my lip. His smirk looked almost cruel. "Why do you think? You're mine, Shay. If I handed you over to your family before you knew this, what would you have done? You would've left me."

"What are you saying?" My eyes glazed over, feeling him between my legs. He wanted to pierce me, shifting even harder against me, into me. I felt my desire there and knew my wetness had soaked my clothes. I wondered if he could smell it. I did. It was intoxicating and embarrassing at the same time. I bit my lip, wishing my body wouldn't betray me while it did anyway.

"I've known about your mother and your aunt since I became old enough to look for them. It's been a few years, *only* a few years, but I couldn't risk losing you. Paint me the bad guy for that, I don't care. I still wasn't willing to gamble you and throw the dice. I brought you to them when it was safe for me. You would've done the same."

I frowned, wondering what he meant, but his eyes snapped to the right. His body stiffened, and he dropped his hands from me, stepping back. I fell against the counter and would've fallen to the floor if he hadn't caught me with one hand. He whispered in my head, "*Something's coming. Demons. They're not friendly.*"

Then he flung me behind him and sent two bursts of black energy at the doorframe. Two dark figures flew in, but immediately were flung backward. They ripped through the house and into the trees outside. Another black figure soared at us from above and something came over me. My head snapped back, all the way back, and my eyes shifted into yellow. I saw the demon and became furious. Yellow energy emanated from me and shot upward, slamming it away from us.

Kellan leapt after the other two and lifted his hand, catching both of them in a paralyzing grip. They floated in the air, helpless to move or fight back, as he drew them to us.

The third demon was coming back. I felt its approach and then flung my own hand outward, palm extended in the air, and I caught the demon in my grip, too. I had no idea how I was doing it, but I was angry. How dare they try to attack us? How dare they think about hurting us? My fury knew no bounds, and I was ready to tear the demon apart. I wanted to torture him one breath after another. I wanted him to hurt. He intended to hurt us. Then Kellan spoke in my ear, "Don't kill him. Not yet. We need to find out what they know, why they came here for us."

I growled, "I don't care." And I flexed my hand, bending the demon in half and it screamed. The agony that came from its mouth was genuine and blinding. I smiled, bending it even more, until I felt him ripped from my hold.

Kellan glared at me, flinging one of his demons away. It hit a tree that caught it and used both sides of its branches to tear the demon in half. It turned to dust and fell to the ground. A wind then swept it up and flung it away from us, far away. Kellan took the demon I had broken, still hanging together by a piece and rested him on the table before us. It was quivering in pain, writhing in motion, but the sound was the worst. It was a high-pitched whimper, sniffling. I wanted to silence it then and there, but Kellan clamped a hand on me, stopping me as he floated the other one to sit at the table in front of us. Its leader was still thrashing back and forth on top of the table, but this one stared at us in terror. His eyes were wide, white saucers with nothing in the middle. The entire figure was cloaked in a black robe.

"They're from the underworld," Kellan spoke in my ear, holding me back. He wanted me behind him, and he spoke in my head, "Remain quiet. They get information from you the more you speak. They can see into your words. Don't do anything. Trust me."

I trusted him, but I wanted to hurt them more. A thirst for their pain had been awakened in me. It was nearly intoxicating, threatening to take over, but I closed my eyes and battled for control. Kellan was right. He'd get the information we needed: why they were sent to us, who sent them, and what they wanted. Killing them wouldn't help us in the long run, but I wanted to. I wanted to so badly.

He stalked toward them, growing before my eyes. I shrunk behind him, but Kellan took on a menacing stance. A black cloak seemed to shimmer over him, covering him before my eyes, and then I heard him speak in a different language. It sent chills down my back, and I gritted my teeth, fighting myself from lashing out. I wanted to stop the words that he spoke. I didn't know what he said, but I wanted them to go away. I wanted it all to go away. I couldn't stand the stench of the demons in the sanctuary's kitchen. I cringed hearing Kellan speak to them in their own language, and I loathed the reminder that he was one of them, more powerful than they were even.

After a few moments of them fighting him, straining not to answer him, and Kellan striking them with his power, one buckled. The demon couldn't stop babbling. The words poured out of him as he doubled over, crying, whimpering, begging. It sickened me. The entire thing made me nauseated and I bolted from the room, dashing upstairs to my bathroom. Within moments, I burst through the door and emptied my stomach's contents into the toilet. I hurled a few more times until something exploded beneath me, under the floorboards, where the kitchen was. Immediately, I felt relief and knew that Kellan had vanquished both demons. Their presence no longer haunted me, overwhelming me with sickness. It wasn't long before he came to the bathroom door and stood there. "Are you okay?"

I nodded and wiped some vomit from my mouth. "I'm fine." I collapsed against the wall and sat there with my knees raised before me, my arms dangling from them, feeling lifeless.

"Your reaction was from her. You know that, right?" He sounded cautious, reserved from me.

My stomach twisted again, feeling how he watched his words with me. It was like he was scared of me, hesitant of my reaction. I closed my eyes, pain stabbing my gut at his reaction, but I choked out, "I know." And I did. My hatred had been tenfold since I had merged with her. Only an idiot wouldn't have known where it had come from, but another feeling took over me. What was I supposed to do about that? I was a hybrid, half-messenger. And that side was more powerful now within me. Some of these emotions were bound to come out, right...

"I know you can't help it." Kellan put me at ease, sitting next to me and then reaching for my hand. "I just don't want you to ever loathe me. That's all I worry about."

I was relieved. I could do that. Hell, loathing was the opposite of what I felt for him. Then I grinned, resting my head against his shoulder. "That's the last thing you need to worry about with me." I squeezed his hand for extra reassurance.

"I have something to tell you, something that you're not going to like."

My stomach twisted again, curled into a ball once more. I

forced myself to ask, breathing out, "What is it?" But my teeth gritted together. I wasn't going to like it.

"They took your aunt. They have her, and they sent them after us. They wanted to take us too."

I closed my eyes, feeling a ball of fury roll over on itself inside of me. Something started to take over me... Then I grated out, "Tell me that you found out where they're holding her."

"I did. I know." He seemed to be choosing his words carefully. I felt his hesitation as if it were my own. And I hated it.

"Well?" I snapped out.

Kellan sighed, his hand now lax in mine. "I'll take you there."

"Fine." I scrambled to my feet, ready for war, but I asked first, "Who took her? Who sent them after us?"

Kellan hesitated before answering. "I don't know. He wouldn't say."

He was lying. I felt it. I knew it. I could taste it, but I held my tongue. This wasn't the time or the place to demand answers from him. All I cared about was getting my aunt back. Kellan would tell me. I would make sure of that, but he could wait. That was fine, but he *would* tell me. As I watched him leave the bathroom, my eyes stuck to his back, feeling his lie within me. It was a betrayal, but there was more in me, a sense of determination.

I followed behind, and I couldn't squash the hope inside that there would be more demons to kill. It was becoming a favorite hobby of mine. The thirst was almost too powerful for my liking, but I couldn't stop the desire. It throbbed inside of me, almost as much as my desire for him, but of that, I held my tongue. I was sure we'd finish what he had promised to start in the kitchen. When that moment happened, I could only hope I wouldn't end up begging at his mercy, but something told me that was what Kellan wanted. It seemed up his alley, and I couldn't stop the shiver of excitement in me.

"You coming?" He came to the doorway, dressed in black clothes that were tight on him. My eyes wandered over him, unable to stop myself. Each abdominal muscle was outlined by the material, tucked inside his pants that showed how trim his waist was. Then he bent and grabbed my hand. He lifted me over his shoulder, and my hand fell out, feeling how his skin shifted over his muscles there, each rippling as he moved me back inside the bedroom and then placed me onto the bed.

Need throbbed inside of me, for him and for vengeance. I couldn't battle both of them, so I let him see the hunger in me when he dropped some clothes onto my lap.

He stopped, frozen, and I felt his desire explode inside of him. Then he retreated, battling his primal side back down. His voice came out strangled. "We can't. Let's go. We have to get your aunt now, before it's too late."

"What will happen?" I scrambled into my clothes, trying not to dwell on my disappointment. How could I even think about my desire in that moment? Aumae could already be dead or worse.

"They could go back to the underworld. She can't go there. The mere entrance will be enough torture for her. They're still here, but not for long. They're waiting for their comrades to return with us, once they don't, they'll go without them." Then he grabbed my arm and whisked us down to the car.

When we got in and Kellan started the car, I looked around with an odd feeling in my gut. "We're...driving there?"

He bit back a smile, but gunned the engine, spitting dirt behind us. "We have to. They won't be attuned to human transportation. They're waiting for anything supernatural to come at them. We can get close and they won't know we're there."

That made sense, but... "What about us? Don't we give off vibes? Won't they feel us, just being there?"

"Grab those bags. I put them in the backseat. Inside are cloaking medallions. Give them to me."

I twisted and saw the paper bags he had brought into the kitchen. When I reached inside, I pulled out a small bag with gold coins inside. They looked the size of a quarter, but weighed what a small child might. As I dropped the bag in Kellan's hand, I could hear whispers of an incantation, in a language that I didn't know, but they quieted in his hands.

He brought them to his mouth and began whispering the same incantation, then as something was building in the air, his other hand grabbed mine. His fingers entwined with mine and he brought it to his mouth, kissing it as he kissed the coins in the same moment. I felt the explosion around us, the air spread out in a whoosh, but there was no difference in us. Kellan looked the same, so did I, but he'd just done something.

"What happened?"

He put the coins back and then put the paper bag behind us. "Our presence, to humans and other beings are now cloaked. No one should be able to find us until the spell ends. We can't cloak ourselves. It has to come from the outside world for it to work."

None of that made sense to me, but I sat back. Kellan knew what he was doing, which seemed too easy. However, I'd keep my mouth shut for now, until we got Aumae back and dealt with my father, not to mention Vespar, too.

The drive took hours, but the adrenaline was still boiling inside of me. Kellan pulled the car over on the side of a street, which seemed to be in the middle of a dense forest.

"Where are we?"

"We have to walk in. They're in a cave, and I can already sense two of them patrolling the woods. We will have to be discreet until we can get inside and find Aumae."

"Then what?"

"We grab her and kill everybody else."

17

Shivers went down my back, hearing the promise in his words. There had been no other consideration. Kellan was going to destroy them all, even if I didn't join in. As we got outside, I smelled a whiff of the demons and my stomach turned over, but then something came alive in me. I'd wanted their blood before, but had gotten sick in the next moment. That was not going to happen this time. I wasn't going to be running to vomit anymore.

Kellan started forward, and I saw the same black cloak come over him that had happened in the kitchen. I wasn't sure what it was, but something shimmied over me, too. I watched, speechless, as something glided over my skin, translucent to my eyes. It felt like armor, but weighed like nothing, like air.

Whatever it was, I felt protected. I felt like I could walk in and raise hell, knowing they couldn't touch me.

The closer we got, the sickness from before built inside of me. It fueled me, and when we looked up to see a demon floating in the air above us, looking around with no idea we were there, I had to grit my teeth. I wanted to kill it, too much, and Kellan took my hand in his. He led me past it and past the

second one that looked like it was perched on a tree limb, with
his white saucer eyes shining a beacon wherever it looked. The
light blinded us for a moment, but it moved past without
missing a beat.

We were safe.

The entrance of the cave wasn't far. I felt the mouth of the
cave like it was the opening to a vortex. Whatever was inside
was evil, through and through. It sucked anything good,
anything pure, and swallowed it whole. Two more demons
floated above it, but Kellan took my hand again and we stepped
around tree roots, over and under. We followed a narrow path
that led around a body of water. I glanced down once,
wondering what the water would be like with so much darkness near it, but it shined blue and bright. It even looked white
in some parts from the sand that was so close to the surface. I
felt it beckoning to me. It wanted me to go inside, take a swim,
but Kellan yanked me away.

*"It's enchanted. The water doesn't look right. It'll draw you down
and drown you, killing anything that steps foot in it. Don't even look
at the water,"* he warned me in my head, shaking his.

As soon as we stepped inside, Aumae's pain was overwhelming. I felt her everywhere, in every corner, behind every
rock. It almost stopped me in my tracks, it was so strong. The
torture must've been tremendous, and I held my breath the rest
of the way. Kellan seemed to know where to go, when to pause
as a demon went past us, and when to sidestep traps they had
laid.

The cave turned downward, and we followed. The sounds
of water grew in volume the lower we went, and soon the
narrow pathway we were on grew slippery. Water dripped from
the walls and ceiling onto our feet. Some splashed up from
below, and the rushing sounds of it grew loud, too loud to hear
anything else.

I turned one corner, but Kellan yanked me back. A floating

demon was right in front of me, would've touched me in the next instant. He passed by and it wasn't until my heart slowed a little bit before I let myself breathe again. It had been close, too close, but rounding another corner, I saw that we were there.

Aumae was tied to the floor in front of us. Her wrists were crisscrossed over each other, bound by rope to two stakes. Her legs had been spread out, also staked to the ground. As we got closer, I saw the rope was soaked in a red liquid. Aumae's eyes were closed and tears had streaked down her cheeks, leaving trails through the dust and dirt on her skin. The white robe she wore before was stained in red. There were clumps of the same red liquid on her robe and marks that looked like she'd been scratched.

I bent to untie one, but Kellan shoved me aside again. *"Don't touch them. They're soaked in virgin's blood."*

"Virgin's blood? Are you serious?"

"The virgin was raped and killed, Shay. It's an old metaphor for purity, but it still has power over messengers. Whatever was pure and innocent that's been violated by the hands of evil will harm a messenger. Aumae is bound just by the blood, not the rope."

I shuddered and moved away, wondering what would've happened to me if I'd touched them. It didn't matter, thankfully, as Kellan had them untied in seconds. I waited, expecting Aumae to spring up, released and free, but she remained on the ground, groaning and writhing in pain still. I exchanged worried looks with Kellan, but he knelt quickly and thrust her robe away. Still, she stayed on the floor.

"What's keeping her there?"

"They soaked her in the blood. It's all over her skin and they might've made her drink it. We'll have to move her. No, I'll move her." Kellan pushed me away when I stepped forward. *"I don't want any of the blood to touch you. Its hold won't be as powerful since you're a hybrid, but it'll still affect you. I need you strong."*

He lifted her and then we turned, ready to leave, but

stopped. Four demons were there, in front of us, just staring at us.

Kellan didn't pause. He threw Aumae at them. As two caught her, he sent two bolts of his energy at the other two, flinging them backward. Then he leapt forward, took Aumae back, and whipped her around. Her feet clipped one in the head. With a hand holding my aunt's head, Kellan started to turn her around so her feet would hit the last one. As he rounded, the demon wasn't there, and he turned to look at me, a question in his eyes.

I grinned and lowered my hands. I'd sent two shots of my power at him and felt the demon die. The anger in me was boiling again, and I felt more demons approaching us, alerted from the death of their comrades. As they came in, we were still cloaked. They didn't know where I was at first, but all of them zoomed in on Kellan. Aumae wasn't cloaked and he held her, making him the obvious target.

One after another, I shot my energy at them. One after another, I felt them die from my blast. Kellan fought as well, but he wasn't the power force that he'd been at the house. Aumae was limp in his arms, barely conscious, but it wasn't long before we were making our way back up the cave. More and more demons flew down to us, but we shot all of them down. As we got to the mouth of the cave and stepped out, an army of demons waited for us, floating in the air above the water.

I looked down. I couldn't help it. The water had been serene and beautiful before. It was angry now, splashing over on itself, boiling upward. Each wave had darker waters than the last until the entire pool was a mass of churning black waves. It fed off the demons. As one dipped down, the water spewed upward to touch it. The higher demons kept more calm water below them, but it was still a rolling mass of evil, in liquid form.

"Shay."

I turned to him.

"*I'm going to put Aumae on the ground. I need my hands free to fight them. Do not touch her. Guard over her. They will try to take her with them, but they can't have her. The minute they do, they'll go to the underworld. We can't follow them there.*"

I nodded. "*I will protect her.*"

"*Don't touch her. I mean it. You'll just hurt yourself, and none of us will make it out of here.*"

He caught my gaze, and I saw the countdown in his eyes. I felt it within me. Three. Two. One. He laid Aumae down and leapt into the array of demons in the same moment. Two of them rushed for her, but I blasted them back. They seemed surprised, and I remembered that I was still cloaked. One by one, a demon tentatively floated toward her, but I sent each back, killing most of them with one blast. A few were more courageous, going almost too fast for me to shoot them. It never worked. I always caught them, sometimes just by a foot, but my power sent each of them reeling.

I stood back and saw how they started to rush around me, around Aumae. They realized I stood beside her, shooting them. They were trying to figure out where I was, trying to touch me. None of them came close, but it was a matter of time. I couldn't move Aumae, a fact they hadn't realized yet. If too many of them overtook me, I wasn't sure if I could fight them all.

As a wave of ten started to get closer to me, I tried to shoot into them. As one was taken down, another one replaced it. The wall of demons kept coming, closer and closer to me, until I feared they could feel my breath.

Then Kellan shouted, "Down!"

A tree was thrown into the group. I ducked just in time, and it sailed over my head, knocking the whole row of demons over me. I spun on my heel and took aim, shooting the tree instead of the demons. It burst into flames, white flames, and engulfed all of the demons still attached to it. They exploded, sending white sparks into the air. As those floated down onto more demons, killing them, I hoped none would touch Kellan. Then I turned again and saw another wave of demons coming at me.

This time I reached for the nearest tree and lifted it. I sent it myself at them and lit it on fire as soon as it touched the demons. This routine kept happening before the demons fell back once again. They couldn't find me to fight me so they turned their focus on Kellan.

The circle doubled in size around him. Kellan drew them above the water and then he yelled to me in his head, *"On three, light the water."*

"NO! It will hurt you, too. You need to get out of there."

"I will. I promise, but count to three and don't hold back. It has to be the exact same time."

I closed my eyes, hating what I heard, but lifted my arms anyway.

"One...Two... Three!"

I gritted my teeth and sent everything I had at the water. My energy sparked it, and it quickly grew into a rolling flame, like an exploding volcano. It burst into the air, wanting to extinguish itself somehow, but it caught the demons. All of them were sucked down into the fire, and one by one, I felt them each extinguish. They died, and as the air seemed to get lighter with the passing of one by one, I found myself praying. Words I didn't know spilled from my lips, and I tasted tears beside them.

I hoped against hope that Kellan had gotten out. He must've gotten out. It had been his plan. As the last demon burst into flames, I opened my eyes and saw another bright explosion in the air. It sucked the remaining evil from the air, the woods, the cave, and even the water. It engulfed onto itself and then vanished.

"Kellan!" I screamed. I couldn't see him anywhere. "Kellan!"

He poked his head out from behind a tree, a few feet behind me. Chuckling, he glided down to me. The black armor that had grown over him disappeared, as did mine. Somehow I knew both of them appeared because of him, but it was another question I'd wait till later to ask. At that moment, as soon as his feet touched the ground in front of me, I threw myself at him. He caught me and it felt so right, his body to mine. I savored the feel of it, the realness of him again.

"Thank goodness," I whispered against his neck and hugged him tighter. I wasn't sure if I could let him go.

He hugged me back for a moment, squeezing tight before he let me go. As he stepped back, I wanted to leap at him again, but forced myself to stay. Instead, I watched as he knelt beside Aumae and rested his hand to her cheek. After a moment, he looked back at me. "She took in a lot of blood. She'll need help. We'll have to take her to someone."

"Who?" Who even knew about this stuff, much less someone willing to work with a demon and messenger?

"There's someone I know. Take my other arm. I'm going to take us the fast way to the car."

"The car? Just take us to where she needs to go. She can't wait for a drive. We don't have the time, Kellan," I cried out.

"I will take her, but you have to drive the car back to the sanctuary. We need it there."

"Is it safe there still? They found us there before." As I spoke to him, I touched his other arm, and Kellan whisked us back to the car on the edge of the road. It had never looked so human and normal to me than it did at that time.

Kellan gave me the keys and waited till I got inside, behind the wheel. He bent forward at the open window, still holding Aumae in his arms. "I won't be long. I hope not. Go to the sanctuary. It'll be safer now than it was before. Nothing can find it now. The trees have grown in height; they protect it. Trust me.

That's the part of it being a sanctuary. Once it's been broken into, it'll never be again."

"Okay..." I still wasn't sure, but he leaned in and pressed a kiss to my forehead. "Go, Shay. You'll be safe."

I drove back, relying on memory. It seemed longer than the hours it had taken to get to the cave. It felt more like an entire day of driving, but when I pulled into the driveway, I wasn't sure it was the right one. Nothing looked the same. In fact, I felt like I hadn't even gone to the same place, but this was where the sanctuary should've been. And then the trees shifted in front of me and allowed me entry. I drove the car through. When I'd gone past the first line of trees, they quickly closed behind me, shutting everything out. No one would try to get past. I even saw a few trees lift up their roots and settle back down in a different spot.

Kellan was right. Nothing was the same. The waterfall was gone, but as I got out of the car, I could hear it. I knew it was there, but I could only see forest around me. Guessing where the house would be, I moved forward, looking for the front steps. A wind rushed forward, picking up some leaves and I was shown the path that led to the house. It went down instead of up, and I found the front door and went inside, I saw that it was an entirely new house. It had been built upward before. This new one was built in a circle, around the waterfall inside now. The kitchen and dining room opened to the pool of water, as did the living room to their right.

The roof didn't look like a roof. It didn't seem like there was even a closing, but I knew there was. There had to have been, and just then a bird tried to dip down, inside of the house. A thick glass barrier kept it out, zapping it away.

Everywhere I looked, the walls were thicker, sturdier. The windows moved for me, where I looked, they appeared. I finally chose a room on the first floor, underneath where the waterfall fell into the pool. It splashed up, but a glass wall formed over our hallway and connected to the door. The water slid down it, trickling back into the body of water. I sat there and watched it. It felt like I stayed there for another few hours before I jerked in place. I'd fallen asleep without realizing it. With a yawn coming over me, I looked up and saw the sky was dark through the glass roof. A few stars could be seen, but not many. It felt like a darker night than normal, and I figured there was no full moon, but that didn't matter. What did matter was where Kellan and Aumae were, and when they were coming back.

After showering, then lying in bed for a while, I got back up. I couldn't sleep, not until I knew where they were. Padding barefoot from the kitchen to the living room, I curled onto a couch and then reached for the remote control. I'd never been one for television, no one in my family had been. Humans were...entertaining enough to me, but before I turned on the machine I was distracted by a buzzing sound. I searched through some bags and then through a few kitchen cupboards until I found a cellphone vibrating in a small drawer. Kellan's name was scrawled over the screen, and I answered it, "Hello?" That was when I realized I had no idea where mine had gone. I couldn't remember the last time I'd even used it.

"We're coming back, and we have another guest."

"How's Aumae?" I didn't even care about the other guest. Kellan wouldn't bring anyone he didn't trust. "When will you be here?"

"We're turning in right now. How's the new layout look?"

I heard laughter in his voice, and everything relaxed in me. It was then that I realized how much I depended on Kellan. Not too long ago, I hadn't trusted him with what I painted and now I was fearful to step foot out of a house without him. Before I started pondering whether that was a good thing or not, I hurried to the door and flung it open when I saw a pair of headlights approaching underneath the trees. One lifted up its roots, and Kellan drove through, underneath to park beside our other car.

As he got out first, I came down and asked, "Where'd you get the new car? And why are you even driving?"

He flashed a grin and then opened his back door, bending inside. As he came back out, Aumae was in his arms. "I couldn't transport as we normally would. She's too weak, but she's better. She needs to rest for a few days."

Relief washed over me.

Kellan turned and nodded toward the passenger door. "And the car's his. He decided to join us."

Damien got out of the car and smiled at me. He stayed there and asked, cautious, "Is this okay? I don't want to overstep my boundaries."

"It's okay with me as long as Kellan's okay with it." I looked over with a question in my eyes, but Kellan nodded before he held Aumae tighter against him and started toward the house.

Damien held back and walked around to the other side of the car. He slid his hands into his front pockets and leaned back, giving him the same aloof quality he had the last time I'd seen him outside of the school. "You're sure it's okay?"

His eyes had such uncertainty that I reached over and squeezed his hand. "Why wouldn't it be?"

He shrugged. "Things have changed between you two. I can feel it. It's much stronger and I'm...not a part of that. I wasn't sure if you'd want me here or not."

"Kellan trusts you, otherwise he wouldn't have let you step foot in the car."

"It's my car."

"He doesn't care." We turned for the house, walking side by side. "Do you have news from home?"

He sucked in his breath and stopped before he reached the door. His eyes grew somber, everything in him stiffened. "That's why I came with Kellan. You need to hear some things."

A knot formed in my gut, once again, but I knew we couldn't hide forever. "Does Kellan know?"

"He probably guessed, but he wanted both of you to hear at the same time."

"Okay. Let's get this over with." And I showed him inside.

18

Aumae insisted she would be a part of the conversation. We congregated in a room on the basement level. One wall was made of glass with the water on the other side. The bottom of the pond was real, but the house had built around it so we were able to see the rocks, fish, and even the seaweed beside us.

"It's beautiful." Aumae rested a hand on the glass as she had been positioned in the corner of a couch by Kellan. She wanted to sit up, and no one argued, even though we all felt she should've been resting.

"Yes, it is." I squeezed her other hand as I sat on her other side.

Kellan stood in a corner. He didn't make eye contact with anyone, nor did he speak. He merely stood there, turned halfway to the corner so we couldn't judge his face, and waited until Damien stood in the center of the room.

"Your father's in town."

It took a split second before I realized that Damien had spoken, and he'd spoken to me. With a quick jerk, I pulled my gaze from Kellan to the other messenger and watched how his eyes looked clouded over. They weren't as bright as normal and his voice was sad, resigned, but there was another touch of something else in his voice. I narrowed my eyes, concentrating, when I realized what it was.

Guilt.

"What have you done?" I asked.

Damien reared back a step, surprised, but then another look of resignation flared over his features. "I feel that I should've done something to keep your father from arriving. I could've sent him somewhere else."

Kellan turned and faced the group. "That would've been useless. Her father went there with the excuse of looking for Vespar and Gus. He stays with the real reason of searching for his daughter. She's been kept from him since she was given life in her mother's womb. He wants Shay, and he won't leave without her."

Aumae sat up slowly, still weak. "Then he has a different sort of fight on his hands, doesn't he?"

Damien looked between the two and cleared his throat, stuffing his hands into his sweater's front pocket. "It doesn't matter. He's in town, and he's watching your half-siblings."

"It's a trap." When everyone looked at me, I nodded. "It's a trap. He thinks we'll swoop in to get Vespar and Gus out of there, but we won't. We'll leave them. I mean, Vespar was going to kill me. I don't want to go anywhere near him after that. My dad will never know. He'll watch them, and we can get away."

"Uh..." Damien sent me an apologetic smile. "That would be all good and everything, but you don't know where your half sibs are... They're being held captive by two humans you went to school with."

"Two humans?"

Kellan groaned. "Dylan."

"Exactly." Damien snapped his fingers at him.

"What?"

"Gus said he was into dark magic. He could've used something to keep me from wiping his memory and then decided to go after Vespar and Gus when we were gone." Kellan shrugged. "It's what I'd do if I were him and I knew dark magic."

"What?" I snapped, throwing my arms in the air. They were both acting too casual about this. "Dylan and someone else captured Vespar and Gus? What are they doing—torturing them?"

Aumae shuddered behind me.

"Probably," Damien answered with a blank face.

"Are you okay with that? They might be getting tortured, and you act like you don't care?"

"Why do you?" he shot back at me.

"Because torture is torture. It's wrong. It doesn't matter what the person or thing did—it's always wrong. I shouldn't have to tell you that." My eyes were cold. He was a messenger, at least half of one. Didn't we stand for the good?

Flinching, I turned away, but I was aware of Kellan's sudden intense gaze on me. He was studying me, watching for some reaction, but it didn't matter. Torture was wrong. I wouldn't want anyone to go through that. As my eyes shifted over Aumae, I shivered at the memory of seeing her tied down by a violated virgin's blood. Her skin had crawled over her, boiling from the inside up. Vespar wanted to kill me, but I still couldn't handle thinking of him going through that same torture.

I lifted my chin and squared my shoulders, turning toward Damien and Kellan.

"We're going back. We have to." My eyes went to Kellan. "What do you think?"

"We could use their help against your father."

"Then it's decided. We go back."

"But—what?" Damien shook his head. "I can't believe this. You're going back to save two demons? Two demons that were planning to kill you?"

"What do you mean 'you're?' You're not coming?"

He snorted in disbelief. "Messengers don't save demons. And I think you're crazy for even thinking about it."

"Well, then I'm not the typical messenger, am I?" I was a little hurt by his decision, but it didn't matter. Kellan and I would handle it. We'd be fine. Then a different thought came to me. "Why did you even come here? You told us about Gus and Vespar. Did you think we wouldn't go to save them?"

Damien shuffled his feet, from side to side before he responded, "I wanted to warn you about your dad. I never thought you'd go back. You should be going the other way—not headed into the lion's den."

"She's made up her mind. We're going," Kellan spoke up and left the room. As he walked past, I met Damien's eyes and saw concern for a moment. It shocked me, but then a blank mask fell back in place. It didn't surprise me. I always knew the other messenger was guarded, controlled, but the concern did cause me to pause a moment. What would he be concerned about—about me? About Kellan? Did he think the humans were going to actually beat us?

Damien left right behind Kellan, and Aumae sat up beside me to rest a hand on my arm. She murmured, "He's not used to being worried about anybody."

When she got up and followed behind the other two, I sat back in more dismay.

What did that mean? Damien didn't have anybody close?

"Shay!" Kellan yelled out. "Come on!"

"Coming!" I jumped up and hurried out to the car. We'd just got back from one mission and now we were leaving for another. I had a feeling that downtime would be sparse from here on out.

On the way back, we were in the back while Damien drove his own car. Aumae was next to him in the front passenger seat. She let a window down and then rested her head against the corner of her seat and closed her eyes, fast asleep. A soft hum vibrated from inside of her, and her skin started to glisten and then roll over her, around her. When I jerked upright, alarmed, Kellan pulled me back and murmured, "She's healing herself. You should rest, too."

"Why?"

"Because you're going to need all your strength." He squeezed my hand and slipped his fingers through mine.

"Why don't we whisk ourselves there? They're human. They won't know we're coming."

Damien glanced at me through the rearview mirror. "Because your father will know."

"Oh." Point taken. And from then on, I kept my mouth shut. Sometime not long after, I felt myself falling into Kellan's side, and he moved to put his arm around me. After that, it was lights out as soon as I snuggled into him. When I woke later, we'd arrived, and I was surprised to see it had taken three hours.

I'd been asleep for three hours in the car, and after a peek, I saw the alertness in both Kellan and Damien. Aumae was still humming, but Damien touched her leg gently and it went away. The glistening, crawling skin stopped, and the soft white color that had surrounded her was gone, too. When she sat up, she looked back and gave me a clear smile.

"You look better," I noted, sitting up from Kellan's side.

"I should be fully healed." She looked at him beside me. "What's the plan?"

"Shay and I go inside. That's it."

"But—" she argued.

Kellan shot back, "That's the plan. You stay. He stays. We go." He jerked on my arm and I only had a second to glance at Damien, expecting an argument from him. There was none. As he sat back in his seat, I realized that he never had any intention of going inside with us. He wasn't going to help at all. And for some reason, that pissed me off.

"What—huh? Why isn't he helping?"

Kellan hissed under his breath, "Because this is our fight, not theirs. Come on."

He murmured as we started toward the house, "He needs to be on watch. If your father comes, I want to know."

"Oh." That made a lot more sense, and then I looked up. The house looked like a typical two-story home, built in the suburbs. There were shrubs neatly trimmed in front of the patio and two wicker chairs on top. The sidewalk had been swept clean with a line of flowers beside it, free of weeds. It might've been a home I could've grown up in as a normal human child.

But when he opened the door, I was assaulted by the evil. It was dark inside, and I smelled sex, desire, fear, torture, sweat. So much more. I felt like I was being choked, burdened down by it all before Kellan touched my arm. Then it was all gone. Looking up, I was able to see inside the room.

"Your messenger side is too much now. It's like a muzzle around you. You won't go berserk."

Shuddering, I glanced around and heard moans from a back room. Kellan stepped forward, and the same cloak from before came over him. He put it on me, too, and we were able to walk around without being felt or seen. And as we went into the back room first, I stopped in disgust. Leah and Matt were tangled together, naked, on a bed with no sheets or pillows. He was thrusting into her, hard. As we watched, she tipped her head back and screamed. Matt thrust harder, banging her head into the wall behind them.

I felt like I should've thrown up, but there were no more emotions. The disgust was short-lived, and now I was unemotional, just there to gather information. Glancing at Kellan, I wondered if he had done that, too, taken away my emotions. I wasn't sure if I should've been grateful or angry. It didn't matter. We turned and went upstairs. When we approached another room at the top of the stairs, I knew I was clearheaded this way. Nothing was going to filter my judgment.

Then we saw Gus. She was naked, strapped to a bed, and bleeding all over. Her head jerked up, but it fell back down in pain with a rag between her lips.

Dylan was shirtless, and he turned with one hand on a fire poker. "What? Did you sense something?"

He clambered off the bed and snapped his pants shut in the same motion, going to the opened door. "Leah? Matt? You two still fucking?"

Leah screamed in response. Her voice was thick with desire.

Dylan looked back and perused Gus for a moment. "What's that mean? You haven't done that since..." Then he turned again, slower this time, and searched the room. His eyes passed over us and kept moving without pausing. I felt Kellan's anger beside me and wondered if I could turn his emotions off, too.

Gus moaned and turned her head to the side, away from us.

"Out there? Who's out there?" Dylan walked to the window and lifted up a corner of the curtain. As he continued to inspect outside, Kellan touched my wrist again before he was moving once more.

The remaining three bedrooms were bare upstairs. Only one had furniture with an empty bed mattress thrown in a corner. All the rooms remained dark from drawn curtains.

Of course, they wouldn't want anyone looking inside. They'd see... My thought trailed off, not wanting to envision the torture of people I once considered my brother and sister.

"Shay," Kellan called to me, and I hurried, finding him on the main floor again. We moved past as Matt let out a guttural groan, arching above Leah. She moaned, satisfied. We were at the stairs to the basement, and when we went down, the floors creaked beneath us.

I felt Vespar's alertness like I'd been whipped in the backside. It was quick, alarmed, and vicious.

"Who's there? You want to go again?" he growled from a corner.

As we stepped onto the cold pavement and turned toward his corner, all the lights snapped on. He was crouched in the corner, held in place by chains, but still able to stand and move an inch. The links were nailed into the walls and I wondered what magic held them intact. Vespar's fury was Goliath-like strong, but he was still a captive.

"Who are you?" he roared this time, surging forward. The chains snapped in place, and he flew backward, hitting the wall. "Who?"

"What the—" Feet sped across the floor above us, and the door was thrown open soon after. Leah and Matt hurried down, pulling on clothes. They stopped, seeing no one, and gazed in confusion.

"What?" Leah's hand dropped from her shirt's strap, and it fell back down to her elbow. "Are you going crazy now?"

Matt grunted, fastening his pants. "He was saying a bunch of crazy shit last night, too."

"What's going on?" Dylan came down the stairs at a slower pace, still shirtless and barefoot.

"Nothing. Demon boy is just trying to make us antsy." Matt shouldered past him, headed upstairs.

"I don't know..." Dylan gazed around, peering into every corner how he had upstairs. "She sensed something, too. Then she tried to hide it, like nothing was there."

Leah sucked in her breath. "You think someone's here?"

"Someone or somethings?" Matt stopped on the stairs.

"I dunno." Dylan narrowed his eyes and started to chant under his breath. He kept looking around, as the words got louder and clearer. Leah joined in, her voice raised with each passing word until she was shouting, stretched upward on her toes.

"It's not working. It's not them."

Dylan stopped and then started a different chant.

Leah looked at the stairs. "I don't know that one."

"It's not them!" Matt was disgusted as he walked down again. "And even if it was, they're strong, Dylan. You're not hearing me on this. They're stronger than you think."

"Then what are we going to do when they do come?" Dylan shouted back. "That's all I got."

"I don't know. Doesn't your grandmother have other tricks or something? The stuff you dipped his chains in, what was that?"

"Saint's blood? It doesn't come cheap. What do you think we'd do with it? Throw it at 'em?"

"I don't know. Put it in squirt guns?"

"What?" Leah laughed. "Are you stupid?"

"I'm trying here! All I know is that Kellan and Shay won't be harmed by some stupid words. They're stronger than that, stronger than these two."

I was starting to be amused by their conversation before Kellan touched my wrist and indicated the stairs. Nodding, I moved to follow, but he took hold of my elbow instead and whisked upstairs. We never touched one step. I opened my eyes, and we were in Gus' room again. Her face was turned toward us, straining against the rags around her mouth and neck.

"You can untie her." Kellan moved to the door, watching out. "I can't."

Gus' eyes popped out, straining even more. I felt her desperation and a flare of hope when she heard his voice. Then, as I knelt and untied all of her restraints, Gus flew upward and wrapped both of her arms around me. She gurgled into my neck, "Thank you, thank you, thank you, thank you. I'm so sorry, Shay. I didn't know—" She gasped and fell limp in my arms.

"Wha—" I looked at Kellan, whose hand was outstretched toward us.

He rolled his eyes. "She would've alerted them if she hadn't shut up. Take her out; get her in the car with Aumae. They'll watch over her."

"And how I'm supposed to do that? They can see me now."

The window flew open behind me, and Kellan smirked. "Fly, Shay. Fly."

I rolled my eyes, but bundled Gus in my arms and climbed onto the window's frame. Perched there, I glanced back once and then jumped. I landed, smooth on my feet, and was across to the car in a hurry. The back door flung open, and Aumae held open her arms, a cloak over her and I placed Gus in her arms. As soon as she wrapped them around her, both of them were invisible to the human eye. I looked at Damien who still sat in the front seat. He stared back, unaffected. It was like we had gone to get groceries, and it irked me for some reason. It should've meant something to him.

"He's going to need your help soon," Damian spoke in a flat voice, watching over my shoulder.

I swallowed a harsh retort and hurried back. Instead of the front door, how we'd gone before, I circled back to Gus' bedroom window. No light shone out of it, so I sucked in my breath and jumped back up. When I cleared the frame and landed on my feet beside the bed, I saw that Kellan wasn't there.

In fact, he wasn't anywhere. I left the room and searched the remaining ones on the floor, but nothing. Then, as I stood at the top of the stairs, Dylan, Leah, and Matt all stood at the bottom, conversing with each other.

"I don't care what you guys think, something's going on. Someone's here."

Dylan cursed under his breath.

"It can't be Kellan and Shay, can it? We did the chanty thing and nothing happened. How can we not see them?" Leah's voice went from excited to confused and ended with disappointment.

Dylan had been watching her as she spoke and then rolled his eyes. "Don't tell me you're excited to see the demon? That's pathetic."

"It's not pathetic," she cried out. "I used to have a relationship with him, and I can't help that I still..."

Matt shuffled to the side, looking disgusted. "Still? You still have a thing for him?"

"But I want Shay dead. Isn't that enough?"

Both guys snorted and looked away.

"What?"

"I'm going to check on Gus," Dylan started to say as he turned to the stairs and then he looked up. His hand had been reaching for the hand rail and then he froze. His hand froze in mid-air as his eyes were locked on mine. "Holy—" As he cursed, he went pale.

I'd forgotten they could see me now. "Hi..."

Dylan threw something at me, and I sidestepped it as it soared over my shoulder and shattered behind me.

"Get down!" he yelled, turning away and throwing an arm over his eyes.

Matt and Leah did the same, but I stood, confused. And then a light exploded in the house, from behind me, and I turned in curiosity. What could produce such blinding light? It didn't bother me, not at all. My eyes were able to see clearer and I bent to scoop up the broken pieces. It looked like a Christmas ornament, one that sparkled and illuminated. It was beautiful.

"What the..."

I turned, holding the ornament in my hands and saw Dylan's mouth fell open.

The light started to fade, and he gaped at me, speechless.

"But...you're..."

Matt growled, grabbing Leah's hand, "I told you. Your stupid tricks won't work on them. They're too strong. Come on!"

He dragged Leah behind him to the back of the house. Dylan remained as I soared down the stairs toward him. He couldn't seem to move, and he lifted a hand to me, pointing. "What are you? That should've—all demons are affected by that. That was some of the Holy Fire. It's supposed to sear the skin off any demon, but you...you picked it up like it's a toy."

I balanced the broken ornament in my hand, rolling it around my opened palm.

"It's very pretty. White mosaic?"

A gurgle left Dylan's mouth as he stood, as white as the ornament in my hand.

Then my eyes snapped to his, cold. "What else does your grandmother have up her sleeve?"

19

Dylan didn't answer. He turned and fled. Everything shifted in me when he took flight. A burst of pure energy rushed through me, spreading throughout my body from fingertip to my hair follicles, and I lifted off the ground in one movement. Soaring over him, I landed in front, stopping him and staring straight into his eyes.

He gasped, reeling backward. "Your eyes—they're black, just black..."

"I know." My voice was different, stronger. It sounded like it was coming from a well, an ancient well that was so deep and water was surging upward at an alarming speed. I didn't know what it was, why my voice was like this, but I felt connected to every messenger that had died before me. They were with me in that moment.

"Demons don't look like that. Their eyes are red, brown sometimes when you see their true form." He kept inching backward.

"Are you trying to run away from me?" I glided after him, moving an inch to his inch. "Do you think you can escape me?"

As I watched him consider his options, run, fight, or surrender, I saw into him. There was a tiny speck of blackness in him. It had a ring of the same reddish brown that he just testified all demons have in their eyes. Dylan didn't know it, but he was becoming part of a demon or a demon was becoming a part of him.

"What are you?"

I stopped in the kitchen's doorway as he continued backward, closer to the front door, through the living room now. "What do you think I am?" But that wasn't what I wanted him to know, so I asked instead, "Did your grandmother prepare you for beings that aren't fully demonic? What did she teach you? What else do you know?"

Vespar and Gus weren't full demons. They were only half. At least that's what I thought, but she doesn't act like one of them. She's more or something else? What else could she be? Grandma didn't teach me this stuff.

His inner voice was panicked, and he still hadn't decided what to do. Then again, if he chose to fight, I wasn't sure what I was going to do either. He was dark, and I felt the messenger in me rearing to attack, rip his head off, but another part held me back. The majority of him was still a human, a very sinister and sinful human, but one nonetheless. A protective emotion filled me at the same time.

"Shay, I—" *he gasped, interrupted by his own thoughts. Where the hell did Matt and Leah go? Is Kellan here? What about—oh God. I can't...*

"What are you going to do, Dylan?" I tilted my head to the side and narrowed my eyes. He had become part of the black and white backdrop that I saw through my messenger eyes. The little demonic part of him flared upward, like a small fire that had been given a burst of oxygen. The smoldering red and brown waved together in a furious motion. It wanted to take over more of him, but couldn't. Not yet.

"What do you mean?" Dylan fought a shudder from coming over him.

"You can't fight me. You can't kill me. You don't even know what I am or what I'm not. What are you going to do?"

He licked his lips in a nervous motion. "I think the question is what are you going to do to me?"

"What do you think I should do?"

The shudder broke over him, making his body tremble before my eyes. "I...I don't know."

"What were you going to do to us? To me? If you could, what were you planning?"

"I—it doesn't matter. I can't take it back, can I? You're going to kill me. I can tell. It's what—" *I'd do if I were her.*

"Where did your friends go?"

Hope flared in him as an idea came to him. "Leah wanted you dead more than I did. I wanted Kellan, but Leah wanted to hurt you. She asked me if she could be the one to torture you. She wanted you to watch her have sex with him."

My, my, what a little whore she's become. I added out loud, "And you were going to let her?"

"No! I wasn't, I really wasn't. I wanted her help. I knew that she'd been affected by you guys, too, and that..." *Leah's a fun screw. Why wouldn't I want her? If Matt hadn't taken over, things would've been fine.*

"Let's be honest. You wanted her with you because you wanted some sex on the side. Didn't you, Dylan? I can hear your thoughts. I know I'm right."

His eyes popped out in horror. "What? You can? I don't—I mean. Holy shit."

"Matt got in the way? She's been with him when you were hoping that she'd be with you this whole time? That's why you planned this, isn't it?" I saw the wheels in his head turning. Each statement I made was true and with each word, the hope in him shrunk. "You didn't even really care that Gus killed your entire family, did you? You liked the idea that you were alone, not held back by human morals. Then when Kellan brought them all back, when Kellan and I brought them all back, that's what really pissed you off. You wanted to be done with them, but you couldn't, not after all of that. And you wanted us out of the way. You want to be top dog around here, don't you? You want to be big and bad and Leah will be all yours? Why didn't you compel her? Use one of those handy magic spells your grandma taught you and make her yours?"

"It didn't work," he gasped out, blanching as he heard his words. "She's too broken from whatever you guys did to her. Her mind can't be controlled anymore, it's in pieces."

"Well, there you go. What were you going to do to Matt? If this had all worked and you'd been rid of the Braden Family, what then? She still would've wanted to be with him."

I was going to kill him.

"How?" I spoke to him in his mind, and he winced from the intrusion.

"I was going to drug him one night and leave his body in the woods."

I withdrew from his mind and moved backward, watching him in condescension.

"And you think we're the demons? Before you know it, you'll be one of us."

"What?"

"You're becoming a demon. I see it in you, and it's thirsty. It wants more of you, and it's going to make you do horrible things to grow. You planted a bad seed inside of yourself. All your pretty words are only going to hurt you." Then I smirked. "You might want to watch what you teach others. It can all be used on you, too, now."

Dylan's face scrunched together, and he opened his mouth with an angry retort on the tip of his tongue, but a blood-curdling scream shrieked through the air.

"What the—" he cut himself off and sprinted for the basement door. I was right behind him. We braked at the top of the stairs. Matt was pointing a gun at Kellan. Leah stood in the middle while Vespar was straining against his chains. His skin was pale and sweaty, white around his mouth, but his eyes were alert, more focused with the sight of help in front of him.

"Matt, don't," Leah pleaded with her hands clenched in tight fists. One was stretched toward Kellan while the other held on to Matt's arm. "Think about this first."

"Oh my God. Why do you care?"

"I love him." The admission was whispered. "I can't help it. I don't know why, but I do. Don't kill him. Don't shoot him."

"You're sick, Leah. You're just...you're so sick. How can you love one of them?

You know what they did, what he did to you."

Dylan was slow as he went down the stairs, both of us watched in silence. The tension was thick in that room between them, so thick I feared the slightest sound would set off Matt, or Kellan, who looked like he was contemplating killing Matt or waiting to see if Leah would be successful.

"I know," she said, quiet as tears slid down her cheeks. "But I can't help it. Don't kill him, Matt. Please."

"I have to," Matt choked out. His fingers tightened around the gun.

"Don't!" Leah yelled.

"Why are we scared of a gun?" I looked at Kellan and saw him hear my question, then shoot me a dark look.

"You were supposed to stay upstairs and distract that idiot. Go back. Make something up."

"Why are we scared of a gun? Can it hurt you?"

"It can hurt you. Go back! You're still half human."

"So are you."

"I'll be fine. Get back! Shay, do it."

I cast a worried glance at Vespar, whose eyes hadn't moved from Matt. He seemed captivated by the threat from him.

"*And Vespar? It can hurt him, too?*"

"*More him than you. The bullets are dipped in the same saint's blood that his chains are. It'll kill him. It might hurt you. Stop wasting my concentration and get out of the room. Take Dylan with you; better yet, just kill him.*"

I ignored him, too concerned for Kellan and a little bit for Vespar. As I watched, Leah started to reach for the gun, but Kellan murmured at the same time, "Leah, you still love me?"

She swung her gaze to his with her eyes wide with devotion. "You know I do. I never stopped."

"Help me then."

"How?"

"I can't touch Vespar's chains, but you can. Unchain him. Let him go."

"But—" She swung nervous eyes to Matt and then back to Kellan. "He'll kill me. I hurt him, too. I was a part of this, but I did it for you. I wanted to be with you."

"Wanted? You don't want to anymore?"

"No! I do. I really do. But..."

"Unchain him. I promise Vespar won't hurt you. I'll protect you. You can come with us then."

"Don't listen to him, Leah," Matt burst out, his hand started to tremble.

"He's lying to you. He loves Shay. You know that. You saw him with her. He won't leave her for you."

At the mention of my name, she sucked in her breath and then pinned Kellan down with her eyes. "What about her? About what he just said."

Kellan frowned. "Shay is my sister. Of course, I love her. You want me to kill one of my siblings for you?"

"You don't have a sister-brother thing. I've seen you with her. It's not right. It's gross. What about her? Do you love her?"

"Of course, I love her. She's my sister." As Kellan answered her, he started to move forward, gliding with each word he whispered. "But I could love you, too, in the way you want me to."

"You don't now?"

I winced, hearing the pain in her voice, no matter how delusional she was.

Kellan was close to her now, close to Matt. "I don't love anybody, not in that way, but I could. I do think I could love you. I was there for you. Do you remember? When your parents died, are those memories still with you? I stayed with you for a week. I was concerned about you. That has to mean something..."

Matt stumbled back a few steps. "Get away. Get away from her!"

Leah didn't move as she lifted her eyes to Kellan's, lost in what he was promising. "Do you mean it?"

Kellan bent his forehead to rest against hers. "I do. I really do."

The surrender was swift in her. Her eyes clasped close, and her body relaxed in one breath. "What do you want me to do?"

"No!" Matt yelled and then pulled the trigger.

Kellan shoved Leah aside, but it was too late. She screamed when the bullet pierced her back and then fell forward into his arms. In two seconds, Kellan had Matt in the air by the throat and slammed him against the wall. The gun dropped to the floor with a rattle, but it was ignored. All eyes were on Kellan as he growled, "I can hear her heart slowing."

His face was pinched together, but Matt tried to respond. It came out as a gurgle instead.

I was frozen on the stairs as my heart started to slow. Kellan cared for Leah. The realization shook me. It wasn't something I had ever considered, but the evidence was before me. For once since we'd entered the house, he wasn't in complete control.

Glimpses of his real demon came out, and his rage was so strong, the house started to shake from it.

Matt looked around with panicked eyes, but only squeaked as he was thrown again into a wall.

Dylan scrambled off the stairs and lurched for the gun.

"No!" Vespar threw himself forward, but the chains jerked him backward.

"Kellan, the gun."

Matt was forgotten. Kellan looked back and watched as Dylan rose from the floor, the gun in his hand. He pointed it at him with a steady hand and hatred in his eyes. "You made him kill her. He never would've done that if you hadn't seduced her with your sick lies."

"I did care for her."

Even as I heard the growl in Kellan's voice, I studied him and saw he was back in control. The momentary lapse was forgotten, and now he stood there, content to watch what Dylan would do.

Why? I thought to myself, but stopped my thoughts when Kellan threw me an irritated look.

Vespar growled, "Rip out his throat, Kellan. What are you waiting for?"

But he didn't. He stood, staring down the muzzle of the gun, with a calm that emanated from him. It was like he wanted the gun to go off, but... I was left with the same question I'd asked myself. Why? It hadn't taken him long to take the gun from Matt and Dylan was closer, but something held him back, something that hadn't happened yet.

Without thinking, my hand let go of the stair rail, and I stumbled to the floor. As I righted myself, everyone watched me, distracted for that moment. It was a surreal feeling in the basement at that moment, like the calm before a storm and then, like an echo in the distance, Dylan pulled his finger on the trigger. A bullet shot out, straight toward Kellan's face, but it bounced off him. The air around Kellan rippled from the force of the bullet, protecting him.

I felt weak in the knees. My relief was so strong. I'd forgotten about the protective armor he could put around himself.

Effing hell! This guy doesn't die. Even as he swore in his mind, Dylan turned in a smooth motion and thumbed out another bullet. This one hit Vespar in the chest and sent him backward against the wall. Dylan shot him again, and his body slumped to the floor, unconscious. Blood spilled out at a fast pace, but I didn't wait to see it start to pool around him.

I whirled back and saw a satisfied look come over Kellan before he shot his arm out and snapped Dylan's neck. The gun slid into his hand as Dylan's body dropped to the floor, limp.

"What just happened?"

"Shay," Kellan clipped out, unloading the gun in a motion that looked like he'd done it thousands of times. "Heal Vespar."

"What? I can't—you told me I couldn't. I don't..." I swallowed, feeling a lump in my throat. "I don't know how."

"Oh my God," Matt whimpered from his sitting position against the wall.

"Ignore him. Heal Vespar."

"You told me I couldn't."

"I lied!" Kellan roared at me. "Do it now or he's going to die. Now!"

My feet were frozen in place as I watched Vespar's body turn different shades of colors. It went from pale to golden tan to a purple shade. As the skin started crawling over him, it turned to blue and then white again. When he started trembling and rattling the floor, I choked out, shaking my head, "I can't. I...I don't know..."

And then the house started to shake again, but it wasn't Kellan. As he closed his eyes, I turned toward the door and something in me wasn't surprised when Damien glided downstairs. He wasn't there in his human form, but as his messenger. His eyes were black orbs, and his entire body had grown white. Bursts of cold air rolled down the stairs before him and swirled around the room. It was a dramatic event, one of too many that night, but then as Damien paused before me, his eyes met and held mine. I felt his request for permission, though I didn't know what it was for, and I nodded, succumbing. He was there to heal Vespar. I couldn't do it...

When he didn't move past me, I followed his gaze and saw he was locked in a heated look with Kellan. They were talking through their thoughts, but I wasn't privy. Neither wanted me involved, and then Kellan jerked away. His shoulders dropped slightly, and I knew he'd given his permission, but I didn't know why. And then before I could think about it, Vespar's body was jerked in the air. It floated toward us and Damien touched it. A bright light burst from him, blinding Kellan and Matt. I was immune, as was Damien and we both watched as the poison from the bullet retracted itself and then poured from the wound. The skin healed itself, and then Vespar's body was laid back on the floor.

It was done as quickly as it started.

20

We put Vespar beside Gus in the backseat and Matt in the trunk. Kellan refused to leave him behind. He'd seen too much, but I wouldn't let him kill Matt. Too much death had already occurred. Then Damien and I climbed into the front with Kellan behind the steering wheel. As we drove off, everyone was quiet. Gus and Vespar were unconscious. Aumae remained quiet beside them and I felt the tension between Kellan and Damien. It was thick, so thick I wondered what would spark it. It was going to happen. I just didn't know when.

"Shay's father is tracking us. I can feel him," Damien murmured.

Kellan kept driving. "I know."

"He waited for us to deal with the humans. He can't interact with them. It's not why he's here."

"I know that, too."

"Do you have a plan?" Damien whipped his head around and glared.

I closed my eyes, just waiting.

"My plan? My plan was to get Vespar and Gus. We'll need their help dealing with Shazaam."

Damien bit out, "That's not his name."

"It is in my world."

"And what world is that, Kellan? The underworld? Where you came from."

Aumae sucked in her breath, as did I.

It was quiet for a beat before Kellan responded, in a quiet voice, "I've grown up with humans, among this world. I consider them family. Where I was born means nothing to me now."

"What about who you were born to? Does your father mean nothing to you as well?"

Kellan grew silent, and I felt his anger start to churn. It was there, underneath his surface, boiling to the top. But then he replied, flicking some switch so he was calm once again, "My father ceased to be my father when I went to Shay. You know that. I know that. My father knows that. And Shay knows now. No, Damien, my father has no bearing on me anymore. He hasn't for a very long time."

Damien went silent this time, but I felt his tension, too. His hand fell and rested beside mine. It was an accident, but he didn't move away, and his pulse started to skyrocket. It was rapid, steady, but now it was sporadic and racing. Something Kellan said didn't sit well with him, but I held my tongue, too afraid to ask the wrong questions at that time.

"He's not going to let you regroup."

I had a very strong feeling that wasn't what Damien wanted to say, but it was what came out. Something was going on between those two, and both of them had made the decision to focus on something else. Which was fine, for now, but I intended to find out what was going on because I had another feeling that it had to do with me, and I wasn't okay with that.

Damien added, "I know you're thinking that we can get

somewhere and rest, but he won't let that happen. Shay's out in the open. He's going to come now and not risk losing her again. She shouldn't have been there to start with."

"I needed her help getting them out." Kellan was quiet as he watched the rearview mirror.

Regardless of what Damien thought, I knew that Kellan was three steps in front of him. Now, where he was going, I had no clue about, but I knew my supposed soulmate had a plan already in motion. We were all along for the ride, for the roles he had slotted us into. When Damien figured that out, that Kellan was the mastermind controlling him, manipulating him to do what he wanted, that was the spark he'd need. Then the explosion would happen after that, but until then—I knew enough to sit back and let Kellan's plan happen. It'd work. It always worked, but I felt there would be collateral damage this time.

"I could've helped instead."

Kellan snapped at him, "But you chose not to. You made that decision very clear, early on, when we could've left Shay in hiding. Deal with it now."

I prayed he would, the interrogation wasn't helping. Then, after another beat of silence, I released my breath, thankful. He had stopped...for now.

"There's three of them," Aumae spoke from the back. "They're close and coming fast. I can feel them."

"I can, too." Damien jerked around and stared out the back window. "Sachiel's not with them. That's what worries me."

"Sachiel?" My heart was pounding in my chest. "Is that—is that my father's name?"

A hush came over the group, and Damien cast me an apologetic look before he turned back to the rear. Then Aumae spoke again, "I'm sorry, Shay. That's his name, it's what the messengers call him, and you should've been told your father's name before this."

I hadn't asked. I hadn't because I'd been afraid to think of him, of what it all meant.

"He's here." Kellan jerked the wheel around. The car skidded to a halt, parked at an angle across the road, and we hadn't come to a complete stop before Kellan threw himself out of the car.

"Kellan!" I gasped, scrambling after him, but he was gone. Vanished.

Damien and Aumae hurried out of their doors, and then Damien yelled at her, "Wake them. We need them."

She went back to the car, but cast a look at him. "You're helping them? I knew I would, but you..."

He jerked a shoulder up and faced where we'd come from. Three white beams of light appeared on the horizon, coming slow. As they drew closer, I was able to see each of them looked like humans out for a nightly stroll. They looked calm, dressed in street clothes. A male was in the lead, taller than the other two, over seven feet. The others were both females. One had long blonde hair, and the other had long black hair. All three of them had high cheekbones and slender bodies. Any other human distinctions were diminished since they were in messenger mode with their eyes as black orbs and a white aura over them.

"Where'd Kellan go?" I looked around, but nothing. We were alone. It was like he became a part of the night and disappeared in it.

"He's not our problem right now." Damien's hands flexed beside him. "They are."

"They're waking." Aumae hurried to stand beside Damien. "They'll help."

"They'll have to, or they're dead with us."

Gus and Vespar stumbled out of the car, exhausted from the coma they'd been in. Studying Vespar, I thought he'd been unconscious from the bullet and then because Damien had healed him. I thought the body needed time to repair itself, but now they both shimmered in health. They seemed toned, ready, and alert. Aumae had put Gus to sleep, and now I wondered if she'd done the same to Vespar, that she had healed them even further somehow. I had never seen them at their peak as I was seeing them now. Like a button was pushed, their exhaustion vanished.

They looked up at the same time, ready to fight, and saw me.

"Shay?" Gus gasped. "What are you doing here?"

I frowned. "What do you mean?"

"We're..." She looked around. "What are we doing here and where is here?"

Vespar growled with his hands clenched in fists beside him, "I was shot. We were in the basement and then..." He looked at Damien and jerked forward a step. "He's a messenger."

"So is she." Gus gestured toward Aumae.

Both of them ignored my siblings.

"Shay? What's going on?" My sister gentled her tone.

I opened my mouth to answer, but Damien cut me off, "There are three messengers coming. See them? Destroy them because they're here to destroy you."

"What?" Gus clamped a hand on my arm. "What are we going to do?"

"Fight." Damien cast a look at her. *Idiot.*

I hid a smile when Gus asked me, "Shay, is that right? Are they—"

"Gus. Shut up and fight." Vespar stood beside her, tense.

"Male demon—" Damien started to say.

Vespar interrupted him, "I have a name."

"—you will fight alongside Shay. Female demon." Gus narrowed her eyes, but didn't make a comment. "You will fight with Aumae." Damien ignored both of their reactions and gestured beside him.

"And you? What are you going to do?"

"I'm going to take the leader." Damien took a deep breath and stretched to his fullest height. "I've met Mayorn a few times."

"*What about the human?*" I heard Aumae ask Damien.

"*If things go badly, we can bring him out. They can't be around humans that they aren't sent here for. He'll repel them, but right now they don't know he's here. They can't sense him through my car's trunk. It's been sealed.*"

Aumae nodded, satisfied with his response, and I cast a nervous look over the other messengers. They looked powerful, more powerful than any of us combined.

"*Don't think like that, Shay.*" Damien looked at me. "*You're more powerful than all of them combined. You're a first descendant from your father. You may be even more powerful than him.*"

I didn't feel it. I felt like a weak human at that moment, but as the three messengers drew close, I knew it was game time. They stopped, and the leader approached alone. His eyes skimmed over all of us, but lingered first on me and then moved to Damien, who had moved out in front of us. He proclaimed himself our leader with those two steps.

"Donai, I'm surprised to see you here." His smirk said otherwise.

Damien rolled his eyes. "No, you're not. You've always known this would happen. You've always wanted it. And it's Damien."

Mayorn wrinkled his long nose and grimaced. "You've become like a human, taking their name for you. Donai is a good name. You should remember your heritage."

"I do." Damien flexed his hands.

He grew tired of baiting Damien, so his eyes skimmed over me, studying. I forced myself to stand strong as I felt him trying to pierce into me, to see my insides. As he kept poking, trying to get past my walls, I started to grow angry. It shimmered over me, up from my ankles and around my waist to my eyes. I snapped them open and knew I'd turned into the messenger they wanted to see.

Instead of Mayorn seeing into me, I saw into him now. I pierced his walls with no fight and sifted through his insides.

He was outraged and battled me to get out, but I refused to move. When he realized he couldn't get me out of him, he became further enraged and lunged at me, snarling. Damien cut him off, tackling him and throwing him to the side of the road.

Mayorn threw his blond locks back, glaring and seething at me. "Get out! Get out! Get out!"

"Mayorn?" one of the other female messengers asked, nervous.

"She's in me. I can't get her out. Get her out! Kill her!"

The other one wasn't as scared. "We can't. Sachiel wants her alive."

"I don't care. She's in me, and I can't push her out." He shook his body, then lunged for me. His eyes pierced mine with red in them, red for blood. *"I will kill you. Take heed of this warning. I will kill you."*

"Like hell you will," Kellan growled, appearing from nowhere. He stood behind Mayorn and plunged a dagger into his back. Fire burst out of his eye sockets, mouth, and fingertips before he exploded. Then Kellan tossed it to Damien, who stabbed the messenger he was beside. Aumae turned to the third one and opened her arms wide. A light came from them, like she had spread wings, and shone in the female's eyes, blinding her. Kellan swooped in, caught the dagger back from Damien, and slit the messenger's throat. She fell to the ground, wide eyed, as blood poured out of her, darkening the gravel around her.

"That wasn't hard." Vespar glanced around beside Gus, who was scratching her head.

"They were the appetizers." Kellan stood beside me, holding my gaze. His eyes were steady, looking into me with a deep intensity. He wanted to tell me something, reassure me, proclaim something, I wasn't sure, but then the look was gone as his eyes slid over my shoulders. They caught on something in the woods behind me and stayed there. I turned, too, my heart pounding, and gaped. It wasn't what I saw, which was a set of twenty pairs of eyes, watching us from behind the trees, but it was what I felt.

They were powerful and ancient. They were together as one and they were angry. Three of their own had been murdered in front of them, and they were ready to enact their revenge.

Everything stopped in that moment. Heartbeats slowed. Breaths were held. No one moved, not even turning over a small rock in the gravel beneath our feet. No crickets chirped, no breeze swept around us. It was the calm before the storm, and holy crap, my bones knew it was going to be the storm of my life.

Then Damien broke the silence. "You brought them here?"

"It was either that or die at their hands. I was outnumbered." Kellan threw an irritated look at him, but no one else said a thing. "I'm stronger by Shay's side. Strong enough now anyway."

"*Shay...*"

I jumped, feeling my father. His voice was strong as he called to me. I felt my blood churn inside, hearing part of its ancestry.

It freaked me out. Without thinking, I reached for Kellan's hand and squeezed tight. He moved closer so our hands were hidden, but he squeezed back, and the other blood in me calmed down. I needed him.

The twenty pairs of eyes moved back, parting waves. Everything moved to the side, and I was staring at my father. He was over seven feet tall with long blond hair held back in one large braid. My eyes were drawn to his clothes, a loose fitting tunic as a top and pants that billowed around him.

"*Look at me.*"

I flinched and looked away, at Aumae who had a resigned expression on her face. She caught my gaze and winked, the resignation switched to an eager defiance. "We'll be fine, Shay. Answer your father."

"Do not speak to my daughter. You've done enough, Aumae, you and your sister," my father roared, flying forward and landing in front of us with a force that was fierce. The earth moved beneath him, and we all moved as well.

Aumae snapped her head to the side as if she'd been slapped. When a red mark appeared on her cheek, I realized she had been slapped. That pissed me off, and I snapped inside. My fury built inside of me like a volcano, boiling and churning upward until I reared back in the air and sent two bursts of energy at my father.

Kellan followed with his own bursts of energy, as did Damien.

My father was slammed back, past his followers. Kellan went with him, and I caught a flash from his hand. He meant to use the dagger on my father. My gut sparked, and I knew it was a bad idea if Kellan stabbed him. I didn't know why, but I flew after them. When my father tumbled to the ground, still dazed from the onslaught, Kellan landed on top of him and raised his hand.

"No!" I caught his hand and clawed, trying to unleash the dagger.

"What are you doing?"

"Trust me," I panted. "This is not a good idea."

"He's going to kill everyone, Shay." Kellan took my hand and shoved me backward.

"Kellan!"

He turned back, but my father was on his feet again. Laughing. "You think that little thing will kill me?"

Kellan fell silent.

I stood, cautious. "What are you talking about?"

"I'm a first lineage messenger. Those things give us strength. They don't harm us."

I hadn't wanted to look at my father. The power in him was enormous, and it drew me in, captivating me. I'd fought against it, not wanting to feel connected to him. Perhaps that had been my fear—that I'd want to be with him and somehow I'd be brainwashed into forgetting everyone else. Aumae, Damien, even Gus, especially Kellan. I couldn't forget them, and when he first spoke my name, I knew that was what he wanted. But now I looked at him. His eyes were intelligent, old, and they spoke of memories. However, when I looked into them, I knew one other thing. Those memories weren't from my blood.

"You're not my father."

Kellan was tense beside me.

Something was coming, something was going to happen, but I didn't know what. I just knew it was bad, very bad, and I had no way of stopping it. And then the messenger's laughter faded, and he nodded. "You're right. I'm not your father. But I am supposed to bring you to him."

He grabbed my hand—Kellan yelled—and we were gone in the next instant.

21

My feet hit the floor, and I rolled with it, coming back up to stand in one smooth motion. I looked around, but Kellan wasn't there. His shout echoed in my ears and it was like he was still there. I could still feel him. No. I was alone. Breathing hard, the sounds almost drowning out Kellan's voice, I hunched forward. My knees were bent. My arms out. I was ready to battle, but I swung my head around and no one was there.

I was in a dark room.

The wood floors creaked under my weight.

Edging forward, they protested loudly, but I kept moving forward ninja-style.

"You think to sneak up on me?"

A loud voice boomed through the house. I gritted my teeth. A piece of hair fell over my forehead, blocking my vision and I swiped at it. "Come on. When you bring a girl to an old house, sneaking's not the first thing that comes to mind."

I had no idea why I said it, but it was out there. My heart was still pounding against my chest, and I waited for his response.

There was none.

I kept moving, going from room to room. I was on the second floor and all the rooms were empty. Coming to what must've been a bathroom, the back wall was completely blown out. It looked like a grenade had been thrown in the room. Black smudges plastered the wall, and half of the sink was gone. I stepped down, and sucked in my breath. The hole was there where the toilet should've gone.

I tiptoed to a stair rail. Oh no. Not the second floor. I was on the hundredth floor. Okay. That was me being sarcastic, but seriously. I tried to count the floors. Six, seven. I was on the eighth floor, and I twisted my head to look...and it kept on going.

I grumbled under my breath, "Couldn't keep it simple, Dad? Had to bring me to the building that never ends?"

"Why? So your boyfriend could swoosh in, grab you, and you'd both be gone again?"

His voice was clearer. The hairs on the back of my neck stood up. I didn't move, still hunched over the stair rail, but my hands let go, and I started looking out from the corner of my eye. It was just darkness. The walls were white with black streaks from explosions. The floors had been stripped down to their oak finishing. Moonlight filtered in from somewhere. I could see enough to move around, but mostly, everything was shadowed. Still, the hairs on my neck were telling me my asshole father was close.

I had powers. I needed to use my damn powers, and soon.

"You are not bonded to him yet."

His voice echoed against the walls, bouncing all around me.

"I am. He's my soulmate."

"Your connection should be stronger. He's been with you almost all your life."

I frowned. Was he upset by that? "Where are you going with this?"

"You're supposed to be more powerful."

I twisted to the right. His voice came from there. It was less wall-bouncy, but I still couldn't see him. "That's your problem? I'm not more powerful? Are you kidding me?"

"You were supposed to have bonded with him by now."

Damien chose his words carefully before. "Just that it would be smart if you strengthened your bond."

My mouth went dry at that. "What do you mean by that?"

Then he grinned, crookedly. "You can take it any way you want. Kellan will know, but if the two of you are strong enough, your father will know not to even try to break the bond. If you two work together as a team, you could be powerful, more powerful than you could imagine."

"Yeah..." I spoke slowly, turning so my back was against the stair rail. I crouched down. "Or so I've been told."

"I can't do anything with you. Not with how you are right now."

One foot scooted back. The other followed behind. And repeat. I moved at a snail's pace toward the stairs, but when I stepped down, the entire floor screamed. I winced. The point of acting like a ninja was to be silent like one, too. This abandoned building wasn't working for me.

"Uh." I raised my voice. "Sorry?"

"I could take both of you." His voice ricocheted from the left now. "I could make you bind together."

"Shay."

I perked up. That was Kellan's voice, but I looked around and it was the same darkness everywhere. I whispered under my breath, "Kellan?" That was ridiculous. Like he could hear that? I rolled my eyes at myself.

"I'm in your head. Your dad shouldn't be able to hear us."

"You are?"

"Just think to me. You don't have to actually speak."

"Oh yeah. How's this possible?"

"*Aumae is helping me. She's strengthening our connection. Where are you?*"

"*Some abandoned place. I'm on the eighth floor, if that helps?*"

"*It doesn't, but hold on.*"

"*What are you doing?*"

"*Shay!*" Suddenly, Kellan was in front of me. I didn't know how that happened, but I wasn't complaining. He reached out, and I grabbed his hand.

"NO!"

My dad roared, but it was too late. We had poofed away. I held onto Kellan's hand, not looking a gift horse in the mouth, but my dad's voice never faded. It kept going, and it was getting louder. I looked over my shoulder, and I could see him.

We were in a tunnel, and he stood at the opening. All white with black eyes. I made out a chin and a neck, but that was it. I could feel his power, and it was reaching out to me. "Shay, come back to me."

"Kellan!" I squeezed harder onto his hand.

Whatever was going on, I wasn't in the safe zone yet. My dad's power was reaching after me and I felt it start to slip around me. It was like invisible tentacles. One wrapped around my neck, another my waist, and still another around my arm. He began to pull me backward, yanking Kellan to a stop.

"Shay?"

He couldn't see what was happening to me. I tried to tell him, but another tentacle covered my mouth. I couldn't speak. Kellan shook his head and tightened his grip on me. My dad was winning. I was starting to go backward.

Kellan's eyes darkened. The same black cloak that emanated from him when we rescued Aumae rippled from him now. His eyes were black, but an outline of bright red formed. I couldn't look away. My dad's hold on me stopped, like he hit a wall and Kellan's black cloak reached over me, enveloping me. He was fighting against my dad. Of the two, my father was more powerful...I thought? But Kellan was winning. He completed cloaking me and trailed behind me, reaching to where my father still stood.

"She's my daughter!"

Kellan's fury whipped back at him. "She's mine!"

"You cannot have her, demon. You are an abomination of nature. You deserve to rot in hell where you were born."

"Shut up!" Kellan's mouth never moved, but he roared back. My eyes clung to his. He wanted to murder my father. If he could've, he would've right then and there.

I shuddered. The pull between the two was exhausting me.

"Shay." Kellan was talking to me again.

"What?"

I hadn't moved any closer to him. I was held suspended between the two men.

"You need to help me."

"Kellan, I'm tired." And I was. My head was falling down. Something was going on in me. I didn't know why I was exhausted, but my hand started to slip from his. "Kellan. I can't hold on any longer."

I felt his refusal. He wasn't letting me go, and my dad wasn't withdrawing either. My eyes started to drift closed. It was too hard... Everything was going black...

"Shay!" Kellan's yell whipped against my face, snapping me back awake. My head straightened and my eyes were wide open. "You have to fight."

"I can't. I don't know what's going on."

"Your messenger side wants to go with your father. The rest of you wants to come with me. You're fighting yourself."

He had helped me before. He could do it again. "Kellan, your demon needs to come inside me. Do whatever you did before."

"I can't. I'm using everything I have to hold your father off."

"Get Gus and Vespar. Everyone needs to help."

"Damien and Aumae are helping. Gus is too exhausted."

"I don't give a shit." I scowled. "She has to help."

Somehow, I focused on Kellan, but then moved behind him. I didn't know where I was getting the strength, but I reached over him. I sensed where everyone stood. The other angels were standing across the road. A barrier kept them out of reach. I didn't question that. We needed to use that. Gus and Vespar were behind Aumae and Damien, who stood right next to Kellan. Both had their hands in the air, chanting, and fusing their power with his. They watched this, but couldn't stop me. The angels behind the barrier became frenzied. They began crashing into the barrier, trying to break it down.

"Shay," Gus looked around her. "What are you doing?"

"Use your powers. We need you."

"What do you want us to do?"

Vespar kept his mouth shut. I was trying to get into his head, but he blocked me out. I couldn't force my way in. I was using too much of my power as it was.

"Shay." Gus began trembling. "What do you want us to do?"

"Touch Kellan. Connect your mind. He'll guide you from there."

I placed both of them on their feet, behind Kellan. He knew what was happening, but couldn't lessen his concentration from holding off my father.

"Gus." She was just standing there, looking around. "Do it now."

"Vespar," she murmured, nudging him with her arm.

He refused to look at her. He was refusing to help.

"Come on."

He turned his back on her.

"They saved us. We have to help."

"She's the enemy."

"She's the reason we're alive."

"Kellan's the reason we're alive."

"So help me instead!" Kellan thundered, his voice crashing down on both of our siblings. They covered their ears. Kellan's fury had reached another level.

I grew determined. The bastards were going to help, whether they wanted to or not. I closed my eyes and began searching inside. My power was throughout me. It wasn't pooled in any one place, but most of it wasn't being used. Kellan was right. Some of it didn't want to move. It wouldn't. It wanted to go back with my father. I bit down on my lip, and I thrust into my own power. It would help me, just like my siblings. I was choosing, and I was choosing Kellan.

"Move!"

Slowly, so agonizingly slow, it began churning. It began circling around, almost sluggishly, but the more it circled, the more it began to pick up speed. It was a steady pace, like the beginning of a hurricane. It was moving faster, just a bit, and it kept going...faster, faster, more and more. It was starting to whip around, now like a full force hurricane and I was keeping it restrained inside me.

"Shay." I heard Kellan's concern. "What are you doing?"

"Helping." I couldn't say more. I was using what strength I had to keep it under control. It was beginning to be too much.

I opened my eyes. The twister was rising in me, but I needed to see if Gus was helping. She was. Her hand was on Kellan's shoulder and her eyes were closed. Her head hung down. I felt her power slip past me, merging with Aumae's and Damien's, too. Vespar still wasn't helping, but he was watching. His forehead wrinkled in fear.

Fine. Forget him.

I was almost ready.

"Shay," Kellan said. "I don't know if this is a good idea."

"Shut up." My hands lifted out to my side. I was getting ready. "Just be prepared. This is going to be fast."

"What are you do—?"

A burst of light exploded from me. It was like a nuclear bomb. It hit against my father like a speeding bullet, slamming him back and cutting him off from us. The rest of my power shot out, disintegrating the barrier, and it blasted against the other messengers. It flung them miles away from us. I felt each of them crash into the ground and all of them except one fell unconscious.

I formed pockets of protection, covering Kellan, Aumae, Damien, Gus, and even Vespar. Everyone else was obliterated.

My power reached out further, traveling farther than even I wanted it, and suddenly, it flung back into me. It was like another bomb that went off, but in me. Pain sliced me as my power smashed back into me. I gasped. A rush of blood filled my mouth and my head fell back like it was yanked from behind. I heard a cracking sound and then—nothing.

The world went to black.

22

I woke up feeling warm and safe, with an arm over my waist. It was nighttime, and Kellan was sleeping with me, his eyes closed and face turned toward me while he held me. I melted. He looked beautiful. There was no sign of the demon in him, and he looked angelic. His strong jawline, his perfect lips, his eyelashes that any girl would yearn for, and his cheekbones—I couldn't help myself. My hand rose, and I rested my fingers over them, trailing down to touch the rest of his face. If he woke, he'd be startled, but I didn't care. I almost wanted that.

I wanted to stop thinking and worrying about what was going to happen. I just wanted to be, and Kellan was in my bed with me. I wanted to just be with him.

As my fingers moved to his lips, it was caught.

His hand moved like lightning. He caught my wrist, but his hold didn't hurt. It was a gentle, but firm grip and then his eyelids opened.

"You caught me."

His eyes darkened, and he said softly, sending shivers down my spine, "So I did." They were the good kind of shivers, the kind that made me want to forget all reason and logic and roll underneath him. Even thinking of that, my legs parted, and I licked my lips. My body began to grow warm.

Kellan noticed the changes, and his hand that was resting over my leg curved into my side. He applied pressure, bringing me forward, turning so we were lying face to face. Both of us were on our sides, and we were close, too close, and I couldn't stop it. I didn't want to stop it. His hand ran down my side, sweeping over my leg, and he applied the tiniest bit of pressure. My leg followed willingly, sliding in between his. My hips shifted, moving closer to him. Our waists were almost touching, and his hand, the one still on my hand, didn't move. It was burning its hold on me, permanently scarring me.

He waited, his eyes darting from mine to my lips, lingering there.

A small groan slipped out. Hearing it, I felt more heat rush to my face and knew I was blushing.

"Are you okay with this?"

"With you sleeping with me?" *God yes.*

"No." He shook his head, his voice a caress in itself. "This." His hand skimmed over my thigh, rising up to my arm and where the bed sheet was covering me.

I wore pajamas. Someone had changed my clothes, but I felt naked. I felt like it was just us, both naked, and the bed sheet, that flimsy little material was the only barrier between us. My breathing grew more rapid, and my heart sped up. I was sure Kellan knew the effect he was having on me. He knew everything about me.

"You're right," he murmured. His hand left the bed sheet and curved around my face, cupping the side of me. His thumb rested on my cheek, a tender touch. "I know a lot, but not everything. I wish I did. Things would be...easier."

"What don't you know?"

"What you hold closest to you." He pressed his hand to where my heart was. "I don't know what you have in there."

I grinned. "A heart?"

"You know what I mean."

He was asking how I felt about him. I nodded, biting down on my lip.

"Kellan," I murmured, but I didn't know what I was going to say. So, instead, I only asked, "What happened?"

"You mean before?"

I nodded again.

"You protected us."

"No," I said. "You protected us."

"I protected you, Shay." His hand lifted to the corner of my mouth, touching my lips in a soft graze. "You protected everyone."

"Kellan, don't act like that. Like you don't care."

"I care about you."

"That's not true. You care about Vespar and Giuseppa." I hated to say it, but... "You cared about Leah."

"Maybe."

He was lying, but I realized he wasn't lying to me. He was lying to himself. "You love so hard and hate so cold."

"Shay." He sighed, rolling to his back. The bed sheet slipped down past his waist. He was wearing gym shorts, but I could see his chest, all the dips and valleys of his muscles as he lay there, breathing in and out. "I'm a demon. I'm more than half-demon, and that means I can only love one person." He watched me from his pillow. "You. Only you."

"Then why'd you save Vespar and Giuseppa?"

"Because they knew too much about you. I didn't want your father to get his hands on them."

"That was the only reason?"

I remembered him in that house, fighting Dylan, yelling at me to save Vespar. He cared. I knew he did. I lay back, too, mirroring him, and I rotated my head on my pillow to look at him. "You're not a normal demon, Kellan, and I know a part of you cares."

"You're lying to yourself."

He believed that. There was no uncertainty inside him. I felt it, as real as if I was feeling my own emotions. I could feel him. That should've alarmed me, or alarmed my messenger, but it didn't. Somehow, it felt right to feel all of him. I started to ask, my mouth opened, and he answered before a word slipped out.

"Yes. I feel you how you feel me."

"So, you know that I know you're lying?"

"I'm not lying."

"To yourself, you are."

"I'm not doing that. You're searching for goodness in me." His eyes were bleak, but a flash of anger sparked in there, just a flicker in the background. "The only good thing in me, is you. If you die, there's no redemption for me. I'll become a full demon."

I frowned. "What are you talking about?"

"I told you I'm not like normal demons. I'm not. The only spark of humanity in me is from you, because I love you. If you die, so do I. The only difference is that you'll become a full messenger, and I'll become a full demon. You go up. I go down."

"Like heaven and hell?"

"Maybe," he said softly, eyeing my mouth. "I'll probably stay on Earth, working for my father. You'll probably... I don't know what will happen to you, but you'll be my enemy. That's all I know."

"So if the human side of me dies, then..."

"...then everything is over. That's the end of us." His hand found mine. My heart skipped a beat at his words. I watched as he lifted our hands in the air, lacing our fingers together. We were together. We were holding on to one another, but I felt the heaviness from what he said. He wasn't lying. He wasn't lying to himself even. I could feel the truth emanating from him and my throat swelled up. A deep sadness pressed down on me, pushing me further into the bed.

"I love you, Kellan."

It was a quiet testament from me, heard perfectly in that quiet room.

"I love you, too, Shay."

He held me for the rest of the night, waiting for the others to wake. I knew two things. One was that I loved Kellan with all of my being, and two, *nothing* was going to happen to us.

Nothing.

23

We were hiding. We drove that night for hours, eventually finding a home set deep in the woods somewhere. It was clean with fresh laundry folded in piles on the kitchen table. Everything inside the house was modern and chic. Outside the glass patio doors, right by the kitchen, let out to a patio overlooking a large lake. Trees wrapped around both sides of the patio, giving the house a treehouse feel to it.

"Do I want to ask if there was an owner here when we arrived or not?"

Vespar and Giuseppa were sitting on stools at the bar-end of the island. They shared a look, both grinning to the other.

"Never mind." I changed my mind. "I don't want to know."

"He's not dead," Vespar offered. "If that helps."

"Only because Damien wouldn't allow that." Gus sneered at the messenger as he walked into the kitchen behind me. "Speak of the devil."

Damien grabbed an apple and paused, shooting her a look. "Don't start, half child. I can eviscerate you with a thought."

"No, you can't." She raised her chin, challenging him.

"You don't think I can?" He stepped next to me, stepping

toward her. I felt the anger radiating out of him. His entire body tensed up and he was ready for a fight.

"Gus," I said, shaking my head. "Maybe not this fight, not today."

She snorted, rolling her eyes. "I meant it when I said he really can't, because he can't. Kellan did a spell. No messenger-on-demon action going on in this house." Her nose wrinkled, and her top lip lifted in a sneer. "I don't think he wanted to get up this morning and find half his backup obliterated by the other half."

"Yeah." Damien grunted. "You guys."

"Let's take this up outside where it's not charm-free, buddy." Gus swung her long and tanned legs off the stool, standing in a sensual fashion. She was dressed, but barely. A white top clung to her, fitting around her breasts and resting a few inches above her waist. She was showing off her stomach muscles and how fit her body was. Sticking her hands in the pockets of her white shorts, which stopped at the top of her thighs, she struck an alluring and cocky pose at the same time. She could've been in a yachting magazine. She looked him up and down, noting how his hand had a tight grip on the apple. "Imaging that thing is my neck?"

And on cue, the apple exploded, but a cold smile told me it wasn't by accident. Damien retorted, "How'd you know?"

Gus cooled, just a bit. A tiny amount of caution entered her gaze and she glanced to Vespar, seeing that he had a bored look on his face. "What? The thought of me fighting a messenger is putting you to sleep?"

"Fuck off, sister. You're not going to do shit and you know it."

"Yeah?" Anger sparked in her eyes once again. The little bit of fight that had left her, returned and it was doubled. "You don't think so?"

"No, because he'll wipe the floor with you. If by some

miracle he doesn't, Kellan will wipe the floor with you right afterwards. This guy has juice. Kellan's smart. He knows we need him around." Vespar had slowly risen to his feet as he talked. He wasn't dressed in the nice clothes Gus was, but he looked every bit as dangerous. He had pulled on a torn black shirt over jeans. Standing next to his sister, the two were striking together. Both blond. Both gorgeous and both deadly, but Damien didn't seem disturbed. He came around the island, regarding both of them. All three were locked on each other. Damien skirted between the two, but he didn't look scared. He said, "So, you think I'll wipe the floor with your sister, huh?"

"Yeah. Alone." A warning was there. Vespar rolled his shoulders back and held his chin up, slightly higher than Gus'. It was obvious who the alpha was of the two. "But there's two of us and one of you. You don't stand a chance, *messenger*." The last word was spoken with such disdain, my own messenger stirred inside. She didn't like that, not one bit, and my eyes cooled.

"Watch it, *brother*." I used the same disdain he had. "You're forgetting he's not the only messenger around."

I'd just declared war, or at least threatened it when Kellan swept into the room. I felt him coming, like a dark cloud that slowly filled the room. His presence was felt long before he appeared from the stairs where I had come from a few minutes earlier. Without breaking stride, he went past Gus and Vespar, placing a hand on both of their shoulders and physically sitting them both back down. Then, he was around the island and he tugged me with him, pulling me away from Damien before he let me go and he went to the patio doors. He pulled the shades and ordered, "Messenger, close the rest of the windows."

It was an insult and command all rolled into one.

Damien seemed ready to protest, but his shoulders lowered, and he went off to do as Kellan said. One by one, all the windows were closed, and all the shades were pulled. I didn't know the reason, but I waited until Damien was done. Kellan was leaning against the counter next to me. His arm brushed against mine, and I knew the contact was on purpose.

Damien saw it, too, gritting his teeth, before he stopped at the other side of the kitchen.

"Aumae?" I asked.

"Here." She sailed in, coming from down a first floor hallway. A long white dress billowed behind her, and her eyes were dancing. She smiled at me, her face almost glowing. "You look so well rested, Shay. That's wonderful. A good night's sleep must've done the trick, hmmm." She cast a sideways look to Kellan at the last part, with the sides of her mouth turning inward like she was trying to hold back a grin.

"Matt." I chose to ignore whatever innuendo my aunt said. "We brought him with us. Where is he?"

"Tied up in the shed outside."

Giuseppa added to Vespar's statement, "Along with the owner of this place."

"Who put them there?"

"I did." Kellan answered him, his eyes hard on me, almost daring me to say something against him.

I frowned at that. "Okay."

"Did you charm that place, too?" Vespar asked Kellan.

He nodded. "They won't be able to find us, for now. We have a few days to come up with a plan before Shay's father finds us again."

"And speaking of my dad," I told them about my encounter with him.

"Huh?" That was all Gus said.

Vespar seemed confused.

Damien was quiet, his face unreadable and closed off.

Kellan didn't say anything either, out loud. He said to me in my head, *"He said you didn't have enough power?"*

The backs of our fingers were resting against each other. I

moved mine, just barely, to brush against his. *"He was disap-pointed. I don't know why he fought for me. Before that, it felt like he was going to send me back to you. He wanted us to bond."* I kept the part where Damien suggested the same sentiment to me. Things were tense enough. Kellan could use that as an excuse to kill Damien and for some reason, I didn't want him to do that. I snuck a look across the kitchen to the male messenger. His eyebrows were bunched together, lost in thought. A nervous feeling trickled through me, but I wasn't sure where it came from. I had no reason to distrust Damien. If anyone, it should've been Vespar. He actually planned to kill me, but for some reason, that same feeling wasn't there for my pseudo half-demon sibling. I knew where they stood, he and Gus. Both were too scared of Kellan to go against him. One would think they'd be loyal because we saved them both, but I snorted at that thought. I wasn't going to hold my breath for that kind of loyalty from them.

"What's so funny?" Gus asked.

"What?"

She told me, "You just laughed at something." She looked at Kellan with suspicion. "Are you two doing the thought thing?"

"What thought thing?" Damien asked.

"They can hear each other's thoughts." She glared. "It's annoying."

"You can't?" Damien surprised her.

"What?"

"You can't hear your brother's thoughts? You two are connected through blood. You should be able to hear each other's thoughts."

Gus and Vespar shared a look, both shifted in their seats. Then, Gus burst out, pointing at us, "She and Kellan aren't connected by blood. What the hell?"

I felt everyone's attention turn to us, and I straightened against the counter. I didn't want the attention, at least that attention. Everyone knew we were close, but the less they pried, the more comfortable I would be.

Kellan said, "Even more reason to learn your place." He stood up and glowered down at Gus, using his body to intimidate her. "We're both powerful, more than you."

And it was working. Gus sat back down, her shoulders lowering, and she seemed almost submissive. "I wasn't challenging you. I was just wondering how you guys can do that. That's all."

Vespar's jaw clenched, shooting his sister a sideways look.

Damien remained quiet, observing the entire exchange. His gaze was clouded over and he cleared his throat, drawing everyone's attention. "Do you have a plan?"

Kellan glanced over his shoulder to me. I saw one lurking in him, but he said, "No, and we have three days, maybe four tops, to figure one out. I'm assuming you'll bring something to the drawing board."

Damien narrowed his eyes, but he said nothing more.

Aumae smiled. "Well, I think if we all put our heads together, we can all come up with something. Three half-messengers. Three half-demons and two captive humans in the shed. That's a recipe for success, if I ever heard one."

She clapped her hands together, amusement sparking from her. But from the rest of us—not so much.

24

"Everyone wants us to bond."

I tensed, but turned around. I'd gone on a walk. It'd been two days of hiding. Everyone was tense inside the house. I knew Kellan didn't want anyone to leave, but I was going nuts. For the last two nights, Kellan went with me to our room. It wasn't my room. It wasn't his room. It was ours, and every night, I lay in his arms. We kissed, but we never went further. The ache for him was taking over. Even the messenger in me was ready to combust.

I couldn't see him now. The walking path I took in the woods shut out the moonlight, but I felt Kellan before I heard him. I knew he was going to follow and a part of me had been waiting for him.

"What took you so long?" I asked.

He drew closer, stepping further toward me so I could make out his silhouette. I saw the whites of his eyes. They were lidded. "Bonding?"

"No. You've been following me since I left."

"Oh." His shoulders relaxed, straightening out a bit. "I wanted to wait until we were farther from the house."

"Yeah?"

"There's a traitor in the group."

Alarm jolted me. The hairs on the back of my neck stood up. "Who?"

"If you were to take a guess?"

I frowned. "Damien?"

"Maybe."

"You don't think it's him?"

"I don't know what I think yet."

"Who else could it be? Vespar and Gus are a-holes, but you think they'd betray us and to whom?" I laughed. "And it can't be Aumae. She's...she's like the only good one out of everyone. And it's not Matt. He's our captive. That doesn't leave anyone else."

"Damien knew where we were at the house when the demons came."

I nodded. "So it has to be him then." A knot formed in my stomach. "He wanted us to bond too, but he made it sound like we needed to do that to take on my dad. But, what if...?"

Kellan was watching me. He knew what I was thinking and when the words couldn't form, he moved so he was right in front of me. I could feel his warmth and he pulled me into his body, folding me in his arms. He rested his chin on top of my head, murmuring, "Everything will be okay. I'll make sure of it."

I heard the dark promise in his voice and closed my eyes. A sensual tingle wound through me, warming me all over and I rested my forehead against his chest, right where his heart was. I could feel and hear it working. My hand fell to his stomach, pressing there, and the longer I stayed in that position, the faster his heart sped up. He was reacting to me, too. I let out a sigh, thinking, *Everyone wants us to bond. Myself included.*

His arm tightened on my hip. "It's what your father wants."

"And that means we shouldn't, right?" I licked my lips because that's not what I wanted. Not at all.

"*I can hear all your thoughts, Shay. The ones you don't think I can hear, those too.*"

"*I know.*" I didn't care. I was starting to not care about a lot of things. And I moved, closing the distance between our bodies. It had been a small opening, but it was gone now. Our bodies were fused together with only our clothes as a barrier. I wanted his shirt gone. Reacting to my thought, my hand slid up under his shirt, lifting it as I explored his chest. I was becoming lost in the feel of him.

"Shay," he murmured, his voice almost a groan next to my ear.

I didn't answer. I pushed his shirt the rest of the way up, pressing my lips to his naked skin now. I was becoming intoxicated, just from this touch, from not caring, from not holding back. I wasn't holding back anymore. I wanted him. I think I had always wanted him.

He caught the back of my neck. "Shay."

"Shut up," I growled, lifting my face. My lips were waiting for his, and I opened my eyes. He was staring down at me, torn. I saw the temptation there and feeling braver than I ever had before, my hand fell to his jeans. My fingers slid inside, touching his skin, and my thumb rested over the first button of his pants.

An animal-like growl came from him, and he snatched me up in his arms. I was shoved against a nearby tree, but I didn't feel the bark. I didn't feel how rough the tree was. All I was feeling was Kellan, his mouth on mine. His hands were on my hips, holding me up as my legs wound around his waist. I opened his pants and slid my hand inside. I was addicted to him. That was the only explanation for my behavior. I was past caring. I just needed him—then his hands were between my legs, and he slid a finger inside.

I stilled, savoring that sensation, and he began to move. In and out. He went deep, then pulled back out, only to go once more inside.

This was natural.

This was how we were supposed to be, except I wanted him, all of him inside me.

"Kellan," I gasped against his mouth.

Desire and pleasure pulsed through me. I felt his darkness cover us, and I even wanted more of that. He protected me. He killed for me. He would do anything for me. The messenger in me was quiet. Kellan pulled his mouth from mine. He rasped near my ear, "She's gone. She's letting us have this moment."

In.

Out.

I needed more.

"Kellan," I started to whimper. Wave after wave was crashing down on me, nearing me to climax, but I wasn't ready. Still. I couldn't do anything. Kellan held me in place. I couldn't move my hips in response to him. He held me firm. I could only be there and endure what he was doing to my body.

"Shay," he growled again, letting me fall to the ground. He caught me and laid me down gently, then bent over me.

The night cold should've covered me, but it didn't. Kellan's darkness was warming both of us, and he had woven a spell over us, and then I felt his lips replace his fingers. My back arched, and I let out a guttural scream. I grabbed his head, but he caught my hands and pinned both down beside me. His tongue began moving, licking, slipping inside. I was helpless again. All I could do was lay there, panting, trying not to scream as he made me come.

"Kellan," I was begging. "Please."

I couldn't take much more.

He was relentless. I wanted *him*, not his mouth, not his fingers. I wanted him, and I wanted to touch him back. I was brazen now. I just wanted *him*. I wanted to give him pleasure, too.

After coming a third time, my body was exhausted and satiated. I was panting, and Kellan lay on top of me, smirking down at me.

I raked my fingers through his hair, grabbing ahold of him. "What did you just do to me?"

His eyes darkened. The smirk vanished, and he lowered his lips to mine. A soft kiss there. He whispered, "I made you mine."

A delicious shiver.

Goose bumps broke out over my skin, but all I could do was shake my head, my lips to his, and I murmured, "God. You're mine."

"Not God. Just me." Then he took control of the kiss again, and he started his sensual assault on me all over again.

HANDS LINKED, we were walking back when suddenly Kellan stopped.

"Kellan?"

"We aren't alone."

I tried to sense out, feeling who was there, and he was right. A presence was waiting for us, just a few yards before the walking path opened back to the house's lawns.

"It's Damien."

I tightened my hand over his, but Kellan pulled loose and strode forward. "Are you waiting for someone else, messenger?"

Damien sighed. "Please. Like I want to smell the two of you together, what you've been doing. I'm waiting for you and you know it."

"Why?"

"There are things at work that you have no idea about. I feel it's time you know."

I waited, expecting Kellan to say something more, but he was only silent. His head turned halfway from us, like he was watching something beyond the woods. He moved forward a step. He was seeing something.

"Kellan?" "What is it?"

He didn't answer me.

My insides began to churn.

Damien filled me in. "He's seeing what I came to tell you guys. When you left, the traitor took advantage of your disappearance."

"What is she doing?" Kellan's voice was tight and controlled.

"You see her, too?"

I looked, but nothing. Just the black of the night and Damien's white aura. That was the messenger emanating from within him. "You guys." I wanted to know. "What's going on?"

A door from the house opened, light spilled out. We could see from where we stood. We were close enough to the house and someone shouted, "Hurry! They're coming back."

Kellan vanished. I felt him beside me and in the next second, he was gone.

"Kellan!"

"Shay. Come on." Damien motioned for me.

I ran and he ran with me. We got to the lawn just as Vespar was running toward the shed. Kellan appeared and grabbed him by the throat. He picked him up, pulled him close, said something. I tried to hear, but Kellan shut me out.

"Stop, Kellan."

"Stay back, for your own good."

I felt his murderous intentions. He was going to kill Vespar, and later he'd regret it. I tried to run faster. Damien was right beside me. Why we couldn't vanish and appear there was beyond me, but I gritted me teeth and kept going. We got there in time to hear Vespar squeak out, "It's too late, Kellan. She already called them."

A deep roar erupted from the bottom of Kellan's throat, and his hand closed around Vespar's throat. We heard a snapping sound, and Vespar's body went slack. He broke his neck. Kellan let the body fall to the ground, and for a moment, it was complete silence in the lawn. I sensed Aumae coming to the opened door. She wondered what was happening, but no one said a word, and in that small break, we heard moans from inside the shed.

"No." Damien tried to rush for the shed.

Kellan flung a hand out. He didn't touch Damien, but the messenger was thrown back. A bolt of static came from Kellan's hand right after and when Damien tried to run back to us, he couldn't. He ran into an invisible force field. I asked, starting to tremble, "What is that?"

"It's a barrier." Kellan turned back to the shed. He only stared at it for a moment.

"Kellan, what's going on?"

"It keeps them out and us in."

Us. He meant him and me... I thought. I assumed the 'them' was Damien and Aumae. He couldn't have meant messengers, because I was a messenger, too. I was a little more than half of one even, but I didn't voice those questions. Whatever was happening on the other side of the shed door—it sounded like sex, but I had a feeling it was more than sex. Kellan wouldn't have cared if it was only sex, and then he strode forward. I followed, and when he opened the door, I expected the occupants to jerk at the sight of us.

They didn't. They kept on as if they couldn't hear us.

"I blocked them before I caught Vespar," Kellan told me.

I saw why as Giuseppa arched her back, letting her head fall backward. She was straddling Matt, who was kissing her breast. She lifted her arms, cradling his head, sliding her fingers through his hair. "More, Matt. Please more," she crooned, urging him on as her hips moved faster. She was riding him.

He grasped her back, jerking his hips up into her. A growl came from him as he caught one of her nipples in his teeth.

Her mouth fell open, and she continued with her moans, but then her hand lifted from his head. It continued, moving all the way in the air, and it reached behind her. Then, the moonlight glinted off something metal, and when her hand came back up, she was holding a nasty-looking dagger.

I started forward, but Kellan stopped me.

"What are you doing? She's going to kill him."

He didn't answer. He kept me in place.

"Kellan!"

His jaw hardened. His hand was firm on my stomach—and then as Matt and Giuseppa climaxed, both letting out loud groans, her hand slashed in the air. She sliced his throat. Matt jerked forward, making empty sounding gasps as blood spilled out from his throat. His hand came to his throat, and he looked at her, shock and revulsion mixing together. She ignored him, coldly pushing his body back from hers, and she stood up. She was naked, blood covering her, and she wiped her hand over her chest, then tracing a symbol on the wall. Once she was done, she stood, facing the symbol and took a deep breath, then placed the palm of her hand against it. An explosion happened in the air, throwing her backward. Heat and fire flared in the air. It would've flung me backward as well, but Kellan held on to me. He anchored me in place and moved so one of his shoulders was half shielding me. Some of the fire grazed my cheek. I felt it burning there, but it wasn't painful. It was like a warm tickle. I frowned at that, but something was coming. Giuseppa had opened a hole in the air and whoever/whatever was coming from the other side.

Kellan was waiting for it.

"What—?" Giuseppa struggled to her feet. The shed had blown up and ash, wood, and soot covered her body, mixing with the blood. She shook her head, gazing at us. "Wha—what are you doing here? Shay?" She gulped, jerking around. "Wait. Where's Vespar?" Panic rose in her voice. "Vespar. Where is he? Where is HE?"

"Shut up."

Kellan silenced her with that, then we felt the presence from whoever was coming.

I felt its darkness before it said anything. It was evil, and powerful, and I was trembling. I would've fallen back or run if Kellan hadn't been touching me. He wasn't keeping me in place. He was enabling me to stand there and tolerate what was coming. It was pure evil. I began clawing at his arm. I didn't want to be there.

"Shay," he said softly. His hand left my stomach and caught my hand. Our fingers laced together and I was beginning to cling to him like a lifesaver.

Black smoke began to waft in. It coated the ground, filling all around our feet and slowly rising up to cover our knees, our legs, our waists. It rose up to my face, and I began choking. I couldn't breathe.

Kellan saw what was happening and uttered a word, "Aysh."

The smoke combusted into fire. Again, we were unharmed, and then the smoke was gone. Giuseppa coughed, falling over behind us. She clutched at her stomach. "What did you do?"

But she didn't matter. I felt his presence. He was there, right on the other side. I couldn't talk or move. I could only hold on to Kellan, but I sensed his fear, too.

Black tentacles began to come through the hole, like black snakes, but they were all attached together. A thin sheen of skin covered them. They slithered all around, feeling the ground, the remaining wall of the shed until they touched the bottom of our feet. Instead of heat, I felt cold. Ice plunged through me, and I began violently shaking now.

Kellan bit back a curse, then suddenly, the snakes/tentacles left. They moved past us, leaving a perfect circle in the ground around our feet. They went to Giuseppa and a shrill scream came from them. It wasn't Gus. It was the snakes/tentacles. Immediately, the rest of them swarmed, overcoming Giuseppa.

I didn't want to watch, but I couldn't not watch.

She had been my sister, then half-sister, and now she was an empty vessel of someone I was supposed to have loved as family. I felt none of those feelings anymore, not after seeing her murder Matt and knowing she had been the one to bring forth whomever this demon was. The snakes/tentacles writhed over her body. She didn't say a word. They swarmed inside her throat, and when that happened, I couldn't look anymore. I pressed my head into Kellan's arm.

Then, I heard a hiss, "Son. You are here to greet me?"

Kellan didn't say a word. His hand had a death-like grip on mine. His entire body was like stone. He was tensing up and I knew something more was going to happen.

"No." Another hiss. "You're not here to greet me. You're here to kill me...for her? You are betraying me for that monster?"

Again, no sound from Kellan. I looked up and saw the torment on his face. His father was in his head, and Kellan's face had drained of blood. No. His father was assaulting Kellan's mind, how the snakes/tentacles were still assaulting Giuseppa. They were loving it, whatever they were doing to her. I wondered if Kellan's father was doing the same to him. Loving whatever torture he was inflicting on his son?

I turned to face his father, and I said the first thing that came to mind. "Stop."

25

"It's you."

As he spoke, the ice plunged deeper inside of me. I cried out from the pain, almost doubling over. That was him, he was inside of me like he was inside of his own son. "You are what my son loves above all else, why he refuses to return to my side."

The rest of him stepped through the hole. He wasn't corporeal. The snakes/tentacles were a part of him as was the ice he had inflected upon us both. The smoke had been a part of him, too. Everything about Kellan's father was to bring suffering and pain. He was thriving on ours, and I could see that he was getting stronger because of it.

I closed my eyes. I had to block out the pain, somehow. I could get a footing then.

"You think to fight me?" He was laughing. "You are nothing. Even the great Shazaam couldn't take me on. I am Darkness. I am Evil. You are a small shadow underneath a rock in my world."

The ice burst through new layers inside of me, tunneling all

the way to my core. He was going for my soul. That was the ultimate destination for him.

"No."

I felt more than heard Kellan's protest. He knew what his
father was doing to me, and he was rallying against it.

'What did you say?"

"I said no. Let her go."

The ice was ripped out of me. I screamed, falling to the
floor and I felt myself being pulled away. There was a vacuum
effect going on, yanking me backward. Kellan stuck his foot out,
maintaining contact with me, and as soon as he did, the world
righted itself. He anchored me again. Without Kellan's touch, I
would've been swept back, and I glanced over my shoulder.
Damien and Aumae were on the other side of that barrier. Both
had wide eyes and paled features. Damien's hands were curled
into fists. He'd been trying to break through the barrier, but
paused, seeing that I was looking back. Aumae clutched at a
blanket over her shoulders. Tears fell down her face, and she
never flicked them away. She just let them fall, like she knew
something we didn't, like she knew this was our goodbye, like
she knew I was going to die.

"NO!" Kellan roared, hearing my thoughts and feeling my
pain. He broke free from his dad's hold a little bit more, enough
so he could lean down and grab my shoulder. I lifted my arm
up and he caught my hand. There. As soon as our palms were
next to each other, it sealed our connection. A wave of strength
surged through me, going through him, too, or maybe it had
been his in the first place. Maybe he loaned it to me. Either way,
I felt a tiny bit stronger.

His father had pulled all the snakes/tentacles back. He
stood in front of us in a corporeal form wearing a black suit,
buttoned in front of him. His body looked like Brad Pitt, and he
cocked his head to the side, a genuine curiosity alighting his
eyes. "Well. That was interesting." He studied us closer, sniffing

the air. "You two are bonded, but not enough. You've not taken her completely, son. What are you waiting for?" He gestured to me. "She is willing. Even her messenger is silent, knowing it needs to happen."

My messenger—she wasn't fighting for me. I tried to waken her, use her power, but nothing. It was like kicking around an empty can.

"Ah." Kellan's father smiled at me. "You're not used to being as one with your messenger, are you? I put her to sleep. I won't have a half-messenger trying to kill me and only killing herself before I'm done with you." He swung his head back to Kellan. "Why have you not fully bonded with her?"

I wanted to die. He was talking about sex. If I weren't so scared, humiliation would be coloring my face red.

Kellan's eyes closed to slits. "Are you joking? What we do is none of your business."

"It is my business. That's why you were sent here, for her. You're supposed to take her power. I want her power."

What? I needed to know more, feeling that this was important, but Giuseppa coughed from behind us, rolling to her hands and knees. Her body was black and blue now, with red splotches all over. There were marks that looked like rug burn, like she had been dragged behind a car. I cringed just looking at her.

"Vespar?" she croaked out, one eye looking to the left as her right tried to focus on Kellan. "Where is he?"

Kellan's father walked around, gazing down at Gus. "Ah yes. This is the foster sister that I sent you to be with."

She wasn't looking up at him. Her head hung low, and her back was spasming from trying to breathe. He kicked her, flipping her over. The front of her looked the same as her back, black and blue with red splotches all over except blood had broken through her skin. It was trickling down her body, making a path among the soot, markings, and dried blood that had already been there. Her head fell back to the ground. She couldn't move. She could only look up at him, and she said, hoarsely, "They did something to my brother."

"Ah. Your brother." Kellan's father knelt down, shaking his head as he took in her form. "You're a mess, aren't you? What did my pets do?"

Pets? I didn't want to think about that. I shared a look with Kellan, who frowned and glanced away.

"Son." His father swung back around. "Your foster sister was kind enough to call me forward. And I have to fulfill part of my end so where's her brother?"

Kellan still didn't say anything.

"Did you kill him?" Giuseppa spoke with such vehemence, she spit out the words. She sat up, her entire body still taking gulping breaths. "Did you?"

Kellan shot her a dark look, but he looked more bored with her question than angered.

"Son?"

He transferred the look to his father. "Are you fucking kidding me? Of course, I killed him. They called you here."

"They have our mom and dad!" Giuseppa exclaimed. She tried to rise, fell, and remained sitting, wrapping her hands around her legs, balled in fists. "Because of you. They took Mom and Dad. Do you care?"

Mom and Dad... My surrogate mother, the one that was human but had her insides carved out from living and loving her demon husband. The ones that I didn't want to see so I cast a spell so I never saw them. Those parents.

"They were taken captive?"

"Yes." Gus huffed at me. "We're the ones who sent the demons after you guys before." Her nostrils flared. "You're not the only ones who have some juice. We can do a freaking tracking spell." She looked to where Matt's body was, now under a pile of wood and soot. "That's how they got the jump on us. I didn't know the exact words to say, but Dylan did. Asshole. We spilled a little blood, he said the magic words, and then I woke up and I was tied to a freaking bed. When I woke up, Dylan said they followed through with the rest of the spell, hoping the two of you would be taken care of and they wouldn't have to deal with you, but they were going to 'deal with Vespar and me.'" She glared at Kellan. "I'm sorry, okay! But they took our parents. Apparently, you were cloaked somewhere—"

The magic house.

"—and they needed us to find you, so we did what we had to do."

"And it didn't work, huh?"

She sneered at him. "You kicked their asses. We had to try again, so yeah, I did what I had to do just now."

"You had to kill Matt?" I asked.

"Yes. The spell required a sacrifice. It was him or the owner of this place, but Kellan moved him so..." she trailed off, shrugging again. She regarded Kellan's father. "You said to deliver your son and Shay. They're here. Where are my parents?"

"They're fine. They're back at your home, packing."

"What?" She grew wary. "Packing for what?"

"Packing to leave. They can't stay here anymore. Too many people know what they are, so they're off again, with little demons to raise all over again."

"What?"

Giuseppa wasn't the only one confused. I asked, "What are you saying?"

He swung those dark and hypnotic eyes my way. I gulped, feeling the full force of him again. I felt my soul being sucked out of me as he began to glide toward me. "I gifted them with more children, more demons to raise. I didn't pull them in to take to hell with me. I pulled them in to give them a job. They work for me now." He glanced to Giuseppa, speaking to me, "As does your foster sister now." He lingered on Vespar's body. "And your foster brother would've, but oh well. My son did what he does so well. He killed." He patted Kellan on the shoulder. "I'm quite proud of you, but don't take this rebellion too far. You were given a job."

Kellan's eyes narrowed. His father pulled back some of his power, freeing Kellan and me even more. I could see the wheels turning in his mind. He was going to do something. I felt his intentions like a timer counting down. In three—Kellan smiled at his father. "I have to thank you."

"For what?"

In two—"For letting me come find Shay. For letting me fall in love with her." He paused one second, his eyes sliding to mine. "And for letting her give me a little bit of humanity."

And one—Kellan pulled out the dagger I recognized from earlier, when he'd been about to use it on the messenger who my father was channeling. I started to fling my hand out. It killed Dylan, but it wouldn't have killed the messenger. It would've only given him power. I worried it could do the same to his father, but instead of thrusting it into his father, he twisted around and threw it toward Damien.

I held my breath.

The invisible barrier was there—the knife sailed right through it, breaking it, and Damien caught it in the air. He paused, staring at Kellan's father, then a cruel grin spread over his face.

Damien and Aumae were back in the fight.

Kellan's father started laughing.

The brief joy I experienced shriveled up and burned away. He wasn't worried, not at all. In fact, he sounded even happier. He pointed at them, turning to Kellan, "You think they're going to help you? You're a demon, son. You're *my* demon. Those two are hybrids. They would never help you—"

His words choked off into a gurgle.

Damien leapt in the air, plunging the dagger through his

back. He backed away after, waiting to see what happened. Everyone did, except Kellan. He didn't seem shocked, amused, anything. He was watching his father with a hard expression in his eyes, like he knew what was going to happen wouldn't work. I held my breath, and then his father started laughing. He looked down at the end of the dagger. The tip of it stuck out of his chest. "This was supposed to kill me?" He reached for it and began to pull it the rest of the way out of him, through his front. "Kellan, you couldn't have thought that would work—"

"No, but this will."

While we were distracted, watching his father start to pull the dagger out of his chest, Kellan had gone to Giuseppa and held her up by her arm, literally lifting her in the air. She was too weak to fight and new blood poured from her throat. Kellan was covered in it. His father realized what was going to happen and he sucked in his breath. His hand fell away from the dagger, and he started forward. "No, Kell—"

He was too late.

Kellan threw Giuseppa through the hole, and as he did, another explosion like when the hole was created occurred once again. "NO!" Then, just as quick as it happened, it was done. This time, instead of exploding outward, it imploded. Giuseppa vanished, and so did his father.

Kellan's father was gone. The hole in the air was gone, and everything was in shambles around us.

"What just happened?" Damien asked.

Aumae started to murmur to herself, stepping forward, clutching her blanket over her shoulders, "One sacrifice to call him—"

Kellan finished, "—one sacrifice to expel him." He stopped, closing his eyes, and hung his head for a moment. He hurt. I felt it from him and because he did, so did I. I was aching. I started forward. "Kellan."

He stopped me, holding a hand in the air. "Don't, Shay. I don't deserve any comfort you're going to give me."

His words hurt, like a knife twisting in my chest.

He added, "She called him forward. If I threw her body in there, he'd have to go. She was the reason he was here and I don't deserve any kindness from you. I murdered Vespar and Gus. They were our brother and sister. That...you're right. I do care and they meant something to me. They don't mean what you mean to me, but they meant something and..." He stopped again, drawing in one more ragged breath. "You were disgusted when you watched her kill Matt. You can't pretend otherwise."

"She *murdered* him. Killing and murder are different. One's in cold blood, and that's what she did. She planned it, and she executed it. That was different."

"No." He shook his head. "It wasn't. I executed her. I executed Vespar."

"But they called your father here. They sent those demons after us."

"And Matt helped torture Vespar and Gus, too. He was human, just like half of Gus and Vespar were. No, Shay. I know you're going to turn a blind eye because that's what you do for me, but I can't let you this time."

"Kellan." I couldn't hear anymore. He was twisting that knife in my chest, over and over again. Tears threatened to spill from my eyes. "Stop." He was going to leave. I felt his withdrawal from inside of me, and I couldn't do a thing to stop it. "Kellan, don't go."

And he walked away...

26

"I don't get it."

I was sitting at the kitchen table with Aumae and Damien later that night. The owner, whose name was Kent Ocean and that Kellan had moved to the basement without telling anyone, sat with us. He was cradling a mug of hot tea between his hands, clenched with white knuckles and shaking arms. Aumae brought him out of the basement and coaxed him to sit with us. He hadn't been tied up or anything. There'd been nothing keeping him down there, except pure fear. When he realized Kellan wasn't with us, he noticeably relaxed, but he was still cautious and every now and then, like just now, his arms began shaking. He couldn't seem to control them, but he offered a trepid apology, "So sorry. So sorry." He kept repeating those words until Aumae reassured him enough times that we weren't going to hurt him.

It hadn't mattered. He kept uttering those words until his shaking stopped and another bout hit him, but this time I saw that the hot tea was spilling onto his arms. He still didn't stop. He didn't even react to his burning skin.

"Oh dear." Aumae took the mug away, patting his shoulder. "We'll just, huh, how about some cold water instead?"

I cleared my throat.

She amended, "I mean some room-temperature water."

He glanced up, pale, and his lips parted to say thank you. He couldn't. His bottom lip was shaking as well. A brief stutter was the only thing that sounded from him.

I pitied him. He hadn't asked us to come here. He hadn't done a thing to us, and we muscled our way into his house, taking over. I wondered what Kellan had done to scare him so much, but rethought that. I'd rather not know, though his parting words still lingered with me.

"...you're going to turn a blind eye because that's what you do for me."

"Excuse me."

Damien and Aumae gave me knowing looks as I stood from the table and headed toward the master bedroom. Kellan left the property, but returned ten minutes earlier. Mr. Ocean jerked away from the table, but Kellan scanned the group, lingered on me, and turned down the hallway. We heard the shower running moments later and when I went in there, Kellan was just standing in the shower. He'd left the door open, and his clothes were still on, plastered to him now.

I knew he felt me, but he didn't say anything. I perched against the counter, watching him.

He stared straight ahead to the tiled wall, so I waited until he spoke, almost dully, "You're the only good part of me, and I'm going to fuck that up."

"Kellan." I started for him.

"No." He shook his head, and I held back. He added, closing his eyes, "I have no more secrets from you. I love you. You love me. We're bonded, and yet, we haven't bonded enough."

I grew warm, remembering how he kissed me, touched me before. An image of him over me again, but this time moving inside of me started an ache inside of me, but it also sparked something else. My own fear. I was scared. What would happen then? Who would come for us? Who else was left to come?

"Your father."

Kellan swung those dark and so bleak eyes my way. As he did, it was like everything clicked in place. When he looked at me, how he was looking at me, made the world make sense. It didn't before, if he wasn't with me or at my side, but now, as he was looking at me—I knew everything would be fine. It had to be.

The side of his mouth lifted up in a half-grin. "How do I look at you?"

"Like you're dying of thirst and I'm the last drop of water."

He grunted. The half-grin grew. "That sounds right."

"Kellan." I sighed, moving closer. I stopped just on the outside of the shower. If I took one step closer, I'd be inside. The water would move onto me, and I'd be at his side. I waited, my chest growing tight. "My father is still coming for me, isn't he?"

He nodded, his eyes growing lidded.

"What does that mean?"

"Someone sent the demons after us, but your father found us when we rescued Vespar and Giuseppa. But Shay," he stopped, swallowing. A haunted look came over him. "We could hide. We could use spells to shield us, maybe go back to that house and stay there. Your father didn't know about it, and maybe he won't find us there, but..."

There was always a but. I grew tense.

"Do you really want to do that?"

"What do you mean?"

"Do you want to hide for the rest of your life?"

My life. He said my life, not his, not ours. Mine. That told me so much—I was going to die, but he was not. We had one lifetime, mine. I knew Kellan could hear my thoughts, or at least, sense them, but this time, he remained quiet. He didn't correct me or deny, and that, too, spoke volumes. It was like blow after blow kept coming. I wanted them to stop. I wanted to be the one to deliver the blows.

"What are you thinking?" His voice had grown hoarse.

"You know what I'm thinking."

He leaned toward me, the water splashing off his head and sprinkling over me. "Are you sure? Are you absolutely sure?"

Was I? Did I want to hide, or did I want to fight? A lifetime with him...or nothing at all? It could all end. I knew the risks. I ground out, "We've been hiding all our lives. I'm done hiding." I stepped inside the shower, the water coating me as well, and I pressed against him. "It's time to fight."

His eyes darkened, and then his lips were on mine, and nothing else mattered. We became one that night.

27

"For the record," Damien said two days later. "I think this is incredibly stupid."

Kellan stood next to me, holding my hand, and grunted. "For the record, no one asked you."

"Shut up." I held tight to Kellan's hand, speaking to both and right then, the ground began to quake. "He's coming."

Two nights ago, Damien came to the bedroom. He stood in the doorway, his hands folded in front of him, and we could both feel the confession coming. It came off him in waves. Shame. Guilt. Embarrassment. And then he started by saying, "I've been lying to you."

I knew a whole lot of shit was about to be laid on our laps and I closed my eyes, just for a moment. I needed to prepare myself, and after a few more seconds, I nodded to Damien. "Tell us everything."

He did, later standing across the table from Kellan and me. Aumae joined us as well. We kept the lights off except for one single lamp that was behind Damien from the living room. It seemed fitting, casting him in shadow and lighting up the rest of us. Damien coughed, looking away before starting. He drew in a breath, and held it there, grimacing. "I have to first explain that there's a war going on in the heavens. I didn't want to be a part of this. I wasn't a part of this, but your father," he looked at me, a wall shifting to the side to show new emotion, "*and* my father, Sachiel, is on one side."

"Wait."

Had I heard him right?

Kellan cursed. "Of course. That makes sense now."

"You're my brother?"

"Half-brother. We have the same father."

My head was pounding. There'd been so many turns and twists when it came to siblings. I looked at one that I thought had been my brother to another that was my brother. I began laughing. There was nothing else I could do. Anything else I was feeling didn't matter. I held up a hand, shaking my head. "This is just becoming ridiculous now."

Damien kept going, an apology in his eyes to me, "I'm not as powerful as you because my mother was full human. I lived with my family until I was little. Nine years old. That's when Sachiel found me. I was leaving the house with my grandpa and Sachiel—"

The vision came back to me. I remembered when I first experienced it. I'd been getting into my car. That felt so long ago now.

"Who are you?"

I held my breath and closed my eyes. The ticking from someone's watch pounded loudly in my ear. When I opened my eyes, I saw an older man across the road. He walked beside his son, and they were headed into a house. The voice didn't come from him, but it was connected to them. I just didn't know how.

I said, "I thought that man was your father."

Damien had been watching me. His eyes were knowing as he nodded. "We've been connected since I first started talking to you. I didn't realize how powerful you were until you slipped into my memories. I had to block you after that. I've been blocking you since, well," he regarded Kellan, "until last night." He gestured beside me. "You and Kellan fully bonded, and that ended the connection you and I had."

"What does that mean?"

"Wait. I have more to confess." We could see the actual pain on his face. He paled, his eyes and mouth straining at the ends. "I'm the one who revealed your hiding spot to the demons. They attacked you because of me. I thought if the other side took you, I wouldn't have to deal with Sachiel."

It was because of him.

I leaned forward, saying softly, "We were protected there."

"I know." His Adam's apple bobbed up and down.

"We were safe there."

"I know." His eyes darted to Kellan's, and his lips pressed together. Flinching. "And you guys defeated them."

"You arrived the next day." Kellan's eyes were narrowed to slits.

"I was there before. I tracked where you were through my connection to Shay."

I closed my eyes. I'd been betrayed through my own blood. I whispered, "They took Aumae."

"Child." She rested her hand over mine. "He's confessing now. That's all that matters."

Kellan grunted. "I'm not that forgiving."

Aumae insisted, "Let us hear the rest from him. He's repenting and he's trusting us now. He's making himself vulnerable when he never had to. We must remember that."

My own blood—I couldn't get over that. A dagger was inside of me, cutting away around where my heart should be resting. It was becoming hollow, more and more, but Aumae was right. I could hear the forgiveness in her voice and I clung to it. I let it wash over me.

"I can't track you anymore, if that makes you feel better."

"It doesn't."

Damien's head hung down, and he didn't say anything more. I knew he had more to say, but for a moment, I needed him to shut up. For once, Kellan wasn't the one ready to commit murder. Damien was my brother, and he had betrayed me. He hurt someone else who was good, who should have never been harmed. I glanced to Aumae and she was watching me back. Her eyes were so loving, so giving. She smiled at me. She was trying to convey the same peace to me, so that I would forgive him, but I couldn't.

I sighed. "You can't connect to me anymore because of Kellan, right?"

Kellan added, "You're a part of my blood now. It's like we're married, Shay. You're my family."

My eyes went wide. Oh. "Okay." I wasn't surprised, not really. "That makes sense." I guess...

Kellan grunted, hiding a smile. "I thought you knew."

"I think I did." I laid my hand over his. "I still would've done it, been with you, if I'd known the full ramifications. I'm okay with it. I am."

He turned his hand upside down, lacing our fingers, and pulled our hands to his lap. They were hidden from the others. Damien had been waiting, he cleared his throat. "Like I was saying before, there's a war going on above, and Sachiel is a big contender for one side." He faltered, his head bowing slightly. "Uh...this is hard to say because this was what I was supposed to encourage. Shay, I told you before that you should bond with Kellan because then you'd be too powerful for your father to take on. That isn't true."

I knew where this was going.

He said further, "Sachiel *wants* you to bond with Kellan, because he intends to take your powers. Both of yours."

I felt Kellan's anger mounting and snuck a peek at him, but he wasn't showing anything. His face was unreadable. His eyes gave nothing away, and he even held my hand in a gentle and loving way, but I felt his demon stirring away. My messenger side was awakening as well, and she wasn't pleased.

"The truth is that neither of you is a match for Sachiel, and he knows that. I was supposed to get close to you, Shay, and get you to bond with Kellan. That was the first part of my job."

A knot formed in my stomach. "And the second?"

"I'm supposed to deliver both of you to him."

"You know how to call him?"

Damien nodded. "The messengers aren't watching like they had been before. He was surprised at how you guys were able to fend him off, and how Shay killed the other messengers. He thought you guys had bonded and to be honest, so did I."

"You told him where to watch for us?"

Damien glanced to Kellan. "Yeah. That was me. I came to get you guys and take you back there. That's why I showed up when I did."

I said, "And that's why you didn't want to help us rescue Vespar and Giuseppa?"

He lifted a shoulder, turning away for a moment. "I worried about what he would say, if it were reported to him that I helped save two demons. That was part of the reason. The other part was because they're both *demons.*" He sneered, saying the last word. "It is beneath our kind to help them."

The ground began rumbling.

Aumae and Damien both started, but I knew the cause. I was holding his hand. Both caught on when Kellan and I didn't move.

"Oh." Damien frowned. "I'm sorry for my part."

"Why?"

"Why?" He echoed my question.

"Why did you do it? You were born to a human family. That means you have family still, Damien, and I'm not talking about me or our father."

He glanced away, his jaw clenching.

"Oh dear." Aumae spoke for the first time, her quiet words splicing through the tense room. She shifted in her seat. The corner of her mouth turned down. "Are they still alive?"

Damien jerked his head up and down. "My mother is, and so are my little sister and brother."

He had siblings. That rocked me. "From a different father?"

He nodded again, his voice growing hoarse. "I'm sorry, Shay."

He had a family. I did not. I tried shrugging. It didn't matter. I had Kellan now, but my shrug fell flat. It did matter. It stung. Damien had a true family. A mother he could go back to and hug. Two siblings that would wind their tiny arms around him. I murmured, "I bet their father loves you like his."

"He does." Damien breathed out. "Yes. They think I was kidnapped, which I was in a way. Sachiel took me in and taught me about my messenger lineage."

"What happens when you deliver us to him?"

Everyone turned to Kellan, hearing his question.

Damien's Adam's apple bobbed up and down. "I'm free. I can go back to my family and live out my life like a normal person."

"But you know that's a lie, don't you?"

Kellan's question hung in the room as he stared at my half-brother. It wasn't a challenge, just the truth how Kellan saw it. A second later, Damien nodded and sighed. His hands fell to the chair in front of him and curled tight around it. "I know."

"He'll never let you go back, if your family is even still alive."

"I know."

"And you've finally realized that now, and that's why you're coming clean to us." Kellan rose from his chair. "You want our help."

With each statement Kellan said, Damien's gaze fell to the

table, then to the floor. He looked back up now, shame brimming bright in his eyes. "Yes."

Kellan narrowed his eyes, "That's what I thought."

The last two days passed too quickly. Damien explained there were only two ways to kill a messenger, and none of us would be free until Sachiel was killed. One way was to use a biblical weapon, which we had none, and Damien didn't know where to find one.

I asked then, "And the second?"

He didn't answer at first, drawing in a deep breath. "You're not going to like the second option."

"What are your choices?" Kellan mirrored Damien, standing at the opposite end and leaning forward with his hands on his chair's backrest. "Spill it, messenger. Let's start getting this over with."

And he began, "Well, you see—you'll have to let Sachiel start to drain your power..."

Here we were. Standing on a hill, feeling the ground shake with my father's arrival, and I knew that I would either live through this or not. Those were the two options. The plan consisted of letting Sachiel start to drain our powers. Kellan and I would be linked. Sachiel would open himself up to us and he would be vulnerable. When that happened, Damien and Aumae were going to connect to us as well, and the four of us would instead drain Sachiel of his power. When that happened, when he had no power left, he would be vulnerable to a human weapon. Mr. Kent Ocean had volunteered for that part, stepping out from a closet, pale face and trembling like the other night.

He raised his hand in the air and tugged at his shirt's collar. "I'll do it."

Aumae made a sound and hurried to his side. She flashed Damien and Kellan a warning, touching a protective hand to his shoulder. "Now, dear, are you sure?"

The owner pumped his head up and down. "If this guy is as bad as you say, he won't be focused on a little human being around. He'll be distracted by all of you guys."

"If you kill us instead, I will come back from hell. I will kill you and every single member of your family."

Sweat formed on Kent's forehead. He wiped it off using the back of his arm, his eyes held by Kellan's during his threat, and he squeaked out, "I won't. I, just... I want to help now. I don't think a lot of us folk ever get called to fight a battle like this. I mean, I'm a church-going man. I don't think I could sit back and not help, you know."

"You're a church-going man?" Kellan drew closer, moving around the table and me.

Aumae snapped at him, "Stay back!"

I caught Kellan's arm. "Stop."

"I—uh—I mean, it's not right. No matter how much of a celestial being your father is. He shouldn't be forcing his son to turn on his daughter. I'm a father too and that isn't right. It's the children that are supposed to be protected. That's my job. That should be his job too."

And so, here we were. Mr. Kent Ocean was tucked away behind some nearby trees, protected by the same spell Kellan used to hide us when we were at Kent's home. Sachiel had no clue the person who would kill him was the least powerful there was and in a way, it was ironic. He wanted power, but he was going to get stripped of his instead.

We felt the earth shaking first.

The winds picked up after that.

The sky darkened.

Then, there was complete silence. It was like a tornado was at our door, and we were waiting for it to ring our doorbell. All breaths were held. Everyone paused, their hearts suspended, and then, with a sudden whoosh, he landed in front of us. As he ascended, the ground thundered once again. It was enough to be a small earthquake.

My father arrived, glancing around—he was alone. That was lucky for us, but I didn't want to question our fortune. He looked like me. He looked like Damien too. Now that I knew Damien was my half-brother, we had the same nose, same cheekbones, and even the same heart-shaped chin. Our father stood tall, closer to Kellan's height, and he was like a Greek god. Long blond hair that curled around his shoulder. Broad shoulders. Thin waist. I looked for wings, but saw none until I glanced down. A shadow of them lay out behind him on the ground. As I watched, they folded up, tucking close to his body. His eyes were blue, like Damien's, and he was watching me, studying me back.

"You look much like your mother."

I frowned. "I thought you would've seen me before now."

He shook his head, then grew still and tilting his head forward. His eyebrows pinched together and his forehead wrinkled. "I've been looking, but I've not seen you until today." He glanced to Damien. "Thank you for calling me, and though I asked for them to be unconscious, thank you for having her awake. Your foresight is commendable."

"Foresight?"

I glanced sideways to Damien, who shrugged back to me. He said, "Uh—yeah."

Our father strode forward, his hands stretched out. A low and deep growl erupted from Kellan, and he moved forward, blocking me from my father. Sachiel drew back, his eyes finding Kellan's for the first time, and his hands went back to his side. "I see. You think to fight on her behalf, demon?"

"You're a condescending bitch. Do you know that?"

I caught movement behind me, from Aumae, but I didn't dare look to see what she was doing. I hoped it would help in our fight, because now that my father was in front of us, I knew it would be a big one. The power emanated from him in waves. It was almost overwhelming, threatening to choke me.

"We can't win."

I wasn't sure if I had the realization or if it came from Kellan, but I shared a look with him. It was true, though. My father was too powerful. The plan wasn't going to work. We'd never be able to overwhelm him, not with all of us.

Despair lodged in my throat. I didn't know what to do now. We were here. He was here. There was no going back.

My father laughed, pointing a finger at Kellan. "You have backbone. Most demons don't. You all are sniveling idiots." he spat, indicating the ground. "Every time I come across one, it's always the same. They start spewing promises. They'll turn in their mother/father/sister/brother/best friend/best mate. Whoever it is that might hold my interest and they fall to the ground. They kiss my feet and start begging. They'll serve me even in hell. They'll search out whoever I wish to be on my side. They'll kill anyone I want. Crying. Begging." He paused, his eyes narrowed on Kellan. "Pathetic." He drew closer, and Kellan's eyes closed to slits. "Are you going to be the same?" He flicked his wrist to me. "You are in love with my daughter, and she with you. I can smell the bond between you, unlike the last time. You both are dripping with it. You've recently coupled. Perhaps four hours ago."

Oh. God. That was embarrassing.

"Yes." My father leaned closer and sniffed the air. "I can smell your love, too, but it's going to be the same. I will strip you of your honor, your pride. You will fall at my feet, and you will be like all the others. You will beg for your life, and it won't matter. I will take my daughter's life first. Make you watch that. I want you to hold that memory in your mind, and then I'll send you back to your father's kingdom. You will fall back to hell, and he'll never let you return to the ground. That will be your ending."

Kellan's growl was deepening, becoming more primal. He was going to act soon, and I didn't know what he would do. I worried, for the first time scared for Kellan's life. Sweat dripped down my back, mixing with the cold shivers wracking down my spine, too. My palms grew warm, and I began trembling. The fear was creeping in. I couldn't hold it at bay any longer.

This was the end. I felt it coming.

"Father." Damien jerked forward. His eyes were wild, skirting between Kellan and Sachiel. "You said I could return to my family after this."

"Yes, yes." Sachiel's eyes were gleaming as he continued to stare at Kellan, hard. "I will uphold that promise once I've taken both of their power." He swung to Aumae, who froze with her hands in the air. "And I see you brought me an extra treat. Aumae, it's been so long."

She had dressed in a black sweater with a hood pulled over. It was knocked off and her hair was blowing in the wind. Her arms froze, blood dripping from her fingertips, and her eyes were wild and dilated like Damien's. I traced the blood. I couldn't see where it came from since her sweatshirt was black, but she was wearing a white dress underneath and the ends were red. She stepped forward, and I saw her feet were barefoot. They were bloodied as well, mixing with dirt.

What was she doing?

As I thought that, she spoke in my mind, "You and Kellan hold on to each other. Hold on to Damien as well."

"What are you doing?"

"Pay me no mind, child. I have loved you like a daughter. I'll not let this asshole take you away, not until your time is done." She *raised her arms. "And it's not done, not by a long shot."*

"Aumae?" Sachiel drew closer to her, his head tilting the other way. "What are you doing?"

"You." She sneered. Her eyes turned black. "You used my sister for another child. You picked her on purpose, knowing she was half-messenger, and then you assaulted her body when you tried to rip your daughter from her womb."

"He did what?"

Damien moved closer to me, his hip bumping into mine. "Get ready, you guys."

No. I shook my head. Damien didn't know something else was going on. The plan wouldn't work. I reached back and found Kellan's hand. I felt his tension. He knew my aunt was going her own way. He tucked me behind him.

I murmured to him, "We all have to be touching."

Kellan nodded, still tucking me behind him.

Damien frowned, hearing me. "What? What are you talking about?"

Sachiel was drawing closer to Aumae. He was curious, but that would shift. Whatever Aumae had planned, it wasn't good. He would kill her, if he were smart. He'd strike first before she could finish whatever she was doing.

"Kellan." I thought, *"We have to do something. We have to stall him."*

"I know." Then he spoke up, "You can't beat us all."

It worked.

Sachiel turned to us, his back now to my aunt. "Is the begging already starting, demon?"

Kellan growled, actually showing his teeth. His anger was boiling up, but he was keeping it contained. "Without Shay, I'm a full demon."

"My daughter is three-fourths messenger. My son is half-messenger. Aumae is half herself, and you, yes, I suppose you are almost a full demon. There's a small sliver of humanity in you. I can see it. It's like a pumping heart. It's doomed to turn black within the hour, but even then, you are no match for me."

"Guys," Damien said under his breath. "What is going on?"

"I thought you were supposed to drain us of our powers. That was your plan, wasn't it?" Kellan wasn't backing down. He moved even closer to my father. I went with him, but clamped onto Damien and jerked him with us.

"What are you doing?" he barked at me.

Kellan ignored us, saying, "But you couldn't take on my father."

Sachiel was silent, not moving for a full ten seconds as he stared down Kellan. "You wouldn't."

"I would."

"What are they talking about?" Damien whispered to me.

Kellan answered for me, "Calling my father."

"What?" he whispered again to me. "That wasn't the plan. Why are you guys changing the plan?"

"The plan?" My father didn't sound surprised. "So you were going to betray me, my son. You were going to see your mother, your siblings, even that human father of yours. They're still looking for you, you know."

Damien froze behind me, growing more still with each word my father said. All the blood drained from his face.

"And now you'll never see them. Now, you won't even go to the above with me. I'll cast you out." Sachiel shared with Kellan the same ominous look. "You'll both be in hell for the rest of your eternity."

"Not unless I call my father forward."

Kellan sounded so sure. Even I paused at that, frowning at him. Was he—no... Would he?

Sachiel shared my thoughts. "You're lying." But there was doubt in his statement. "You wouldn't. You'd need—"

And as he said that, Kellan reached around me and jerked Damien forward. He wrapped an arm around his neck, the other holding a knife to his throat. Damien went completely still, his chest barely moving, and Kellan pressed the knife harder to his skin. He lowered his head, holding my father's gaze steadily. "I would. I need a sacrifice mixed with my demon blood. That's all I need, and he'd be here. I have no problem

taking the life of the guy who betrayed Shay." His arm tightened over Damien.

Thunder erupted, and lightning smashed down behind us.
It wasn't close, but close enough where I felt the electricity go
through my body, jolting me.

"Kellan." Damien's Adam's apple bounced up and down.
"What are you doing?"

"Shut up."

I moved to their side, grabbing on to Damien. Aumae said
we needed to maintain contact, all three of us.

"You're a part of this, Shay?" Damien asked me.

I ignored him, staring at my father. "Kellan will do it, and
you know it."

"I don't believe you. His father is as much a fan of his as I
am of you. I have no problem killing my own child, not if it
betters me. His father is more ruthless than I am."

"You can't take all of us on, and I'm sure once his father
arrives, he'll go straight for you. We'll get away. You won't. The
odds are not in your favor." Something new had risen up in the
air. I felt it now. It was low, but building in power. It was like an
invisible river. It was first a small trickle, wetting our feet, but it
grew and grew. I felt it growing and its current was a strong
pull. It was sweeping around us, threatening to pull us away
with it, whatever it was. I glanced over my father's shoulder and
saw Aumae there. Her arms were in the air. Her eyes were
black. The wind was picking up just around her. It was circling
her, whipping and snarling. I was shocked my father hadn't
heard it yet. Whatever she was doing, it was new power, power
that wasn't there because of him. He should've noticed, but he
was still locked on Kellan. He believed his threat and he was
focused on what would happen if Kellan's father did arrive.

He was saying something to Kellan.

Kellan replied, a savage retort.

I tuned them out. I could only focus on Aumae now. The

wind stopped. The current was all around us, zapping against my face, my hair, my back. It was completely enveloping us.

"*My child,*" Aumae thought to me, walking toward us. Her hands lowered, and she dripped blood onto the dirt.

"*What are you doing, Aumae?*"

"*I am saving you.*"

"*How?*"

"*This is why I sought you out. Kellan thinks he sent for me, but it was the other way. I sent a suggestion in the wind for him to seek an ally. I knew he would come to me. This is why I remained on Earth after your mother left. You are that reason. This moment is that reason.*"

"*What—*" I started shaking my head. No. No. Sadness, grief, pain. All three rolled into one, and I felt them low in my gut. I was going to live. I felt that joy, too, but the mourning was already there. I felt her intentions before I fully knew. "*Aumae, please don't. We'll find another way.*"

"*There is no other way. This is the way. This was the reason for me being here. There was never another way.*" She lowered her head a fraction, so her eyes could look right into my core. "*The other plan was never going to work. Your father is too powerful. Now, my child, I will tell them above about you. You will be protected, and your father will be persecuted. Do not worry. I will watch over you from the other veil. I will be there, along with your mother.*" Then, she called out, her voice strong and clear, "Sachiel!"

He whipped around. "Wha—"

She held her hands in the air with a knife poised at her throat.

The throat—it was always the throat. I winced, feeling the blade against my own throat, even though it wasn't. It was only against my aunt's.

My father put two and two together. "No!" He looked around, feeling the new power finally. "No, no, no." He kept whipping around. "You couldn't have done this."

"It is done." And with those words, my aunt sliced her own throat.

Blood gushed from her, and my father began clawing at his own throat. As her blood rained out, so did his. His was darker, almost black, and his entire body was soon drenched. He fell to his knees as her body went to the ground. Her eyes had rolled inside, but I felt her touch on my shoulder. It was a gentle touch, a goodbye and a reassurance. She whispered into my ear, "Goodbye, my sister's child. Until you may join us in another life."

Then, she was gone, but the rest of the spell was only starting.

My father's blood was draining out of him at a racing speed, but he was fighting it. Whatever she'd done, he began to chant, summoning his power to break it. Wind began whipping around us again. The thunder and lightning started crashing, filling up the darkness. This was why she warned for us three to remain connected.

An arm slid around my waist. It was Kellan's, and he pulled me into his chest. He yelled into my ears, sounding like he was far in the distance, "We have to become anchored."

I yelled back, lifting my mouth to graze over his ear, "How do we do that?"

"You guys!" Damien was yelling to us, too.

I clamped my hand tighter on his arm. Kellan grabbed his other arm. He pulled us even closer and yelled at Damien, "Use your power. Secure a hold in the ground."

"What?"

"Just do it!" Kellan yelled back and crashed his forehead to mine. As he did, we were linked in mind, body, and soul. Together, we sent our magic down into the earth, going further and further. We were roots, growing out like a tree, claiming our stand where we were. It was working. We weren't going anywhere. And the farther our roots spread, along with

Damien whose root was right beside us, the stronger we were becoming.

I could hear my father raging. He was fighting the spell. He reached out, grabbing me, but Kellan shoved him back. As he did, the power grabbed my father's body and swept him away, far away. The farther he went, the wind began to fade.

Suddenly, it was done. We were there. We were alive, and my father was not. His body was a hundred yards away, but no. As we pulled back, withdrawing our roots until they were back in our own bodies, we separated and went to stand over Sachiel's body.

He opened his bloodied eyes and coughed.

"He's still alive."

"Not for long," Kellan thought, bending by my father's head.

Sachiel met my gaze. "Your aunt bound her life to mine." He coughed again, blood spilling over his lips. "Bitch."

Damien fell behind us, becoming silent.

I had no words. There was nothing to say. Unprecedented grief sat on my chest. Aumae sacrificed herself for me. I'd never been loved like that, but my eyes fell on Kellan. That wasn't true. I had been loved like that, since I was six years old when Kellan saved me from his father, saying, *"Dad, let her go."*

Kellan took out the same knife he'd held to Damien's throat and laid it against my father's. I held my father's gaze for just a moment. There was no sadness or regret there. I thought there might be. There was just anger, and without a word, Kellan moved his hand—and I turned. I didn't have to see my father die to know I was freed.

Finally.

EPILOGUE

We went to the sanctuary house again.

We stayed for a long time. I'd like to give a certain amount of days, or weeks, or months, but the truth was that I lost count. I didn't know if Damien would want to come with us, but he did. He admitted one night when all three of us had too much to drink that he wasn't ready to see his family again. He was ashamed of what he did to us, even though he helped make up for it. I was fairly certain that Damien blamed himself for Aumae's death, but that was ridiculous.

It was my fault.

I should've realized how powerful my father was. I should've known our first plan wouldn't be enough. But I hadn't. I went there that day filled with arrogance that we would defeat Sachiel. Aumae paid the price. I held that belief in my heart for so long, until Kellan realized I blamed myself.

He kissed me in the shower, whispering, "She knew." A kiss to the corner of my mouth.

I shook my head, but he said again, "She went that day knowing."

No. I wouldn't let him make me feel better about this.

He kissed my cheek, sliding his mouth to my throat. "She knew your father. We didn't."

"Damien did."

"Damien's an idiot." His hand trailed down my back, curving into my waist. He trailed kisses down my arm. "Aumae loved you."

I choked out a sob. That was the problem.

"She was here to protect you."

I couldn't keep my eyes open. His kisses were becoming intoxicating, and I leaned back against the wall, my hands moving to his hair as he knelt before me. He kissed my stomach, his hands framing my hips, holding me steady in front of him.

He said, "It was her decision."

It should've been mine.

He stood and caught my face in his hands. He leaned over me, lifting my head so I had to look up at him. I still refused, closing my eyes. "Look at me."

I didn't.

"Shay."

I did then, but I couldn't hide the agony in me. I knew he was feeling it, like he'd been feeling my guilt since Aumae died. It'd been there, always inside of me, but I refused to put it in words. I refused to say anything because once I did, I knew what he would do. He would do this. Making me accept her passing. Making me accept her sacrifice, and thinking that, tears slipped out. They trailed down my face, camouflaged by the water in the shower.

My throat felt like it was rubbed raw on the inside. "She died because of me. She was the one good thing about all of this."

The corner of his mouth lifted up. "What about me?"

I corrected, reaching out to rest a hand on his chest, "She was the second good thing that happened because of all this."

"She loved you, but it was her decision. It wasn't yours. You have to see that. She made the choice. She could've told us our plan wouldn't work. She didn't. She could've told us what she was planning. She didn't. She chose, Shay. She did. She didn't give you the choice. Do you get that?" He was whispering those words, his eyes searching mine, and I could feel his love. It was so strong, so powerful. It wanted to slip inside of me, warming all the pain I held, but I couldn't let it. Not with this.

I shook my head. "Why?"

"Why what?"

"Why did this happen? Why now? Why not later when I was more powerful?"

He shook his head and pulled me into him. His hand cradled the back of my head, and I slid my arms around him. I hung onto him. He said, his words muffled against my hair as his head rested on top of mine, "I don't know. We may never know."

"But you have a guess?"

He stiffened, then relaxed as he answered, "Your powers were too strong for you to suppress. You couldn't deny them any longer. If I were to guess, it'd be because of that. He wanted to get your powers before you were too powerful, and maybe you would've been able to fight him off. I don't know, though. I don't know if we'll ever know."

His answer shouldn't have appeased me, but somehow it did. And over the next few months, the rest of his words had taken root inside of me. They helped heal the wounds from losing Aumae. Maybe it wasn't completely Aumae either. Maybe it was the loss of everything. I'd been lying to myself before when I cast that spell. I was only six years old, but I didn't want to accept who my parents were. They were evil and I couldn't grow up with knowing them, seeing them, feeling them, but I also couldn't leave. I would've had to leave Kellan, and even back then, I knew I couldn't have done that. So I cast that spell and wiped out anything that would've reminded me about my parents, or the two demons that raised me.

I thought I could live like that. I couldn't. Going through all of this, it was like I was becoming clean for the first time. All the lies, deceit, mystery, jealousy, everything bad that I had to endure because of what family I lived among—that was all gone.

And I mourned it. I shouldn't have. I shouldn't have missed Vespar, or Guiseppa. I did. I shouldn't have even missed Matt, Leah, and Dylan. I did.

I should've been furious with Damien for betraying us. I wasn't.

Everything was mixed up in my head, but the constant was Kellan. His love. His presence. Every time I felt that vacuum inside, of where I didn't understand the world I was in any more, I reached out for him. He was always close by, and if he felt that same dark vortex in me, he'd appear from wherever he'd been. Once I touched him, I felt steadied. He grounded me. We were that tree once again, our roots strengthening with the other next to it.

That went on and on until one day, I didn't miss Vespar, Giuseppa, Leah, Matt, Dylan, my old life. The anger, confusion, sadness was gone, and instead, I was able to realize why I missed them. That'd been my constant. It was what I knew, and now with the threat of my father gone and no more lies anymore, could look ahead now.

I assumed Damien was going through the same struggles as me, over what he did, until the day he must've worked through his own battles. He announced one morning that he was returning to his family. We were welcome to come. We were half-brother and sister, after all. I nodded, with no intention of seeking him out. I'd held on to my anger toward him for a few months, but it faded when Kellan reminded me Aumae wouldn't want me to hate my last blood relative.

I snorted in laughter that it was Kellan who pointed that out, but I knew he did it for me. He promised to be angry for me, and slowly, I started to look at Damien like a brother. Started to. Those were the operative words. We were a work in progress as well, but I wasn't ready to leave the sanctuary home when he first made that offer.

"You sure about this?" Kellan asked me now.

I glanced at him from the passenger side in our car. We had just pulled over in front of Damien's house. Even though we just arrived, I knew Damien was aware we were there. Once Kellan and I fully merged together, Damien and I could block each other, but spending so much time in the sanctuary together, that connection had grown. I opened my end when I decided I wanted to meet the rest of Damien's family. Damien knew we'd been coming even as we began to pack our stuff for the road trip. I wasn't surprised when the front door opened a moment later.

Kellan gestured behind me. "He's coming to the car."

I turned around. Damien's smile stretched from ear to ear as he hurried across the yard. He waved with one hand. I saw an elderly woman appear in the doorway behind him. A little girl stood in front, holding a teddy bear.

I was suddenly nervous.

"Don't be."

I didn't look back at Kellan, but I replied, "They might hate me."

"You're Damien's half-sister. They'll love you."

"Hey!" Damien was at the door. He motioned for us to get out. "It's so good to see you guys." He pulled me in for a hug, and I hugged him back, but I couldn't stop looking at the people in the doorway. What did they know about me? Had he told them anything?

"It's so good to see you guys." Damien stepped back and

nodded to Kellan, who'd come around the side of the car. "Kellan."

Kellan nodded for his greeting.

"Are you guys staying for a while?"

Damien's gaze fell on me as he asked the question. I knew Kellan wouldn't answer. It was for me to decide. I shrugged. "Depends on you, I guess."

"On me?"

"What do they know?" Kellan gestured to me. "What do they know about Shay?"

"They know everything."

My eyes widened. Kellan didn't react, but I could sense his surprise as well. I said, "Everything?"

"Well." Damien laughed a little, one of his hands sliding inside of his pocket. He lifted up a shoulder. "My mom knew about Sachiel, so they're aware of that more celestial world out there."

"And demons?"

"They know about them, too."

Kellan's eyes narrowed. That wasn't what he was asking.

I sighed. "Are they going to have a problem with us?"

"Oh!" Understanding dawned now. Damien shook his head. "No. Not at all. They know you're my half-sister, Shay. They've been asking me every day when you're going to arrive. I told them that you were coming."

They knew.

Maybe hearing that shouldn't have rocked my world, but it did. I felt like my stomach opened up and all my guts spilled out.

Kellan started to laugh. "You'll take on our two demon siblings, cast out two demon parents, square off against my father, and your father, but you're scared of meeting those humans back there." He added, "Good humans, too. I can smell the love they have for you already."

I was terrified.

"Come on." Damien threw an arm around my shoulder, turning me toward the house. "I only got a few minutes alone with you. They're going to be coming out here in two minutes, and my grandmother can be loud. She doesn't hold back anything. I don't think we should be talking about demons and messengers where my neighbors can hear." He looked over to the house beside his. "They already suspect too much anyway. My grandma drinks whiskey. A lot. I told you she gets loud, too, right?"

She did.

She liked to drink, cuss, joke, and she liked to love, too. So did Damien's mother. His father that raised him. His grandfather and his two siblings. They all loved us, Kellan included. We stayed with them until Kellan and I decided to get our own place. Well—Kellan got us a place the next day, but he waited until I brought it up before letting me in on the secret. He didn't want to pressure me to leave Damien's family since we just got there, but once we moved out, I couldn't lie.

It was wonderful.

Damien's family welcomed Kellan and me into their family. They were more reserved with Kellan, but who could blame them? Dark, mysterious, gorgeous, and powerful. Damien's grandma was the only one who took to Kellan immediately, making him drink whiskey with her. The two of them formed an instant friendship, along with Kent Ocean. He began to visit on a regular basis and Damien's grandma thought he was a hoot.

It was an entire year later when I woke up and felt pangs in my chest.

Kellan was already awake. He was propped up on an elbow, looking down at me, and he raised an eyebrow. "Are you ready for today?"

"No."

He grinned. "You wanted to do this."

"I was stupid."

"Be human. That's what you said."

I scowled. I knew where he was going with this. He laughed, tugging at my bottom lip until I started laughing with him. I slapped his hand away.

"I was being stupid. I don't want to go anymore."

His hand went to my side, and he began tickling me. I rolled over to stop him, wrapping my arms around him, and just like that, the laughter faded. His eyes darkened, and he rolled me back so he was on top, lightly resting there. His eyes fell to my lips as he asked, "Do you really not want to go, or are you just scared of leaving your family again?"

Family. Again.

I shivered at those words.

I answered, "It feels like I just got this family, like we finally fit in with them."

His hands smoothed over my forehead, tucking some stands of hair back. The touch was so loving and soft, I melted inside. He murmured, "They've loved you since the second they found out about you."

I knew that. I had felt their love so much over the last year, but we were leaving once again.

"It's not going to go away."

"What's not?" I knew what he meant, but I wanted to hear the words.

"We're going to college, with Damien. We're not even leaving him. We're all going to the same school, but that doesn't mean they'll stop loving you. They love you almost as much as I do." His eyes bared into me, looking right to my core. "And you know that love will never go away. Ever. Nothing can shake it. No one can break it. It'll hold. No matter what." He lowered his mouth, grazing softly over mine, and he whispered, "It'll hold, Shay."

Like his would hold. Like mine would hold. We were strong separately, but when we were together, we were impenetrable. Just like our love for the other. I let his reassurances wash over me. He was right. Everything would be fine, and feeling the unease fade away, I opened my mouth under his.

For more information and stories, go to
www.tijansbooks.com

DAVY HARWOOD

CHAPTER 1

"Mr. Moser is not happy."

That was my greeting as I dropped my books on the library table and plopped down next to my roommate. She was the originator of my stupid hotline volunteer career. The career that was *finito*, done, and over with. I snuck inside that morning, slipped the envelope underneath the door, and bolted.

There are occasions where I'm very much a coward, and this was one of those times.

"I'm not surprised," I muttered and bent to grab a pencil out of my bag. The location of the bag was just opportune. It was on the floor so I was able to turn and present my back to my roommate. I hoped she'd take the hint.

"What do you mean you're not surprised? Why aren't you surprised?" Emily hadn't taken the hint. Then again, she never did.

She had been my roommate for the last three months. Her entire life plan was written in detail with bulleted expenditure costs, but it all revolved around her career choice in social work. She was the one to volunteer at the hotline. She was the one who dragged me there. She was even the one that pointed out Adam. Emily wasn't the reason why I stayed. Adam was that reason.

I like boys. Most people would say that I'm boy-crazy, but the truth is I just find them entertaining. I would never ever kill myself over a guy. They're not worth that much, but they are worth a fun activity or a cuddle during a movie. When I saw his rich chestnut hair and almond eyes, I knew that Adam would make a great movie-cuddler.

"Davina!" Emily called out sharply. She was being ignored. That made her pissy.

I sighed and fought the urge to bury my head in my book. No. Why fight it? I buried my head into my book and groaned dramatically. I knew one thing. It would make Emily shut up. If there was one thing that made her uncomfortable, it was when someone was in need of emotional reassurance. I once saw her spill a drink and use that as an excuse to leave a group when one of the girls started crying. I highly doubted Emily's social work career would make it past the paper it was written on, but I wasn't going to be the one to tell her.

On another note, I hated being called Davina. It's Davy. It'll always be Davy. It'll never be Davina. Then I realized there was silence. Emily had quieted. I risked a look, and saw that her eyes were downcast on her own pile of books. I thanked my own quick wits for this reprieve.

"Davina."

I stiffened at the name, but when I looked over my shoulder I melted into a gooey feeling inside. Adam was approaching with an eager stride. His almond eyes sharpened with warmth, and I saw the earnest grin on his face. Tall, dark, and just pretty. That's how I'd describe my perfect guy, and Adam easily fit the bill. Plus, he wore Abercrombie. What girl didn't like that? Well, probably a lot, but it looked yummy on him.

"Hi, Adam." I was warm. I was always warm around him.

He stood at the end of our table and seemed riveted by me. I wondered why and then let it go. Obviously, the guy had woken up and realized his love for me.

"I heard about the suicide last night. Are you okay? You were there, right? That's what Shelly said."

Shelly. All the gooeyness dried up. Shelly was my competition. I cheated on my empath rules and took a peek inside her once. The feeling was mutual. She hated me even more and I didn't need to be psychic to know that she planned to murder me.

I was only joking...somewhat.

I was a short girl at five foot six inches with an average build, not slim, but not big either. I had brown curls on a good day, and a frizzy fray on a bad, but I knew my dark brown eyes and my full lips were my best features. Guys liked to stare at both of them, but Shelly was a tall willowy blonde with absolutely beautiful blue eyes. I always felt like I was swimming in a lake when I looked at them.

Shelly liked Adam. I liked Adam, but I wasn't sure who Adam liked.

"What else did Shelly say?" I couldn't hide my sarcasm.

Adam's smile dimmed slightly, but he pressed, "Is it true? You answered the phone and she was on the roof?"

The boy was goal oriented. "Yes. I was there, but she jumped."

Emily looked up with wide eyes. Adam shifted a little and his eyes skirted from me to Emily. "Are you... are you okay? Shelly said that you quit the hotline."

Emily harrumphed.

"Um..."

"I can't believe you quit." Emily had to put her two cents in.

"Yeah, I mean..." Adam took the seat next to mine and lowered his voice. It was soothing and seductive to my ears. "I mean...the place won't be the same without you, you know?"

Of course I knew, but that was the point of it. I wanted to get as far away as possible. It would always remind me of the girl from last night. I wasn't freaked out with agony and so forth, but the truth was that I was freaked out by the gut-wrenching feeling that something worldly awful had happened and that it was connected to me. "I just... it's too much, you know? I can't handle—she died in front of me. I can't...it's just too much for me."

I saw the sympathy in Adam. He placed his hand on mine. "I know exactly what you mean. If you ever need anything, call me. Okay? I want to help you through this tough time."

Emily fled the scene. I almost caught a back draft from her sprint. "I'd really like that, Adam."

He squeezed my hand. "Any time. Remember that, Davina."

I'd remind him another time not to call me that name.

Then the happily-ever-after feeling was gone as I felt a vampire walk past us. A cold wind slapped my insides and I looked up. Normally, vamps ignore me. They can't feel me like I can feel them so they just believe that they're not noticed.

Not this time.

I gasped when I saw a pair of coal-black eyes staring right back at me. The vamp was tall with jet black hair. He wore a white buttoned-down shirt over jeans. He kept going, but I still felt his eyes after he turned the corner.

"Davina," Adam said sharply, confused.

"What...what were you saying?" His hand was gone. I wanted his hand back.

"I..." He frowned again and asked, "Are you okay? You pushed me away and I mean, that's okay if that's what you need right now. I just thought..." He trailed off and looked away.

I didn't have to be empathic to see his insecurity. "It's not that. That guy scared me just now. I'm sorry. I want your help, I really do."

His eyes twinkled.

I sighed again. How could any girl not fall in love with how adorable he was?

"Can you two stop with the sappy moment?" Emily returned with a storm at her backside. She slumped in her seat. "I'm trying to study."

"Oh, yeah," Adam laughed, a little embarrassed. "I-uh—I'll talk to you later, Davina?"

I nodded. Hell yeah, we'd talk.

"Good. See you later then."

I glanced at Emily as he left and saw her sharp green eyes on me. She narrowed them in disgust.

"You make me sick."

"What? Why?" I was innocent.

"You totally lied to him just now. I had to run to the bathroom to keep from barfing. Really?! You can't handle it? She died in front of you? Mr. Moser told me that you need to get back to the hotline. You broke protocol and that's why you quit, not because you're 'emotionally shaken.' Seriously, Davina."

Maybe my roommate knew me a little better than I realized.

"Can you blame me?! Adam is to die for." I could not believe I just said those words.

"I can't believe you said that." Emily reiterated my thoughts.

I flushed, embarrassed, and leaned back in my chair. "What am I supposed to do? I didn't quit because of protocol, okay? And I need any advantage with Adam. You know Shelly Whistworth has her claws in him."

Emily was annoyed. "You have to go and talk to Mr. Moser. You did break the rules and he's worried about a lawsuit. And Adam Darley is not worth your time to lie and lower yourself. If he's a stand-up guy, he'll recognize that you're much more fun to be with than Shelly Witless. If he's not and he goes to her, he's not the guy that you'll want anyway."

"I'm not lowering myself," I remarked, and crossed my arms. "I'm just being manipulative."

Emily looked at me knowingly. "Well, stop. It's annoying."

"It's fun."

Emily opened her mouth and started to say something, but I felt the blast of cold race through me. My heart slowed as the vamp walked towards me from the opposite direction. His eyes were on me again. He seemed to look right through me, but he didn't slow his pace. He walked right past.

I hated vampires. I knew what they could do from personal experience. However, there were a lot of good vampires that liked to hang out on campus. Some of them even took classes and wanted to learn. This guy looked like a regular college student and he walked like one. Right to the computer lab, and back out again for a Mountain Dew. Typical college behavior, but I was betting he wasn't one of the 'good' vampires.

"Do you know who that is?"

"You interrupted me. I was talking."

I watched as he returned from the vending machines and sat back down at a computer. "That guy. Do you know him?"

"We're at a school with six thousand students. Really?! We're freshmen, Davina. How can you expect that I'd know him?"

I turned and regarded her. "Do you know him or not?"

She shifted uncomfortably in her seat.

"Who is he, Emily?" I leaned closer and hoped he couldn't hear us. There were two glass walls between us and the computer lab always buzzed with conversations and printing papers. If he tuned in, he could hear us, but for once I hoped that I wasn't a speck on this guy's radar. Correction—make that this vampire's radar.

"He's in my social work class."

"Intro?"

"Yeah. He's a junior and he's fulfilling a requirement." She sounded like she'd practiced that. Something felt off with her.

She liked to share her opinions on people, but she didn't with this guy.

"You like him." I couldn't fault her. Vamps had seductive appeal down to perfection. Emily was a girl. Even *she* would fall under their power whether they intended it or not. The only way you could fight against their pull is if you knew what they were.

"I do not!" Emily cried out. She started to gather her books back up, but I laid a hand on them.

"It's okay. He's dreamy. I understand." I glanced back over, but sighed in disgust.

He just sat there at the computer. His hands didn't move on the keyboard. "Who is he?" I asked again, still watching the back of his head.

He sat rigidly.

"Luke Roane," Emily sighed. She'd be mortified at how dreamy it sounded.

"Roane?" I arched my eyebrows.

What kind of name was that? I'd heard of a Roane back home, but the name was only spoken about as a legend. Most of the vamps didn't believe he existed. I didn't like this new twist. My college life wasn't supposed to deal with supernatural things like this. I wanted an Adam in my life, not a vampire named Roane.

"He's really intelligent." Emily had opened her floodgates. Now her opinions flew freely. "He cares about the world and he's got some super insights into humanity."

I bet he did.

"Even Professor Sulls asks his opinions on matters. Luke's like no other guy that I know. I mean, I respect him. I have really high standards and I only respect two other guys," she said, casually.

"I know." I said dryly, "Jesus and Martin Luther King Jr."

"Can you believe it?" Emily sighed again. She was on the

fast track for her first college lovecrush. It was my little name for those crushes when a girl thinks she's in love. They were annoying... to everybody.

Lovecrushes aside—or maybe front and center—I hadn't moved my eyes off Roane's back, but then my eyes slid past his shoulders to his black computer screen. I found myself staring smack head-on with him. I gasped in mortification. He'd been staring right at me the whole time. This was not good, not at all. He knew that I knew. I knew that he knew I knew. I could've pretended that I didn't know he was listening to us, but now all bets were off.

He'd seen.

I smiled smugly and whispered, "I know what you are."

His face didn't move. His eyes didn't react, but I knew I'd made him angry.

Keep reading Davy Harwood here!

MICAELA'S BIG BAD

JAY HAPPENED

The only thing standing between me and me getting drunk was a naked four-year-old.

He was my best friend's nephew, and he was swinging his little penis in the air, staring at it, smiling and giggling, and clapping his hands with glee. He was also standing just inside the door, and I was standing on the doorstep, a full bottle of whiskey needing to be drank, and he wouldn't let me in.

"Heya, Bud."

More laughing.

He clapped.

He was shaking his little hips as if it were the first time he'd learned how to shake those hips.

"Bud."

That was actually his name.

"What?"

I nodded to the doorhandle. "Let me in."

"No." He hit the lock—shit, my hands were full, but why hadn't I just grabbed for the handle, anyway?—and took off running.

Crap.

I had a bulging backpack on me. Three grocery bags were hanging from one of my arms, the same one I had my coffee in. My other free hand held the whiskey. I knew my priorities. Also, the grocery bags were filled with my clothes, or at least what I had been able to grab in a desperate speed-round of packing.

I went so fast. If there was a speed packing race, I could've been a contender.

Not a winner, a contender. After all, I was realistic about my abilities.

The most extraordinary thing about me was my long hair. I had long dark hair.

Jay used to whisper how he liked to twine it in his hands when he—nope. Not going there.

But this was me. Micaela Nadeem, an energist who didn't use my energist side. Middle of the road. Some might say boring. I played everything safe. No risks in life. Not great at anything, but not bad at anything either.

Even leaving my boyfriend, I half-assed it. I took what I could, and bolted.

And I threw a fork.

I should've thrown a knife. At least a knife? Why not go totally lame and toss a spoon instead? Nope. A fork. I was a fork girl. A fork non-energist energist.

My car was full of blankets, what bathroom toiletries I'd been able to grab, and all my schoolwork, because this fork girl still needed to finish two courses before I had a bachelor's in communications. What I planned to do with that? I hadn't a clue. See my theme here.

I barely knew what I was going to do past tomorrow, so the future was totally up in the air.

I was not, what someone would call, a *planner*.

Who are those people?

They're a species I'll never understand.

I tried hitting the doorbell with my elbow.

Nothing. I chafed against the wall instead.

I tried a second time.

Rin—

It cut out.

Great.

I had two options. Put my stuff down, find my phone (I had no idea which bag I'd stuffed it in) and try her that way. Bud was here, so chances were high that Nikki was babysitting, but her phone always seemed off so the probability of that working was nil.

My other choice: "Nikki! *Nikki!* NIKKI!"

She came out from the back hallway, her shirt hanging down one arm, doing up her pants, and her hair was all frayed everywhere.

I—

I couldn't.

Not at all.

Her eyes went wide seeing me, and she cringed.

Her face was all red and splotchy.

Her lips swollen.

She came over, cursing under her breath, and unlocked the door. She opened the door, stepping back. I stepped in, and hissed under my own breath, "You just got laid! While you're babysitting!"

More cringing from her, but she shut both doors and swung around to me. "I—" She took in my bags, and surmised the contents in my bag, and her eyes got round all over again. "Oh no, Cale."

I wrinkled my nose at her. "Don't 'Cale' me in that tone. Babysitting. You! Bud locked the door on me."

"Bud?!" She whirled around.

And Bud decided to come running back down the hall, yelling at the top of his lungs, arms in the air. Still naked.

"Bud!" she gasped, rushing to him. "What are you doing here?"

She lunged right.

He jumped left.

She jumped left.

He dodged, then climbed up on a chair.

"BUD!"

Still giggling, he got up on the kitchen counter, and ran the length of it. He was fast approaching the point where he'd be caught or have to jump because across from him was the refrigerator.

I heard Nikki draw in a swift breath of air, at the exact same time as I held mine.

He launched—

"BU—"

He was caught mid-air by two muscular arms.

He was curled up to a very manly and shirtless chest, and he was carried the rest of the way into the living area where I was still standing, still holding all my bags, still clutching that whiskey because I was still hoping to crack this sucker open tonight and drown every last sorrow.

"Uncle Cream!" We were *still* on the high-pitched theme here. That was coming from Bud, and he was pulling with all his might at his Uncle Brad's hair.

There was a story behind why Brad was nicknamed Cream, but I never heard it—actually, I never wanted to hear it. I was hoping to go through my entire life not knowing...and now onto the weird family awkwardness here.

Brad and Nikki were not boyfriend/girlfriend, or at least I hadn't been updated on an official relationship status.

What they were, though, were siblings to Bud's parents. Nikki's sister married Brad's brother, and their first shindig that resulted in my best friend having to do up her pants happened the night their siblings were married.

Do the math.

Bud was four.

Nikki's sister didn't get preggo until the honeymoon.

Brad ending up in Nikki's bed, on and off, had been going on for a long-ass time. I say it like that because there are always after-shocks whenever Brad comes around.

Then, he would leave.

Nikki had tried closing up the bedsheets to him, but he could charm and seduce her and say all the nice words to her to get those sheets back opened pretty much any time he deemed her worthy.

He'd hotfoot out, and Nikki would get a text from one of our other girls (we had a lot around town), and there'd be a picture of Brad curled around another girl.

They were back and forth so much, and it'd been going on for almost four years.

This wasn't my drama, but I was her best friend, and I was pulling the best friend card and admitting only to myself that I was tired of the Brad-drama. Also, not shocked that he'd bring Bud around when he was hooking up with Nikki. How he got Bud into the house without Nikki seeing him before the bed-capades was something I also didn't want to know all the details about because Nikki was all looking shocked at seeing her nephew naked.

And in her house.

"What's up, Nadeem?"

I grimaced. "Don't speak to me."

Uncle Cream was the most real-life version of someone who reminded me of Billy Hargrove from *Stranger Things*. The difference was that Uncle Cream had straight hair, not curly hair. That was it. He could've been his twin, both physically and personality wise.

"Brad," Nikki snapped, but my best friend wasn't paying

much attention to her recent lay. She was back to looking at me. Studying my bags. Studying the booze in my hand.

She noticed before, but got distracted. She was back to noticing and she was figuring it out.

My best friend was catching up here.

"Jay?" she asked.

Nope. That most definitely wasn't a frog in my throat. And it hadn't doubled in size when I nodded back.

"Yeah," I rasped.

Another cringe from her, mixed with a pitying look. I hated the pitying look.

The frog just did a loud-ass *ribbit*.

I looked away, and shuffled back because I knew what was going to happen. She would herd Uncle Cream and Bud, no— she'd make sure Bud got clothes on first—and once they were gone, she'd take my whiskey from me. She'd go to the kitchen. She'd pull out some drink glasses, put in some of the nice cubed ice she always keeps on hand for me, and we'd pour ourselves a drink. After that, it'd either be a veg-out night, which I was now wondering how that phrase came about? Because we'd sit, talk, fill each other in, and we'd drink. Pizza would either get ordered, or we'd go the other way.

We'd drink. Talk. And decide we needed to go out.

It was Halloween, a night we both avoided because we were usually insulted by how humans viewed us, but... Jay happened.

Keep reading Micaela's Big Bad here!

ALSO BY TIJAN

More paranormal:

Davy Harwood Series

Evil

Micaela's Big Bad

Series:

Fallen Crest/Roussou Universe

Fallen Crest Series

Crew Series

The Boy I Grew Up With (standalone)

Rich Prick (standalone)

Frisco

Other series:

Broken and Screwed Series (YA/NA)

Jaded Series (YA/NA suspense)

Davy Harwood Series (paranormal)

Carter Reed Series (mafia)

The Insiders

Mafia Standalones:

Cole

Bennett Mafia

Jonah Bennett

Canary

Sports Romance Standalones:

Enemies

Teardrop Shot

Hate To Love You

The Not-Outcast

Young Adult Standalones:

Ryan's Bed

A Whole New Crowd

Brady Remington Landed Me in Jail

College Standalones:

Antistepbrother

Kian

Contemporary Romances:

Bad Boy Brody

Home Tears

Fighter

Rockstar Romance Standalone:

Sustain

More books to come!